AN ILLUSION OF SUN

Also by John Fraser
and published by AESOP Modern:

Animal Tales
Black Masks
Blue Light / Starting Over
The Case
Down from the Stars
Enterprising Women
Hard Places
The Magnificent Wurlitzer
Medusa
Military Roads
The Observatory
The Other Shore
The Red Tank
Runners
Soft Landing
The Storm
Three Beauties
Wayfaring

.

AN ILLUSION
OF SUN

John Fraser

AESOP Modern Fiction
Oxford

AESOP Modern
An imprint of AESOP Publications
Martin Noble Editorial / AESOP
28 Abberbury Road, Oxford OX4 4ES, UK
www.aesopbooks.com

First edition published by AESOP Publications
Copyright (c) 2011 John Fraser
First paperback edition published by AESOP Publications
Copyright (c) 2014 John Fraser
Revised 2020

www.johnfraserficion.com

ISBN: 978-0-9572061-2-0

Introduction

IT WAS A COUNTRY proud of its railways: officials were
decorated with enamelled miniatures, extravagant diptyches
of patriotic scenes encrusted with gilt and seed pearls. The
politics of railwaymen were as important as those of the police
or the army. The workers were soft-eyed, arrogant, and they
gave directions with intense courtesy and inefficiency: the trains
were swift, dangerous, and as intriguing as the artists who
decorated and drove them. At the stations, you could buy thirty-
year-old postcards, small bottles of warm water, and miniature
bananas: foreigners saw little of interest in these familiar
details. But they did notice that the stationmasters twirled their
ebony batons, and manoeuvred their greasy armies with greater
pride and pretension than elsewhere. 'A good railway means a
bad government,' sighed old men who went everywhere by car,
and who had never been abroad: but the saying was popular and
the railwaymen oiled and scraped with sentimental satisfaction,
and the services grew unusually erratic.

The passengers failed to live up to the standard of their
servants: there were men who undressed their scabbed, thin
children on the seats, slyly smiling with shy pleasure. Old
women, who at forty had put themselves into perpetual
mourning, sat like intelligent vegetables beside their husbands.
As the years went by, they seemed to grow more remote, wiser,
less accessible, until they fell like the overripe fruit to be buried
in the long grass. Embarrassed peasants who had forgotten the
intricate decencies of public life fumbled with their buttons and
clumsy parcels: archaic families, used only to journeys in the
discomfort and pomp of the Rothschilds' continental coaches,
wondered at the bad manners of their companions. Lovers and
little girls sucked sweets and gazed dully from the dirty

windows.

At night, the small bright boxes, spaced like rare gemstones, were tugged through the desolation of a pagan countryside. Stark trees and rabbits could be seen from the intimate compartments, where men pretended to sleep. A ploughed field in the dark: wells, winding gear, stretches of somnolent water: the distressed, ravaged, unquiet countryside, in contrast with the domestic confabulations of bored travellers. These men were unremarkable. Among them one night came Torgano. He was of medium height, and hated tall, intelligent women: he was a dealer in common rarities, and though a romantic realist, lost his nerve when he found himself in danger of emotional ambushes. He was travelling with his friend, Pierrina: she suffered from a cosy chronic inertia, going quietly, delicately, like an invalid, to save effort. She liked heat, boredom, and combing her hair. Thus, she was like most women, except that at eighteen she had written an article on Malipiero: however, she could never again bring herself to work: she liked the pure surface of her ignorance.

'Pastoral piety: the two most unpleasantly evocative words I know,' said Torgano. 'Perhaps that is because you were destined to pass from a fleeting insensitive childhood to a permanent neurotic adolescence. You have stored up your little fantasies and associations until you are too old to become anything but a frustrated dream artist.

'For six years you have called me an old child: since some emotion is indestructible, that can be no reason for treating it as if it is unfeeling: emotion which can be terminated at will is likewise easily hurt, perhaps even more defenceless because it is irresponsible. Not for the first time, I beg you to stop exercising your malign playfulness. Perhaps you say that the prisoner under torture finds his convictions and his defiant formulae beaten and branded on his body as if they were scars, which could only slowly grow livid, then fade. Perhaps you say that your torments strengthen a loving reaction, that the more I am hurt, the more I shall resolve to stand firm against your cruelty.

'Or do you see that I do not shamble and grope along the bright boulevards, that I do not shout and fight myself as I sit aloof over lucent drinks in the expensive cafés, and do you consequently pretend that I simulate my unhappiness? Do you want me to leap about in the squares, screaming to the pigeons like a madman, or a Neapolitan carpet-seller, sending the grunting flocks from one roof to the next over the heads of the angry but mechanically spendthrift German tourists? Do you want me to abandon my antique shop, which you effect to despise? And if I do leave it, what will you do about the so-rare barber's poles? The poles which make a hazard of the squalid approaches to the unsafe, and equally squalid, landing stage of your so unusual palazzo – these do not come to any antique shop but mine, remember, and this is not Venice!'

'Perhaps I just do not like you very much,' said Pierrina quietly.

Torgano laughed scornfully.

Pierrina relied on his antiques to fill her palace, from which, every day, slipped plaster unicorns into the clear water below. She relied on his recommendation to fill the faded rooms with bored tourists; there could be no reason why these two should not love. One day, the water, overlaid with metallic bars and curtains of shifting blue, green, petrol, and broken stucco, would receive the whole weary palace, as it slipped from its foundations. All this, the two reluctant lovers realised and feared; they travelled miles to find antiques to hang from every irregularly protruding nail, before the walls fell away.

'Private transports in public transport,' silently smiled the girl. 'That is how I shall remember him. He is so afraid to stop talking in case silence bores me, that he has become a miraculous spring of boredom.'

Torgano stared rude and ashamed at his scandalised neighbours: they would have liked to cover the ears of their aggressively unchaste twelve-year-old daughter. Soon, mother and daughter awaited the station in the corridors, while the man looked at Torgano and Pierrina with an irritating, frosty pity. Then the station: the sudden, breathtaking shock of animation, as officials poured from private coffee-houses on the platforms, to greet passengers, like a partisan band welcoming foreign liberators. The departing passengers leaving a few penitents who had to sit in the waiting rooms all night for absolution, stiff-backed and resigned; Torgano stared at these familiar unfamiliarities with a sleepy carelessness.

The trains would keep him awake all night now; they would throw garlands of trucks round the contortions of the track. They would lob clusters of wagons like bunches of grapes to one another in tired, aimless railway games. He was angry: he knew he could not lose Pierrina, for he guessed that she was quite fond of him, so it became pointless for him to rage at her, since it would only inspire her to reply with unkind truths.

They parted. Torgano thought, 'To be without responsibility: to abandon this half-happiness, the fetters of affection, and to go forward in selfish efficiency. But then that is merely to look for years worn smooth, made soft and anonymous by betrayal and sadistic enmities. And in this little town, sadism will always return in a day, a month, as masochism. Much better to see my future through a dissatisfied incomprehension. This is a colourful, if lonely, existence. The other day, says the ironmonger, a woman asked for emerald paper: a charming, if ridiculous alternative.'

Pierrina was not whimsical: a decrepit palace, amateur historians, an ungainly antique dealer who ranted about emerald paper, this did not make her happy with the sophisticated enthusiasms of one who sets out to enjoy the mysterious, the irritating, and the illogical at all costs. She forgot things quickly: another ugly antique animal had fallen from the roof that day: another shattered building would give up its ornaments to replace those of a less ruined home.

One day Pierrina's animals would be taken in their turn, and stuck on some fresh façade; meanwhile, it did not help to consider the endless bizarre progresses of the ancient and the elusive. Like one's emotions, plaster animals were things to be considered only after they had sunk in the elastic waters of tidal basins. She liked Torgano because he was always there: he seemed to her like a well-tried metaphor: exciting, but tiresome when used too much in company. She saw that his personality was in danger of disintegrating under her playful torments, but that this was by auto-suggestion, not her unkindness. The palazzo and she would survive anything he could devise: a pity, for she admired men who argued quietly and could convince you of anything, but anything! Thus she lied to herself.

She went out on the balcony and watched large vegetables and small dogs tossing and gesticulating in the water: 'Death is the same as life for those who have never lived,' she thought, then, 'What a tiresome person I am,' angrily.

There were stars: the ghosts of old and incredibly corrupt politicians failed, as usual, to make an appearance. She grew old: a train called to another in the inconsequential cadences of smashed gongs, steam whistles. The dogs still padded on stiff legs towards the wharves and the palaces: Pierrina realised that she would find nothing in this scene to steady her precise, irresolute mind. She closed the shutters.

Torgano was asleep already: a mile from Pierrina, he carried to his dreams the happy but slightly disgruntled look of one who has predicted falsely a sleepless night. He always had the disagreeable expression of a novelist who remarks to himself that his audience will no doubt be bored, but that his writing has sufficient obvious talent to ensure publication.

It was three o'clock: policemen and cats patrolled the streets or gazed stupidly at dying fires. In two hours, water would be sluiced down the gutters, washing in muddy confusion the bodies of beggars and dead gangsters, wealthy partygoers, and children who would wash in no other way. In four hours' time, the first of the next day's playboys and destitutes would lie once more on the roads: the very small children who played out their fantasies at the expense of the department of hygiene would be replaced by lovers of eleven and twelve. These would walk to school hand in hand, embracing with practised passion: old ladies would scowl and grimace, wishing they had such memories of their education. Workmen would begin work after breakfasting on brandy and coffee: the waiters in the empty tourist cafés would call knowingly to their comrades in the cheap, crowded bars used by the townspeople.

Torgano and Pierrina forgot their journey of the previous evening: journeys are to be forgotten; they met in the square, where the pigeons awaited their generous visitors.

'Let us buy little paper cones of grain for these birds: that will let you believe we are lovers,' said Pierrina.

Torgano kicked slyly at the creatures: they pecked and shuffled like insects on the glazed tiles which covered, most unsuitably, the square. Generations of dictators had plundered and wheedled: families of masons and robbers had accumulated and coaxed: statues of histrionic generals on soiled horses, screens, towers, poles, these had all been wrought, or stolen, to embellish reputation and public places.

'It is not right to be apart so long,' said Torgano, who constantly embarrassed his companion with sentimental truisms. 'How long can this go on?' he asked her.

'Any situation, however unlikely, can be prolonged indefinitely: that is how novels are written, that is how I have known you for so many years.'

Pierrina was sad that she should have to speak like this: she was afraid of Torgano, or at least anxious about the impression she thought she made on him, and indeed on everyone. She scarcely dared move hurriedly, or act warmly; she had so little experience that it appeared a technical accomplishment only to be perfected by years of private practice.

'We cannot spend our lives making idiotic wisecracks about life,' she continued. 'There is, or should be, a limit to the permutations of human relationships. You must write your propositions about abstracts on neat cards, type them, perhaps, on that machine which is too big for your hands. You could send them by messenger or small boy to the palazzo in the early morning: I could take them instead of breakfast.'

Pierrina smiled: it was not a bad idea at all. She could even reply with printed notes: 'Pierrina Tarrault thanks you for your attentions, but regrets she will be unable to pretend.' Most people seemed to pretend, certainly seemed to be able to do so: she, however, did not really know what she would have to pretend to be successful.

That is how the two thought, and spoke. Each had friends, but concealed them in mutual respect for their mutual jealousy: they gave time to no others; they felt guilty if one talked to a shopkeeper without the other. It would have been hard to find more complete devotion, and more complete distrust and self-deception.

Torgano said gloomily, 'I want to talk about the palace and my shop: may we walk under the petrified palms, where red marble spreads out into stone leaves and the flickering signs spark in the restaurant windows? Perhaps you would like an exotic bun, or a gilded biscuit? And a cheap, but local, liqueur, strong and pervasive as perfume? And we shall talk sensibly, do let us be serious?

'We shall sit in the café of the Benevolent Triumvirs, and watch the beetling pigeons and the hot tourists. Everyone will believe we are quaint and happy: they will tell their friends that in this country, young men are voluble and bulky, that the girls are disdainful and may drink spirits before midday. They may even try to find out who the Benevolent Triumvirs were: certainly they would not suspect that they were conceived by a lame hotelier who used to keep a collecting box for the Falange behind the exciting football-game table.'

Wearily Pierrina prepared to listen; still she looked at the sacred birds and the visitors who had come so far to admire them.

Torgano grinned and moved about on his chair: 'I have never spoken to you of money before: I have not worried about finance, and I prefer you not to be concerned for it either.' In fact, he had known that confessions of poverty would have meant little to Pierrina, that she might have taken them as admissions of contagious spiritual illnesses, or unrealistic self-pity.

'But you must have realised that I was neither rich nor flourishing: you buy animals, carved wood, striped poles, yes, I am grateful. But I travel a lot, I have to find new stock before I have exhausted the old, because I am an impractical perfectionist. I do not like to see yesterday's mistakes obscuring today's bargains. We may not be friends.'

He paused for the affirmation that they were, indeed, almost lovers, which, as he might by now have expected, did not come.

'Very well, we will not discuss that: but you can surely see what I mean, what I need? Let me live in the palazzo, with my antiques, let me sell them to your visitors. Nothing improper, but a most profitable arrangement.'

He waited uneasily for the answer he had rehearsed for her. Slowly, disappointingly, she replied, 'I cannot say: it is not a thing I could have thought of. Perhaps you think me tedious and pompous; perhaps you think the matter obvious; perhaps you are right. But I must consult advisers, friends.' Torgano reflected on the sudden emergence of business associates and rivals, now that he had found a question which had to be answered.

'Where would you sleep, would you pay me rent, or would I receive a share of your profits, will I be given a reduction for antiques I want to buy?' The questions stumbled out, confused, even angry. Torgano was slightly shocked by the shrill eagerness with which she demanded concessions he would have slowly given her unasked.

'I suppose we are all like her,' he thought. Then abruptly he asked himself if they were indeed right for one another: years of refuge in fond clichés had accustomed him to asking everything of himself with a patronising sentimentality. Now, as usual he reassured himself that whatever his unseen counsellors might whisper, he would not relinquish Pierrina. This decision, taken with a sense of religious firmness and penance, made him happy. He realised that Pierrina was not preparing her reply: the pigeons marched and countermarched, and after a brief struggle with the sun, a morning partymaker lay down beside a table, and rested without embarrassment or reticence.

Pierrina sat thinking about her palace: at the moment, she felt like calling Torgano a disgusting little boy; possibly that was what her father had resembled in his last months in expensive disease in the palace. Her brother had died, she thought, in the war: an unsuccessful coward, he had only known the beauty and squalor of his home. She thought he had been shot by his own superiors, but he might have fallen off a lorry, or slept in wet clothes.

Anyway, his was one of the tragedies of which no family boasted: he chose to die as a civilian, disobeying, being careless, wilful or unfortunate. If his death had given her father something to exaggerate, the old man might have lived: her brother had died as he lived, with an ill-defined, immature, casualness. She had never cared for him: this recurrent dislike bothered her only slightly. Torgano wished he could be in some silent place: he thought of himself as a conductor, able at will to smooth with gesture and grimace the puckered surface of a massive score. Mentally, he stilled the waiters, the adjectives of the domino-players, the machines which made coffee, pigeon-food, and cocktails.

'Give me a week on my own to think out your proposal; it will be good for both of us,' said Pierrina.

Torgano knew how much more she meant than she had said. For once he did not argue.

A foreigner sat near them; to his wife he said, 'If this is another Venice, where is the other St Mark's?'

She searched for references in vain, and Torgano and his girl smiled wearily, as if they had planned the square many centuries ago. On their right, camouflaged with Romanesque obscenities and lives of medieval merchants and devil worshippers in mosaic, was the building which all knew, but none confessed, to be the point of interest in the square.

Protected and much tended, little noise escaped the sleek masterpiece: it was the central railway station.

Pierrina left the antique dealer: he sat and watched the black polluted birds scuffling and kicking at the leaves. A remembrance of the lonely week to come disturbed him.

Chapter 1

PIERRINA AWOKE: content in the five-minute ignorance which protects the newly awakened from realities, she did not think of Torgano, whom she had left the day before at the Benevolent Triumvirs. Then slowly, comfortably, she remembered.

'Perhaps he is still there,' she thought; he would have stayed to brood about many things, his love for her an erratic punctuation to other intimate failures. Now, she had a week, free from emotional stimulation; she could do so much: write a description of a battle, for harpsichord. But that had been done before. She could write a sonnet sequence about the mating of mayfly, she could found a party devoted to the recovery of her country's ancient colonies. All these possibilities seemed attractive, though a trifle passé; a week devoted to nothing in particular should produce something unusual.

Then she remembered the antique dealer's proposal. With whom should she pass the days? The Director of Public Monuments was despicable, but accessible and would be either in his office, or sitting and watching beautiful buildings, the property of princes, shudder into the water. The public buildings were propped and shored: possibly people expected them to be expensively spoiled, but the Director was not inefficient; most of his work was done by subordinates. Men called him the Director of Monumental Publics, but feared this might be too near the truth.

Below, the fruit barge went past: gravid and fermenting, the gross boat looked like a bad parody of a rococo pediment. Grapes were draped from the thwarts like carnival beards: melons rolled and wallowed in the bilge; simian boatmen poled along this heap of goodness. Pierrina looked at the disgusting succulence with all the righteousness of one who has not breakfasted. Cardinal plums, crocodile-skin cantaloupes, bananas amber finished in ebony, the men chanting and straining. They saw Pierrina, their boat drove forward under the stimulus of an obscene improvisation in their quaint plainsong. They bobbed and nodded, winked and swayed, little knowing how ridiculous appeared their foreshortened bodies from the window.

Pierrina, soured, closed the window. Still singing, the punctual crew reached the noxious vegetable mud: their poles no longer crunched on gravel, their chants sounded louder, more commanding as they came among the mysterious sinuosities of the town canals. Even the visitors, miraculously appearing at ten in the streets, affluent and rested, at six were woken by the bargemen and stayed awake to listen. In rooms heavy with the incense of sunburnt flesh, tourists had lain awake and frightened till dawn.

Then, forgetting they were abroad, anxious, swindled and incoherent, they had slept. Now an hour later they hung from the windows: they did not understand the songs, they were angry; the part of their minds which stored such memories to be retailed when they were safely home, was dormant. Innocently the boatmen moved on to the heart of the city; they were at work; they despised the foolish idlers who looked out in indignation at those who sang and toiled in the streets. Pierrina began her day remote and jaded.

The Director of Public Monuments sat in his office, a lazy predatory insect, he leered comfortingly at the small girls and boys who ran to him with files and information long overdue. Pierrina began to wish she had more questions to ask: when he had listened to her lame explanations, the Director appeared to ponder.

'Now why is it, but exactly, that you have come? Perhaps you wanted, as is quite natural, to discuss your personal problems with an official. Well, that is in order, that is to be expected and encouraged. I have so much work to do that I have unlimited time to discuss anything. Especially you,' he finished with a disconcerting smile, which destroyed the effect of his earlier sentences. But he knew that whatever he said would be interpreted as a sign of brooding power.

He continued, 'I take it you wish to ask whether you would be discreet and businesslike in setting up this romantic antique dealer in your palace?' His eyes twinkled and he poked his tongue quizzically from the corner of his mouth. 'A simple question, you may think: if it were one of our buildings, I could say at once "no" and that would satisfy you. As the palazzo is yours, I must be rather more sparing with my experience. But as you have asked, it is my duty, as a public servant, to answer.

'You will think it is unnecessary that I should tell you what you know, but it is right that you should remember. This is a democracy – this was an empire. There is our history for those who can interpret it; but what has brought us to our present eminence? Planning – we have planned, we have accepted planning as an end in itself. That is the only reasonable solution. Two thousand years ago, we drove out the sheep farmers; they had filled the towns with their agents, the countryside with their greedy animals.

'There were fields within the city walls; the fortifications crumbled; sheep skulls lay in the purple weeds which grew proudly in the squares. Yet we were great; our galleys were flogged over the seas, we exploited geography to the full. But because we were proud we expelled these monopolists. Then our empire: we built metalled highways for camels, we divided continents, suppressed religions, always aware, I believe, that our destiny lay elsewhere. When we perceived that we were not welcome, when our tasks of civilisation was finished, when too many frontier forces had been grotesquely mutilated, we withdrew.

'All the time, we were accepting the forces of European reform: we fought the barbarians who, in their brief occupation, built the palace of arts and sciences. We slew prisoners, we respected no international convention to advance the ideals on which ourgovernment now is founded. I am no cynic: our country has always been the first to reject oppressive forms of government: sometimes they are a convenience to men; otherwise, they must be replaced by the benevolence and foresight of a democratic system.

'For instance, though I might be called a part of government, really I am the embodiment of the people's love of their history and their buildings. And for their interests I might fight: whatever our constitution, we are designed to set an example to our neighbours; however much it costs us, that duty we must fulfil. How do buildings and destiny go together?

'We have a history which explains us and everything about our town; we owe the water supply to a general, the swamps were drained by prisoners; a treaty gave us the Western duchy, and gave me my parents. We have a mission, as a democracy; now war is the will of the people. Empire enslaves, democracy liberates; that is what the prime minister ordered the dear schoolchildren to shout instead of effete prayers before lessons. When the time comes to liberate the lost colonies, the people must be conscious of the need to expand the circle of free nations: we must establish a protectorate based on our historic mission. That is, one which expressed the inherent democracy of our ancestors; that is what syndicalism is all about: brotherhood, the control of relatives, with a government as loving parents to the little, eagerly producing, technocratic communities.

'Some will not agree with me, but what are they but the tiresome brothers and nephews in any family? Any amalgamation of political systems is possible, as long as the people are convinced of the power and uprightness of their government. We must organise for efficiency, that is all; everyone must plan. Every part must go to make up a coherent whole.'

'You have a torture chamber?'

'Yes, we do not show it to visitors; we had a guide who frightened a lady from Heidelberg into hysterics, and since then we have used it as a tearoom for large parties, especially for the

English!'

Pierrina was glad to be spoken to at last.

'Our task, then,' the Director continued, 'is to condition our people to see that the lost colonies must be rescued from danger of foreign influences; perhaps we shall have to occupy them by force; I do not know, I am a humble official. But I can say that our leaders make no secret of this, as they might have done once. How shall we prepare men to die? Death is not easy to face, even if you are free. Here we come to my job. When you see an old building, do you not think, "How easy it was for men to die, to find causes to which they might devote their lives," and does this not make you ashamed of your cowardice which presented with more noble ideals to safeguard?'

Pierrina could have confessed that no feelings, pleasant or unpleasant, came to her at the sight of extreme old age. But she did not, perhaps through cowardice before ideals she knew to be respectable and popular.

'You see,' said the Director, 'you must get men to see their place in history not only in perspective, but in a glaze of heroic humility: tiny heroes, every one, taking their place beside these palaces with their plunder. How do I present this? In my work, in the dramatisation of our history, I remember that men must be shown weapons, the rewards of service, the penalties of disobedience. The tapestries which seem to be counterpoint studies in leaf-mould, these are representations of peace treaties, and the monotony of bucolic festivity. No one looks at them: they have no part in our history, so they have no purpose now in the unrolling of our unquestioning devotion to the development of our national responsibilities.

'When I see a palazzo like yours, I ask myself, "Have the universities a student selflessly devoted to his country's democratic interests, who can put across the message of the, er, building?" "Is its history honourable, or did it belong to collaborators, or communists, or foreigners?" "If it belonged to imperialists, did they accept the loss of our possessions with fortitude, and are they now trying, with us, to win them back to liberty and civilisation?"

'These are the preliminaries; then, when my department is organised, the refinements: on national holidays and Sundays, no foreigners, no radicals, just honest people like you and me, anxious to preserve our country's heritage. Let the people drink in without vulgar intrusions the achievements of their frustrated ancestors, and let them resolve to correct the mistakes of their grandfathers.

'That is why I say you must not install a cheap, a deceitful shop in an historic palace. It would, I think, be almost unpatriotic. You may think me an idealist, but I think, don't you, that our ideals are worth sticking up for?'

Too late, he dropped into colloquial understatement; Pierrina was still admiring his feet. She could not be sure if Torgano could have followed the arguments, though these seemed, on reflection, if not obvious, at least simple. The Director leant back; he had obviously made a great impression. He smiled, became aware that Pierrina had been looking at him in wonder all the time, and had the grace to blush.

Without dismissing her, he turned and summoned the proud, sexless messengers. Pierrina felt that she would need many hours of the antique dealer's company to compensate for this highly intelligent insect's frantic demonstration of nest-building. She would only realise the power of his inhuman attraction when she came to criticise her more earthy men friends later: then she would wish them heroically dead, democratic noble corpses twisting and jerking on iron wreaths of barbed wire. Now she had to leave gracefully:

'I shall think about what you have said.' She went out, watched by a girl who guarded her master with virginal jealousy. The Director did not seem to acknowledge that she was leaving.

'Prepare me a report on the palace of Pierrina Tarrault,' he said quietly to his respectable, childlike servants, 'and bring me the volumes of the Civil Code on Desecration of Public Buildings, and Compulsory Purchase of National Assets.'

Pierrina had not impressed him, she was too immature to be trusted with such treasures. Still, his explanations might delay her decadence. He would stay to see her educated in democracy, provided he was not displaced, pushed up and out, like a fat sweet from a tube, pushed up from beneath to hang poised, offered to a friend. It was a defect of the system, this impersonal promotion and demotion: but at least it replaced other defects of other complexes of power. It had to be endured, it was like having a Borgia blind you with your own blood by slashing your forehead with a ring.

But all the same it was tiresome, and that was why, one day, steps would be taken to make appointments permanent; then they would give the government another name. It would be another step forward: to encourage a period of national emergency, that would speed the process. For even if you did not believe in progress, you had to believe in process: development was inevitable, he would make no moral judgements. Here, he was merely a public servant: a boy brought him a bowl of coffee and he sucked at it like a dog.

Pierrina looked confusedly at the traffic as she stood outside on the steps, a child involved for a moment in a lunatic, adult conversation, she felt inspired and depressed. She thought of Torgano, who would have got up feverishly at eleven, opened the shop with the precision of a sleepwalker, and blinked aggressively at scornful customers. He would think of her, and his face would assume that retarded hairless appearance. His eyes would seem to close, the lower lids swelling up, as if his cheeks were bruised. There would be sulky self-pity, a defiant invitation to her to wound his conceits. She felt vaguely aware that she would not see this for some days – another year, and these weeks would become in her mind another part of a protracted adolescence. Other people could recall events of adult life clearly; she, however, saw her time at university so indistinctly, that she recalled it with the disbelieving excitement of one whose parents describe a forgotten infancy.

In the streets walked opulent young men: they were only

sixteen or so, but wore clothes so uncouth and ill-kempt that they must have been expensive and fashionable. They had aluminium rings, and great signets whose muddy stones were like moles on the exquisite fingers. Only in an English country town had Pierrina seen others like these. They had the faces of luxurious old men, ravaged and pocked, yet unhealthily full: they played much tennis, they danced, felt no jealousy, pain or fear. They were most repulsive: Pierrina was glad when cars roared them back to their house parties. Bored with the signs of a healthy civilisation, she walked to the canals.

The water was so clear that the filth which accumulated was as visible and recognisable as if it had been in a glass case: this small capital was not a rendezvous for the gipsy-barons and their town girls, the musical filmmakers, and extravagant Viennese confidence tricksters. Idly, she looked at the street's blue nameplate; she had wandered near Torgano's shop. She went home, and lying on the bed, watched the sun and water making patterns on the ceiling for her amusement, erasing them carefully with a puff of wind when they were likely to bore.

Torgano sat in the shop, waiting like a condemned man for the prison governor; his hands hung between his knees, he gazed at passers-by, his vacancy concealing a cruel professional efficiency. The ironmonger looked across at the apparently guileless dealer; he might die or faint, and remain propped in that position, yet ready to leap up in a warped *danse macabre* of trading enthusiasm. Few penetrated the deep ranks of chairs, the sensuously reclining sofas, the tables with sensible, homely feet. Men stood outside, looking through to the rear of the shop, while their wives leapt and stumbled among the eccentric piles of wood and fabric.

Occasionally Torgano would stand, and shout a conversation or a bargain across the impersonal furniture: although the hearts of many homes had been removed to beat quietly in the shop, it gave no illusion of life, of having connections with human organisation. Little was sold: the ironmonger smiled haphazardly in at the window nearby where women sat puzzled but dedicated, with their heads under vast electric domes. He stepped skilfully among paints and plasters; few would have realised the uneasy alliances, and distances, in a row of shopkeepers. Torgano was supposed, despite his well-moulded dealer's beret, to be a dilettante, an amateur, never quite to be trusted.

There was no custom: he closed the shop. That afternoon there was to be a carnival to amuse the tourists and absorb the unemployed who made a nuisance of themselves by spitting into the water near the seat of government. Sensitive members of parliament anticipated happily seeing them thrown in the canals, in fun, of course. As the morning went on, visitors would no longer even walk past the shop: Torgano decided to lunch early. In the afternoon, he might contrive to see Pierrina, for she would not open the palazzo today, would not welcome the crowds of perspiring doubters who usually took up her time.

A carnival! There would be a film made here next; masks, boats, flowers; a film public interested only in holiday games and sententious comment on them! Torgano went smugly to lunch; he had not thought about Pierrina yet; he had had no breakfast, and the thought of her on an empty stomach was too disquieting. Besides, if she were not at hand to listen to him, there could be no profit in encouraging fresh unhappiness. Secretly, he had begun to accept that it was only pride and self-pity which prolonged the situation. But he knew that everything could be restored if he could find the formula to break open the nervous reserve of his girl.

Hesitantly he strolled past the restaurants, pretending to wait for someone, until he had determined to go in any sit down. He chose the nearest, as usual; the waiter looked at him quizzically. In that country, they drank wine rich and sluggish as melted butter; it poured itself reluctantly from the thin, ascetic bottles. Torgano had never grown used to it: that day it was hot, and he toyed with scorched embryos in thick batter, galantines which had a strong farmyard smell: a cream cake; a modest bill.

He felt heady and nauseated; he thought, 'Pierrina is so polite to those she does not know, at this very minute she is probably submitting to the unsubtle advances of a stranger, because she does not like to hurt his feelings by refusing him. She would be shocked if I did this to her, yet this intruder gets away with it initially, and then she actually comes to enjoy it.'

This thought so upset him that he had great difficulty in mustering the scattered forces of his body to drive him, rocking and reeling through the door. He felt like being sick, or committing some other nuisance. How he hated himself for enjoying the sensation.

Like a sick man, he glided among the carnival faces of the crowd, preoccupied with his own symptoms, he paid little attention to the giddy angles and exaggerated enjoyment of the spectators precariously poised. He strayed to the enclosures where the unemployed and the unemployed were dressing up.

'Where are the dwarfs, no not the Austrians, they're asleep in that cardboard box – I want the Carpathians. Ugly drunken little freaks, all spiky hats and receding chin.'

'Splash some paint on those grins, they look like dysenteric Alsatians.'

'If I could find your silly head in that giraffe, I'd make it into a papier-mâché doorknob.'

'You just get into that crocodile, you're going to make those stinking bourgeois happy or by God …'

Then out of carnival conversation: '*Animals* to the boats,' over the loudspeakers. Weak men crawled into the great frames of nursery birds. Torgano watched fascinated as they pushed their way through policemen, grotesque and forbidding, the trunks and beads of men picking, or thumbing, their noses. All forms of perversion were catered for: even the audience was startled by the parades of disability and deformity.

Obviously some secretary in the Ministry had enjoyed himself too thoroughly with the catalogues. Bulls, cocks, hippopotami, lions, squabbled in human voices, drowning the delighted cries of small children and old maids. Torgano hoped the carnival would keep well away from the palazzo: already actresses were being thrown in the water by burly photographers' assistants. A man next to Torgano addressed him; Torgano turned, the man was wearing a devil's mask, but spoke with such measured seriousness that one knew him at once to be drunk or eccentric.

'Fascists,' he said knowingly. 'I saw it all in Germany, mixing up sex with the police force, juxtaposing animals and humans in unfavourable situations, and the crowds ...' The man swayed expressively, and imitated, 'Hurhurhur ... harharhar ... laughter, then. a minute, surprise, cheeeaauuow ... tension, burrrzzz ... anger, haaarrsscchh ... triumph, blaaarrhhh, doubt, szeeng, jealousy, fuff.'

At each sound the devil mask hung threateningly over Torgano.

'I know the noises of the crowd, you see, the more complex the emotion, the more noncommittal and uncertain the sound. This lot, fascist, I should know. My wife don't like me to come out these days, but I don't like seeing all the people enjoying themselves, bloody fascists.'

Torgano could imagine the tolerant, self-satisfied lunacy behind the mask, which was an excellent likeness of someone or other. Hot, sweet breath came to him through the nostrils and eye holes of the mask. The voice was that of a man behind a door, or a partition.

'I was on the council for ten years.'

Torgano said he could quite believe it.

'Then they threw me off, that is the Commies did. I saw a lot of them in Germany too, I did. Shocking, it was, what they did to the women: talk about having them in common. You'd see two or three nice, friendly little girls, no more than schoolkids, giggling and talking in an alleyway of an evening. Then these rotten Red Front fascists would come along in their cars, or just walk up to them, and take them off. Just like that: the poor little kids didn't know what was happening, of course. And then I thought: that's what they'll do to our daughters, perhaps even to us. Foreigners, ignorant beasts, it was they put me off the council, you know.'

'Really?'

'Oh yes, sir, very many foreigners around, in our affairs; seeing we're gentlemen, I can be straight to you. Shocking lot of fat greasy little northerners, all potbelly and Bradford, as an English friend used to say. I don't trust them an inch, the English I mean, supercilious drunks I call them.'

He had lost the thread. Torgano could sense the quick change of emotion behind the mask.

'You're just a scheming pauper like the rest of them. Effete, played out.'

He turned on his heel, and Torgano could see the scruffy bald head sustaining the naïve intelligence of the terrible mask. The dealer was now sober.

Well, this was carnival – better make the most of it. Where would Pierrina be? He came across groups of embarrassed, slightly shocked tourists, who felt the local colour was being splashed about by an insensitive jobbing artist. The town dandies appeared wearing the by now familiar satanic masks, and tried unsuccessfully to embrace the raw-nosed matrons from Bruges.

A child was being sick, apologetically, at the foot of the war memorial. Torgano thought that all this was really unpardonably overdone, the heat and the sordid human processes. He moved on to a happier part of the crowd. He felt strangely heavy: he grudged the crowd their unthinking involvement in tiny pleasures. He felt old, corrupt; he wanted a girl, an uninhabited island controlled by complacent forces, which would sustain and serve him.

He thought pityingly, as he watched the water tournaments with interest, how shallow must be the minds of those excited by the sight of men thrown inevitably into the canals. He himself, he lied, would prefer to stand all day, just to see one hilarious accidental ducking. Below, the hired retainers pranced and posed in their unlikely liveries: some, finding their adversaries too eager, had poled to the bank, and were talking bravely to the town police. No one took offence at the caricatures of themselves which mocked from the dyspeptic launches.

A policeman said to Torgano, 'We should have no complaints that the public's money is wasted: everyone can see this must all cost a fair bit. The pickpockets'll do a good day's trade with this lot.' He spoke as if pickpockets were a superior class of detective, men to help and guide an honest municipal policeman.

'I've left a mile of cars jammed from here to the Cockatrice Hotel. If they want to see the carnival, they can. I'm not going to stand in the middle of the road, miss the carnival, and have the drivers peer over at the canal and run into one another. Let the rotten riot police do our job when we get a chance of entertainment, that's what I always say. What do you always say, sir?'

Torgano saw that this nonsense was merely an excuse for the policeman not to notice various carnival tasks. A car had stopped with a spurt of hot oil, and the foreign driver was looking for help: a boatload of dwarfs had stuck on a mudbank: children were being lost or abandoned, and were reacting to their distress in all the unpleasant ways they could imagine. The policeman looked at Torgano as if he were at least a murderer:

'Usually, when you folks have a holiday we come behind and clear up the mess you make of yourselves: can't move a step, you lot, without you want to have a fight, or know the time, or have a fit in a public lavatory.'

'He has a remarkable mind, I fear,' Torgano thought.

The man continued until there was a little crowd round the two of them: the dwarfs were refloated, and Torgano seemed to the onlookers to be the nearest person in distress. By the road another policeman was reluctantly lying in the oil looking up at the engine of the foreign car: over at the café two happy policeman and a sergeant were trying to support one another. Torgano slipped away. As it were, thumbing through the piles of girls he saw all around, he looked for Pierrina, or someone like her. He thought he saw a hand, a smile but nothing of this remained when he arrived. He wandered solemn and detached and was absurdly affected by the tinsel and sentiment of the guild floats.

Agriculture: cornucopias, a tin cow from a milk float, dropsical marrows, flowers, a welfare officer off-duty in a smock. And, as a frame, seven healthy minor film stars. Leather workers: brief cases, blotting pads, some old fire buckets from the town hall, an imitation alligator, an inspector from the harbour board in an apron and carrying an awl. And, after much argument and haggling, three minor, but expensive actresses. And so forth.

Torgano thought this easily the most interesting thing he had seen. He felt like trying to conquer his dislike of conversation and crowds, partly self-induced, partly assumed because he wanted to behave as if Pierrina was possessively in love with him, and resented him talking to anyone but her. Of course, it was plain that Pierrina was only slightly flattered by such behaviour, and not at all in need of it. Still, it helped Torgano to feel that he was needed, even if he supplied his girl's affection himself. But at this moment, the effort of acting out the love he wanted Pierrina to feel for him was too great.

He would talk to anyone, as the policeman and the councillor had spoken to him. He would say that in the fourteenth century at just such a carnival, in the capital of the largest of the lost colonies, their troops had been tugged round the streets in the floats and tableaux, and with the aid of a fifth column had successfully attempted a coup. If he told this to a journalist, he might be quoted; perhaps they would search the offices of the League of the Unemployed in the hope of finding material to prove attempts by the Menace over the mountains, to make political capital from the carnival.

Or perhaps he should merely tell some girl, as a prelude to a cynical explanation of his problems. For he had the reckless feelings of promiscuous desire of many who find themselves deeply committed to illusions. Soon, he surrendered to his reserve and walked to a hill, all sand and glossy yews, just outside the town. Pierrina had gone down to the carnival, hoping that if she did meet Torgano, he would be enjoying himself with someone else, she was prepared to relax in the coarse, unlovely way of women unobserved.

She thought of Torgano's proposal: his shop would doubtless do reasonably well in the palazzo, but it would be in the way, fewer people would come hoping to find an unspoilt showpiece. And she would have Torgano all the morning, and at lunch: he would constantly be having his pride or his dignity wounded. He would eat more than his share of the fried peppers she loved.

His mournful declarations would spoil the evenings, when she took a portable wireless down to the landing stage and played dance music to the poignantly beautiful motor-boat mechanics opposite. Then she would take the cards, the Tarot cards which bore her name – Tarrault, misspelt – and say to herself that she was impersonal as chance, that in her, men might read the truth about themselves. This was scarcely true: men do not look for truth in women, nor in a pack of cards, unless they are dramatic critics or makers of documentary films. This is what Torgano said.

No, really, Pierrina could not face him. The Director of Public Monuments was quite right: men like that always were. She walked close to the canal bank; a group of men, absorbed as goldminers, were playing some inscrutable game, squatting and shuffling, chasing pieces of bone and wooden jewels with their long arms. A man came up to her, after making many nervous ploys, pretending all the time to watch the animals and comedians in the boats as if they were relations.

Pierrina thought, 'He is going to be offensive,' but at last he merely remarked, 'What perverted imaginations we must have.'

Coldly, she replied, 'I think it all rather delightful, but I admire gothic grotesques. Are you a part of the carnival?'

The man lied, 'I trust you do not think me ill-mannered, and no, I am not a carnival attraction: I am a sociologist. I wanted to study your reactions.'

'What a coincidence,' Pierrina said. 'I too am a sociologist. Yours must be the more interesting job, to study professionally the reactions of strange women.'

'Yes, I suppose so,' stammered the man.

He left her. Coolly she continued to look at the players, who were now throwing streamers of crepe paper over slow-eyed children, who screamed, and trampled them in the dust.

A woman peered at the girl, as if to decide if she were truly respectable. Then, 'That's right, girl, you wait and choose the one you want. Some would have gone with him, I might have done when I was young, but now you girls are so fastidious – but there, you must make your choice.

'But you should try to remember that a man likes a girl who can talk to him as an equal, wants her to have had men friends, both for his sake and hers. You must be sociable, you know, and talk to people. Especially at carnival time. I'm looking for my boy: he's a student, you know, does imports and exports, and capital cities. They'll make him a professor yet. I spent days sewing his costume, cementing the cracks and bruises in his head.'

'What is he, then?'

'That I can't say. He's one of those geographical animals, like, well, like exactly something you've never seen before. He said they're a mean bray, and immensely powerful hind legs: like an emu, and like a giraffe. Yes, he's a wicked boy, bless him. Hits me! Yes, I could show you the marks, he never helps his poor old mother, just swears and kicks at the wall, I could show you the marks … One day I'll show him, I'll hit back, and then he'll give me the affection he should,' and all the time she was holding on to Pierrina, craning to see her son, her true son beneath the false heads.

'You tragic old fool,' thought the girl, trying to free her arm. The woman was laughing at the antics of the animals as she poured out her classical paradoxes.

'And he doesn't care for his poor shambling old father; he takes up with these politics, and had them home, not doing anything, not drinking, just shuffling and giggling in the dark. I should know, I stay and wait for him to come upstairs: ages he is, in the dining room, just a murmured word now and then, and these politics taking his time and his money, that he should be giving to me. The year before it was art: a different lot they were, but laughed on the doorstep, and kicked the pile off my new carpet.

'But for all his faults, he's a dear good boy, but he never has anything to say to me, and you don't know how depressed it makes me feel. I know what it is, of course, it's all this culture and coddling. He's afraid to say what he wants and feels; it's not natural, carrying eagle banners for the Young Democrats, talking about sewage farms to those girls till two or three in the morning. Ah well, perhaps he'll be different when he's a professor.'

Pierrina wondered if this was how she had appeared to her mother, or to Torgano; she decided that this was unlikely, and continued the search for the brilliant philanderer in the bestial costume.

The woman's small daughter had stood mute and interested, uncomprehending and heedless as only those can be who knew everyone loves them. 'Perhaps I am more like her, this nascent schoolgirl,' thought Pierrina with interest.

'Do you enjoy your school?' she said.

'At four I leave a world of hygiene and incipient hysteria,' the girl replied scornfully, 'the stress of a society based on perverted romantic friendships between girls and mistresses. I leave the wearing sadness of a formal education: tears in deserted cloakrooms, the monotony of autumn, the pain of winter, the frustration of spring, and the boredom of summer. Don't you remember? The leaves, the concrete, the heroic games, the headaches? You must remember the headaches? And the books, the library, the pain you had when you laughed silently for too long? And returning home in the trains with men who would have the evening free to love and drink themselves to sleep, when you had hours of work to do?

'You surely can't have forgotten all this, the work, the unhappiness, the incompetence of staff and parents, the empty hilarity, the examinations? If you have forgotten all this, you must have absorbed the rare toxins they slipped in your chilled milk, or been battered by the foul innuendoes and exhortations which they loaded into every abstract, every conversation. And the holiday reading: the guilt when you did no work, the boredom when you did, did you enjoy all this? Every friendship and ideal warped and eventually destroyed by the pressures of a quarrelsome unprincipled society. And you ask, do I enjoy it!'

She obviously goes to the wrong sort of school, thought Pierrina, it is exactly like mine. To have had sufficient formal education to be able to distrust it, and to have heard the biased interpretation of enough books to be able to ignore reading completely. To be taught that there are intrinsic qualities, moral superiorities in forms of government, yes, now I remember why I hated my teachers. In the ideal school, we would have classes in Pareto.

The girl's mother said, 'There now, that's her civics, I expect, or her domestic conscience. I don't understand all the rubbish they teach her. She's a good girl, but she'll go just like her brother. You can't know my life: my husband, he coughs blood, and he can't, you understand, control himself as he should. Just lies in bed all day, cutting up the newspapers and pasting them in books. My eyes are red with weeping when I go to bed, and swollen with wakefulness when I get up.

'All the tragic lyricism of an idealised motherhood is mine: my son is dead because he is dead to me. My daughter is another woman, I begin to fear that she will enslave my husband. I work all day, and in the evening, I prepare unexpected dishes from unusual foods for an unheeding family. I never asked for a return but I did not expect hostility. I find cherry pie, which I used to eat with enjoyment, now gives me indigestion. Ah God, what is to become of me?'

Pierrina said she could not guess: perhaps a fortnight at a music festival, or trampling grapes with groups of mother-loving students? The woman smiled: it really was pointless trying to explain anything these days. Pierrina left the woman and her daughter; how many times had the boats been round? Weapons of pressed cardboard, showy formations, the mock soldiers were so small beside the mock animals.

'Which are the Derivatives and which the Residues?' Pierrina said half aloud, and then was ashamed in case anyone had heard as she had intended them to. Pareto and carnival went too well together to provide the tingling discomfort of inspired analogies.

She thought of the Director of Public Monuments. Would the people through him subsidise her palazzo? Ah, but one could feel respect for a man like that, masterful and despicable, so unlike the humanitarian circumlocutions of her father were his probing theses. The country would be all right as long as fanatics like that were in high positions.

The afternoon entered its period of expansive decadence: the cider stalls were protected by a haze of wasps; they crawled over the warm, sweet counters, caressing the sticky patches with their slender black arms. Against the tall wastepaper baskets lay the cider drinkers: arms crossed, alcoholic beards thrusting through the wet skin, they slept. They were drenched in the liquor, but the wasps let them alone; they looked like men who had danced all day before vigorous gods. The owners of the stalls which sold sausages in rolls sneered at them; little boys eating the rolls were stung by the insects, but still tore savagely at the bread through their tears.

Cohorts of girls linked arms and rushed forward, brushing aside those in their way, lone debauched soldiers, couples of all ages, fashionable little girls carrying monstrous poodles. The fierce detachments shouted and dared; the crowd was breaking up, they were breaking up the crowd, such was their formula. Policemen at first stood aside and laughed. When it was too late, they made speeches, struck attitudes but could not use their batons. This proud, nubile elite seemed to be making some protest, some last ineffectual demonstration against the world of tiny weak men they were destined to console. Youths timidly watched.

Torgano wondered why it should take a week for Pierrina to decide about his shop; then he remembered that she did not like him, and he sat down and threw stones at a tree. He was alone, he played an imaginary trombone in a jazz band; he lurched and shuffled; he showed every morsel of his artistry in his dumb posturings. On this mound of sand he could do anything, could forget Pierrina.

From far below came rapid choked cries, as from a trapped rodent; journalists were formulating their tired visual images; that was all reporters were good for, describing what they had seen in the cinema a hundred times.

His silent music came to an end; idly, Torgano wondered who Pierrina would choose to dictate the future of the shop; she was as likely to follow the advice of a court usher with red-striped trousers and a machine gun as a noble accountant with an imitation bayonet for a letter-opener. Walking in tight circles, talking to himself about the absurd precautions taken to give the impression that advice is taken and thought given when making decisions, the dealer eventually saw that someone was watching him.

'I'm sorry, I thought I was alone,' he reassured her, but she did not look reassured. She looked unnaturally clean, as do all girls of her age, as if they have inhaled deeply from a rose, and must walk and talk carefully in case they lose the precious perfume. She was dressed with no regard for her anatomy, but did not appear to be aware of the acute pain she must be causing herself.

'Must I convince her I am not mad,' he thought, 'or does she think I am drunk? I must proceed with exaggerated care.'

'I was just thinking to myself, pacing about as I would at home, you understand,' he said aloud to her. 'My bedroom is about the size of the clearing between these two uncompromising pines.'

She was not convinced – she had seen too much.

'And of course, I am a professional trombone player,' he lied.

Happily, she said, 'I knew it must be something like that.'

Now she will ask me to take her out, thought Torgano. How tiresome!

'Aren't you the antique dealer by the, er, the railway station?' he said. 'I have often admired your exquisite head through that gateleg table, your mean eyes trying to pierce the gloom.'

A high unfeeling laugh.

Torgano said, 'Yes, I knew I remembered you, I thought. How strange! I was escaping from the carnival.'

Surprised, the girl said, 'Would you like a walk?'

Torgano hid a smile in which resignation fought anticipation. I knew she would ask that, he thought. Guiltily, he trotted by her side: a thin gauze of suggestive black shapes was pulled smoothly up, over the sun which acknowledged the loud regrets of its admirers with a few sweeping bows. Torgano frowned at this exhibition of bad taste.

They reached the top: there is the sea! Barren, old and unlovely, its dangerous embraces slyly drew in the litter and lost property of the tourists on the beaches. Cold and miserly, the water hurried about its eternal, petty business of scavenging and washing. Incurious fish wandered through featureless countryside, nosing aside fern forests, their flat eyes gazing ahead through an opaque mixture of sand and water.

Torgano and the girl evaluated one another beside the careless beauties of nature.

'Hair, Roman; nose, indistinct; jaw, amenable; eyes, brutish, unsatisfactory; mouth, delightfully weak. What a fortunate child I am!' The girl gazed frankly and with all the irritating conceit of girlish experience at the dealer, who looked like an unsuccessful attempt to create an entirely new type of handsome man. His features had, she decided, the look of a rough sketch of a head in clay. And perhaps the clay was too wet, and was slipping under its own weight from the careful wrappings.

Torgano squinted towards her: for one who had chosen him, she was not too unpleasant. When he was six, he had been kissed by the most repulsive and kind-hearted girl in the town, just as his father was finishing winding a grandfather clock. Neither he nor his father had recovered from the shock: his father had believed Torgano to be the worst immoralist that could exist. One who might let the valuable clocks run down, one who might forget to endorse cheques, or forget to drown the correct number of kittens or puppies from a litter. He might grow up to be a disorderly liver, tactless, unpredictable.

Torgano had found since then that those who befriended him were usually indiscreet and certainly given to excuses of a more or less inexcusable variety; that was why Pierrina had so impressed him. He thought: the strain of loving Pierrina had conditioned him to act haltingly, perhaps to suffer from illogical behaviour. A strain lasts so long, then it becomes a temptation. The executioner dreams of suicide, the lover of coarse, unlovely liaisons. Most reprehensible and refreshing, thought Torgano.

The sea and sun went about their business: Pierrina sat in the palazzo, writing to a young relation. The ideal letter writer, she called herself:

Yesterday in the municipal park, I saw children riding high above the trees on inflated rubber horses: three, four, five colours I saw, little nebulous men with whips driving them on. I do not think you would like to ride on one of them, for you are not very strong, or very brave, are you? There were edible dogs as well, all flavours, just like your own Carco, they were. People just picked them up and ate them, idly and with evident enjoyment.

I saw a little girl hitting a tiny boy-child; you must never do this, for little boys cannot hit back, or if they do, they get many friends along to watch them and good girls never show off, as you know.

Would you like one day to come to the picture gallery, to look at the unfortunate men with their entrails blown out? I am sure if you wish very hard, some benevolent fairy will help you, though not for the next week or so, I'm afraid.

Respectful greetings to your parents,

Pierrina

The child's mother was to intercept this, sensible woman, but it would have had no great effect on the child either way. Meanwhile, Torgano walked with the girl, stopped, and walked on again.

'You know,' he said, 'I can convince myself that it is immoral to eat soup, for example. The capacity of the mind for self-delusion and self-condemnation is very great. I remember seeing schoolboys come out of telephone boxes weeping for some wistful adolescent pleasure. And I thought, why do we torment ourselves, why do we fabricate these childish tortures and tests of endurance? Because of the elusive absolute? Because we say to the god who runs his fingers up our spines at insufferably sentimental concerts, "I am very bad, I suppose. Will you be satisfied if I undertake so many years following the social myth, the intellectual heresy, or the sexual schism?"'

The girl thought, 'You can always depend on a man to give a new eccentricity to natural functions. Lovers are a good idea, but unfortunately immune to the laws of natural selection. I too am quite intelligent, but I do not enjoy discussing ethics when the sun has gone down. Soon, he will tell me he is in love; fortunately, I have a sense of humour, and will not be rude. Then he will notice that the pure eye of the sun has closed in an hygienically lecherous wink, and all at once he will become disgustingly human.'

Torgano decided that the girl looked too knowing; he thought of the lovers who fought outside his shop at night, the men giving little excited belches to show their unspoiled sincerity. And he would smile the irony of the omnipotent insomniac, as they switched off the street-lights.

'Life,' he sighed, 'has not much to commend it.'

Impatient girl, watches the moon swim up: shabby light clots in the trees like bacon fat. 'Prose poets never really look at the moon, you know.'

'Really?' said Torgano in an ecstasy of politeness. 'They must be in bed, I suppose.'

Then he turned, and walked towards the town; a band was playing; angry youths threw cardboard bombs at one another; at that distance the noise of the explosions was lost. The girl followed him; she could only hope now for a later meeting, she almost admired Torgano for his cowardice. He was lonely, but he was also lazy; the decision made, they became friends.

'Wednesday?' asked Torgano.

'The clock tower, yes, of course,' the girl waved away, the lacquered lips gay, deceitful, the skin heavy, carefully preserved, the eyes obsessed and contented.

Torgano regretted everything; the meeting, the parting; he stood and watched the tide isolating and swallowing small piles of offal in the harbour. There was no one in the streets, except the revolutionaries and their fireworks. Sad, but it was so sad: the cafés, smelling of kerosene and sawdust; shops full of dirty engines; gaunt cats prowling in barrels of cereals. A group of lost tourists? No, it was only a congregation of shadows, happy, nodding, well-fed. Torgano imagined them as tall, solid cylinders; he would have rushed kicking and screaming on the shadows, toppling them, trampling their smug conspiracy. Instead, he sneered at himself.

Pierrina imagined parties, intimate gatherings, where several hundred people might gather to look at her dowdy clothes, and compliment her on her interesting French accent. Torgano would not be there; he always talked to her and other people – it was most unsatisfactory. There would be dancing, and quite a new kind of alcohol, without odour, and she would be seized by wicked men who would pierce her feet as they danced with needle-sharp hooves. Intricate social ciphers: really, they were interesting. The opportunities for being humiliated so many. The authors told to revise works which were definitive versions of all emotions and situations: the turbulent genius whose academic wickednesses were taken for confused thinking.

To hear their stories – unhappy people are so wonderful at parties – this was the function of women. The publishers drawn to the ballroom in carts of red wood by enormous dogs. Actresses with pumas, entertainers soaked in the filthy white wine which smells like superior perfume. And these men of power, at three in the morning being hit in the face with obsessive regularity by their rivals. This was the life she craved, the life Torgano could not share. Those who mattered, the unhappy, the rich, the precarious, offensive and bleeding as they lurched onto boats at dawn; this was the empire of a woman. The palazzo once more in history, like an ambitious child Pierrina saw cardinals and courtesan poets preening themselves on the balconies.

Outside it was dark enough to make her feel lonely: she dined. She broke open the beautiful eyes of two eggs. Tender mushrooms, agile and shy in the fields, the secret sweetness of young animals, those she prepared. Shrivelled, black and solid, she cooked them, and pronounced them delicious. An evening before her; outside, policemen danced in their handsome jackboots to the accomplished timekeeping of the café girls. The police motor-cycles lay like a tangle of thin limbs on the pavement. Pierrina felt sad, as did Torgano. Cats flickered over the streets, grey against the grey pavements.

Torgano knew he would not meet the other girl. Pierrina felt suddenly that it would make her most unhappy to see Torgano with another woman, perhaps slipping carelessly down the river in some grimy stolen barge. She shut the window; her dreams of society dispelled, she filled glass globes with small yellow fires. It was gloomy in the palazzo: onion skin wallpapers shone with musty purple; mahogany negro statues glowed like split plums. The brown juice and the discoloured, old flesh seemed to collect in corners and behind chairs. Shabby gilt peered from the shadows; oak and marble were opulently discreet.

Torgano visualised his antique shop in the palazzo, and the delightful feminine comforts to which Pierrina would treat him. Little dishes of herbs, penetrating tisanes when he was ill, sly embraces when he made himself pleasant. Anything, but not this chilly loneliness which drove him to prowl the streets like a sick scavenger. Always he felt nauseated and tired. The disgust he had felt on being told by an adviser reading an article of his, 'Yes, that should impress people,' now struck him each time he went into the public squares and gardens.

The lovesick wistfulness with which he greedily watched the careless lovers made him curse and stagger in the streets. There were many like him, it is pathetic and incurable. To call on Pierrina would be as useful a cure for loneliness as studying the fine features of a corpse; unless Pierrina agreed to accept him, to visit her would merely be a symptom of his unhappiness, possibly a symptom which had to be cured before recovery could begin.

He knew very little of the myth to which he longed to devote his life; he hoped the evening would soon start to move towards its unusually banal anti-climax. Tomorrow would be such another joyless day, enlivened perhaps by the municipal personae, or a journey to the factories which produced antique furniture – but legally, under government licence. It began to rain, a fine drizzle like a spray of paint, or exquisite lacquers on the scarred trees.

The Director of Public Monuments sat in his office, the one bright cell in a dead hive: reports came in detailing damage to national shrines. It seemed that a child had desecrated every chair in the fire station: the Palace of the Tenth of September had olive stones trodden into the soft wood floors: window boxes had been toppled or stolen. A guide had been burned on the neck with a cigarette; there were sandwiches of garlic sausage in every urn and vase; there were bottles in the escritoires.

'Quite like old times,' said the Director grimly. 'That is why we had to remove the owners in the first place. I suppose we should not have opened the public monuments on a day when so many people would want to come and see them.'

The young children who worked for him would be full of indignation when they learned of this vandalism.

Then, 'Palazzo Tarrault', he read. 'Built by a schizophrenic who disapproved of architecture because he despised the functional: thus says Professor Zigeuner. Thirteenth century reconstructed in the eighteenth, when some of the oubliettes were removed. A staircase made of bricks, in the shape of loaves, commemorates the present owner's grandfather, who was a railway contractor. There are some conventional animals on the roof, the linen cupboard has a frieze of goat women. There are colonnades of finger-thin pillars made of dirty jade. The door handles are inlaid with the unusually vicious fingernails of Serbian prisoners.

'In 1787 Szivacs Tarrault, sheep expert, was born here; in 1848 the committee of students discussed revolution next door, but on attacking the professors of the legal faculty who had taken refuge in the Palazzo Tarrault, they were apprehended. They were put in an open boat, towed out to sea till they should apologise. Some of them died, so the professors of the legal faculty were denied the opportunity of defending them, an opportunity they had demanded with suspicious enthusiasm. Nothing much is known of the present owner, except that she came to see you today.'

The Director was displeased with this report: it gave him little reason for dispossessing Pierrina. Without emotion, he learnt that a man named Salo had cut off a finger in the art gallery to prove his patriotism: 'We Latins are too deranged to be really excitable,' he said.

To write reports was what the university claimed to teach; this last stronghold of Platonic fascism, its dynamic intellectual elite, self-styled, was monstrous and moribund. Preaching petty scholarship, it had achieved a petty conformity. The Director despised the futile pretension with which professors chased a butterfly truth.

'So, old and impotent they've become, how quickly are the gifts of the young snatched away by formal exercises. And now, they cannot even write a report – disgusting! The Palazzo Tarrault is an interesting architectural fantasy. My poor little university girls and boys look as if they need a fantasy to fill the great empty intelligent pools of their eyes.'

The Director remembered his time as a student: disillusion, boredom, the arguments he did not want. Perhaps, his teachers would say, we all find these exercises dull: but they should incorporate all the latest research. And so, four years of study, and you became out of date. Then again, they would say that if you did not like what you had to read, you were perhaps idle – even possibly were you mentally ill, were you conceited, pretentious, or insincere? Certainly you could not just be bored: 'Sleep is also a form of criticism', but with that exalted criticism, professors are not disposed even to argue.

But when the academic deceits are far behind, you find men still unable to concoct an elementary, schoolboy piece of chicanery. Obviously, the system was not even successful in teaching these infants the elements of immorality. Angrily the Director turned out the light, and looked out of the window. He knew his head would appear monstrous and noble in the darkened room. Below, there would be someone, some tired bankrupt, or a thief to admire the shadow of that wonderful head, heavy and splendid as a ball of polished blood.

In the square, the Director saw the impedimenta of municipal efficiency. The umbrella frames which bore his electricity, the child's bins for sand and water, the traffic lights with their unheeded harlot's eyes. A few late pigeons were kicking through the gutter paper – or could they be tiny, bent, scavenging men?

The Director shuddered: so small, so silent, so far beyond love and reason. In the shadows, were those men? The cardboard facades of the shops opposite, exquisite angry men in the shadows: it was like a jazz ballet. A car passed amusedly through a red light; the Director heard the drunken twitters float slowly through the glass. In the square, embarrassed policemen slid into doorways beside genteel destitutes. Street lamps dropped their light round their feet: it spread and pooled like ripples in water. The pavements were moist and cold; the stars still shone ... rain?

Anything could happen at night: the Director thought of legends of night fliers which had persisted up to a few years ago. Obviously, men could never really accept that for half the time. they could not see where they were without artificial means. They must think there is something they must not see when it is dark: probably there is, mused the Director. Below, the police strutted in their capes, like toadstools they struck attitudes: drunken men on bicycles carefully protected themselves, as if they were made of china, as they steered erratically through the square.

The Director thought of the women he had known, who had demanded everything, until he had known they would only be satisfied with his life: how often he had given them his life. Now politics were more concerned with a life and death than ever love had been. And when you were used to surrendering to a woman, you could never really resent capitulation before another set of myths, religious or political. The Director no longer thought of happiness: happiness was to be not unhappy, it was all one could expect. He switched on the light, and thought of the Palazzo Tarrault.

The Director talked too much to be able to like people: everyone was silent, or tried constantly to interrupt. Pierrina had seemed quite neat and comprehensive in an unattractive way; she had been the sort he had expected: intelligent in the odd, incomplete way of people who had been to schools and universities he had not heard of. She could not really be considered as a compact problem for which there was a patriotic or legal solution. She was yet another dull woman, who might

be made to scream gently and inoffensively by what the
Director called 'departmental pressure'.

He almost enjoyed dispossessing these women in an
offhand, cursory way; it was so much more meaningful and
bitter to steal with a sneer than a frown or a threat.
Departmental pressure: that was the mixture of planned
inefficiency and official competence that was calculated to
unnerve the least perceptive aristocrat. The Director smiled
wearily as he thought of the shabby comedy to be played out at
the palazzo.

He left the office: all night, reports of damaged traditions
would come in, but then, that too was a tradition. Three hundred
years, the lipstick inscriptions under glass, the idle knife scores
labelled sabre cuts, damage had become history. The Director
thought he would like to write a book on the great vandals, to
whom we owe so much of what we see. His tired brain flogged
itself forward: look, there were cats in those bushes: their eyes
like the petals of green flowers, malevolent, busy. He
remembered the stories of medieval churchyard dancers,
condemned to dance until they rotted. Cats at night, they were
like that: obsessed and violent, yet mechanical and afraid.

Once he would have told all this to his psychiatrist – that
was when there had been women … Now, when he was
unhappy he elevated his misery into bureaucratic sadism. His
psychiatrist had been a delightful lunatic who loved each
fantasy as if it had been a crippled child. They had helped one
another: the neurotic telling the lover that nothing really
mattered. The Director remembered the consulting room, it was
a midnight room, used to dreams, the gentle pattern-making of
inflamed minds. The psychiatrist had made tea, sharp, varnished
tea it was, with synthetic lemon juice. And his wife would come
in to listen to the Director's exotic oriental stories of the
attraction of suffering, the need to live in ruins like marble
teeth, and yet to pretend that a word could re-create the
incinerated princesses, the mahogany kings.

And the psychiatrist would look at his wife as if to say,

'Please go, I can only consider one patient at a time. Drink your tea, and go and play with the familiar animals in the jungle in the kitchen, and later, I will come and talk to you, and there will be love in my mad eyes, and all will be well.'

And the Director would regret that he himself was weak, rather than deranged; and he would see the street lamps awakening, opening their weak, cheap eyes; he went out, and the other man would sigh; how well the Director remembered that sigh. Full of antiseptic despair, the sigh of the incurable. Now, it was so much easier to please a world than a woman; the Director clenched his face into a sad smile. His house would be lonely and preoccupied; in the morning he would have to persecute Pierrina Tarrault, and men would call him vindictive. It had long ceased to matter that he no longer had to argue with his accusers: little enough had changed.

Torgano awoke: in the distance he could hear the glissandi of shunting trucks. In the streets two boring men were walking away from one another, shouting the last formalities of a forgotten conversation. When his companion had gone, one of them stood under Torgano's window and breathed as if his whole body was a perished lung, as if he were full of air like a leather sack.

He must be drunk, Torgano thought, or tired, even if he is ill, he will be offensive, certainly demanding.

Soon the man walked off briskly, as if nothing had happened. And Torgano felt himself slipping towards another joyless argument with Pierrina; those midnight dialogues were unsettling, they seemed always reasonable and sane, until in the morning, he would remember how unlikely it was that Pierrina would ever wake up to think about him. In the morning, he would remember that Pierrina was not to see him for a week, that his shop was at the mercy of her irrational rationality, that by the clock tower on Wednesday he would join the lovers who always met at this meaningful landmark.

But now, here was a sharp, imaginary Pierrina, to explain what she meant by her waking evasions: Torgano asked, 'How

can you doubt our tradition, one which any schoolboy will trace
to the twelfth century? Is it not established that the concept of
selfish love, as you call it, is a delightful and practical aim?
Surely the combination into one desire, of two complementary
wills has a certain precision, an attraction not merely
geometric?

'Yet you question my principles when I ask you to have no
friends but me, you despise the jealousy which would once have
led me to kill the most fantastic dragons. You know I am not a
Christian, that rather than trying to making myself into a god I
would worship you. Yet you refuse to let me: be sensible, you
say, be self-sufficient. Where will all this lead? Yours is a
perverted attitude, a decadent confection, in which, because you
have defined the correct attitude, there is no room for expansion
or tolerance. At least my definition was a wide and antisocial
one. Yours is social, it considers the reaction of people who do
not care anyway.'

'Whatever you say of your emotionalism,' Pierrina replied,
'however strongly you oppose me, my tradition is bound to
defeat you. I have so many more telling accusations to make, I
support a painless pride, the pride which denies emotion the
chance of dramatising itself. Mine is an hygienic affection: I
wear you and your influence as I would an expensive but rank
perfume. You wish to be worn like a knee-length veil made of
sequins. Whatever I feel, it is not right that you should know: it
is not fitting that you should trespass on my personal liberties,
with talk of faith and eternity. Only a primitive man would wish
such a world of flint and shattered bones. You must make use of
all the amenities of your tedious life: to be involved in to be
childish.

'When you were young, you wanted people around you,
you wanted to discuss things like heaven, and magic, and
beautiful snow women. But now, you must be mature: you are
too old to come to rely on other people: not until you are senile
will you again bore women with your frustrations. Have you not
seen the grandfather lacemakers, in the Eastern province, they

sit in the sun which strains through the lace umbrellas of huge weeds. They need, and profess to be ready to give, all the things you talk of: protection, comfort, secrets of eternity, complete isolation. They sit before their lonely hovels, and offer these things to the girls who go by.

'And the girls are slick and scornful as little ornamental glass lizards, and they flicker past, and the old men gape after them, with their ugly, empty mouths. And perhaps their eyes no longer fit well in the sockets, and as they stare stupidly, an ancient hoarded tear may drop unnoticed onto the lace. And so they go on, until the winter comes, and the girls go about their work by another route, and the lacemakers move slowly, like winter flies waiting to be killed. And then they die, or fall and smash themselves, and the police came, and all is sordid and pointless.'

Torgano knew the arguments well: he always liked to say that Pierrina could not really mean what she said, could not be happy in her tradition. But he had no reason for saying this, and he himself got little comfort from his projected despotism. There was little to please him either, in that there were many obvious remedies for their deadlock. Torgano would say to himself that when you were about to gas yourself, you did not welcome gentle advisers who recommended, or even urged, that you should instead shoot or poison yourself. The clocks struck; soon too it would be Wednesday, and there would be that demanding girl to avoid or scare off. And there would be, before that, all Tuesday to fill with unhappy expedients, or irrational commitments: every day, there seemed to be less reason for getting up in the mornings. Torgano slept.

In the Palazzo Tarrault, expensive Florentine-looking dogs yawned and snickered at inscrutable animal witticisms. Pierrina lay sleeping: outside, the watery laplets smacked their lips against the palazzo's foundations. The empty fruit boats were moving down towards the sea. Now they were full of crepe beards, shattered carnival heads, streamers and exhausted noisemakers: the cheap toys could be sold, the paper too as salvage. The boatmen were tired and ill; the envied the tourists their sweaty beds. Grotesquely distorted and arched, they punted, stiff as scythes, with their rubbish trailing behind them.

That day they had been cider-drinkers; they had charmed all with their witty lechery. But now they felt old and dissipated. Their symptoms were disquieting and unusual; they did not talk to one another, lost in morbid speculations. They passed beneath the mottoes of proud families, whose sprawling, and often unforeseen litters had governed the country until so recently. The boatmen were neither impressed nor encouraged by the stone exhortations, on which pranced all manner of freaks and hybrids. On the Palazzo Tarrault was the motto of the cynic and speculator 'Wait and die'. Opposite, 'Repentance is hypocrisy', to the right 'God will preserve the fugitive', that was a professional renegade, and on the left, 'He destroyed their vines with hailstones', that was the admonition of a belated teetotaller.

The girl with whom Torgano was to talk on Wednesday looked from her window. She could see the lights of the café opposite; dimly they shone through the wet glass, on which even then, uncertain fingers were writing syllables and scraps of conversation. She knew that soon women would spill through the door, fighting and laughing. And their competent mates would follow them, pulling on their flashing gauntlets, fastening their crash helmets like elephant skulls. Then they would all climb on their exotic motor cycles: pure-bred beasts they were, fierce and lunging, probably they ran on cherry brandy.

The men and women on the machines looked like bright double-centaurs: the engines argued and asserted in swift alcoholic dialogue. The café closed – a neon sign advertised that that was indeed so. The girl was sad: the street sank back into its daytime images, obscure telegraph poles, breweries, a post office. She drew the curtain and looked round her room: the pictures, sentimental. *Spring beneath the Sea*, a still life of a flock of opal sheep and a suit of armour for a ram, *The Line*

Returns Returns Returns Tentatively, and a doom-stricken *The Islands Are Returning.*

With increasing distaste she looked at her books: *Splinter in Weimar, Mockesz, The Pits of Paradise, The Harp Factory* – so trite and obvious. She was less annoyed by the orderly confusion of her scores – Wellesz, Blacher, Bentzon, Jolivet, Petrassi – but the pictures! She had seen the day before a pleasant lithograph in which eviscerated stars had staggered and died throughout the sky: very moving. Or there was the picture of that aqueduct full of limbs and curious iron implements.

The girl sighed: it was difficult to afford to keep up with things even though there was no longer the problem of changing ethics to be fashionable. Not that she minded about fashion, being too ignorant and well-educated to see the advantage of such sensitivity. But she did sometimes read a book, so that the bored poets who talked to her did not feel completely disgusting when they were condescending to her. She was seen as nearly talented, though she did not actually do anything: she was promising. She looked permanently disgruntled and dissatisfied, as if she knew she was too beautiful to mix with men who were constantly looking for attractive girls and images to deflower in their novels and poems.

'Life,' she mused, as she felt the sickly attraction of the specious once more exerting itself. 'Life is being bitter, and hearing your friends scream and shudder away from you because you are a brilliant bore. It would take a century to tell anyone your bitterness, but who cares, it is like describing the sensation of breathing to an old man; everyone has worked do long at it, they have no more interest. I do not mean very much when I say that I am not bitter: when men have known me for a day they call me sweet; a week, they say "bitter-sweet delicacy".

'And then another week, and I am myself bitter. Self-pity is all we have left; that alone is not frightened, that relies on no one, no circumstance. If we truly pity ourselves, we may at last stop looking for others to comfort us. Yet I suppose I am very silly: sympathy is a myth, but we must follow the myth, if only to ensure for ourselves a heroic life, death with our unsatisfactory children snivelling and deceiving at our bedside. I do not want a child: I would have nothing to tell it.'

She frowned at herself, could not make the effort to question her remarks. At least, she thought, Torgano is so bitter that he has passed through bitterness to inspiration. The fine ellipsis in his mind, a little web of taut string like a cradle – this had grown and been shaped with the malignancy of a bitter masochism. It was intriguing. The girl was happy that there was a new man to be considered; it was the least exacting of hobbies.

Chapter 2

THE NEXT MORNING, straggling storm clouds swung over the capital: long streamers of rain dragged behind the heavy cloud-canopy. At first you could see the sickly yellow of a storm sky behind the storm, but soon the convoluted masses obscured the false dawn. The rain seemed an element different from the water into which it pricked, with eager, irritated pen strokes. Around the motor vessels a layer of oil like mica slowly drifted, and lost its beauty. Workmen were removing wet paper which had clung to the lampposts: silently they emptied bins of refuse into complex lorries. Passers-by fancied they could hear exclamations of disgust, guiltily, they remembered the excesses of the day before: they might have gone up to the grim scavengers and apologised for their untidiness.

The Director of Public Monuments was addressing a small action group: powerful, stark, the campaign Tarrault was his world. He thought, even failures are interested in failures; almost blushing, he asked himself why he thought himself a failure. And was forced to admit that to do so was a convention, a titillating pretence. True, some things had been successful, but now, when he was in command, he knew that he had found what he could succeed in. And that, in the last resort, was all that could be expected.

'The palazzo can most easily be approached by water: a boat—'

'Is provided, Director.'

'The lane at the back ...'

'Yes, Director?'

'God and man! Police, roadsweepers, beggars, comic officials with the wrong forms – surely you go to the cinema! Anyway to accomplish everything in one day, to prevent an idiotic appeal, with its enthusiasm and expense, against our dispossession of this misguided infant. Legally, we are in the right: she will be compensated, no warning is required. We must prevent the attacks of decrepit retainers who have become purblind with unthinking loyalty. We must take over the building intact: we must prevent damage, theft, violence: we agree that to do so warrants an amount of deception?'

The men, tourists would call them honest men, looked thoughtful: it was always flattering to pause before agreeing with leaders. The leaders themselves believed it showed loyalty. Slowly, they agreed: they scratched their long elegant noses; they tapped their cigarettes on the Director's desk, and swept the loose tobacco onto the floor. They did not think of anything.

'You have done all this often enough: publicity, the time it takes for a reporter to get anywhere, that is so dangerous. Which of you, being a reporter, would not write a story if you had claimed travelling expenses from me? You would write a story to justify your extravagance, no doubt. If you have a liqueur, you write a good story, I will have paid for it, you reason. That is what we must prevent. The chance to let men from newspapers sit and drink all the morning while some lackey threatens the department's officers with an archaic weapon, that must be avoided. Take over the building, make an inventory, let the owner pack up and go. What questions can you have?' Knowing that the answer would be: 'None, Director,' the men and their leader felt that they were entitled to another exciting pause.

Eventually the party moved off; grumbling with anticipation, they jostled and chattered in the buses, like invaders they insulted passengers and bus-crew. The Director did not look at them: like a schoolmaster in charge of large, violent pupils, he did not acknowledge his wicked assistants. A number of them went aboard the boat: an elderly, feline man with a cutlass and a briefcase, the whipping white hair of a nineteenth-century French schoolmaster, started the engine. The rain cracked on the canvas awning of the boat: the Director pushed overboard paper hearts and horseshoes, left by some wedding party.

In the bows, two inscrutable inspectors were discussing women of the department in awed, vicious voices. They were huddled together beneath one umbrella, scraps of conversation were washed back to the others.

'... Told her she must not let her enthusiasm for Romanesque obscenity influence her policy on schoolgirls ...'

'... puts suggestive flowers on my desk. It's gone on too long for me to admit now I know what she wants. Besides, I should miss them ...'

'... tells me my own jokes a day after I tell them to her. I daren't not laugh, yet how embarrassing if I do!'

'... Told her that if she wanted to take baths during office hours, she must be careful not to be electrocuted.'

'... I didn't know they had a bath in the department.'

The Director smiled: obviously the communal life and difficulties of his subordinates made them a different class, even a different nation. He had often thought that the canteen inspired the same loyalties and warlike spirit as the communal meals of Crete and Sparta. In the water he could see tiny oil-soaked fish: if he could let them spill through his fingers, he felt the pollution would rub off, they would be naked once more, silver, gilt and flame. Beside him sat his assistant, an amateur cellist, to give expression to points in conversation; he would emphasise the shape of phrase or cadence with nods and absorbed grimaces.

It was a profound aesthetic experience to suffer this leering and bowing, to be avoided by those easily embarrassed. It was bad weather for cellos, it appeared, bad weather for everyone. The Director was tired of problems, palaces in the thick rain, shored and chained together like drooping cedars. He stared up at them: because they were nearly his, they were completely his. He had the joy of owning them, much more than their real owners could ever have: and what a cabinet for his collection. Propaganda and education, that came to his department too:

really, there could be no more successful and plangent position. The Director propped himself on his umbrella, greedy, nervous.

A dwarf with a correct cane and a florescent imperial, hoisted himself onto the seat. Swinging his miniature legs, he told everyone he could, about a literary party he had been to. How Czarnon had been there with his women, and talked of nothing but psittacosis. How Vilny had been carried in by two tender females, propped on a legendary sofa: he had whispered, 'Art, poetry, television, I utterly despise …' mute with ecstasy, he let women and little boys massage his right hand. Brodman had said he hated the Russians, and English editors had rushed to foster his hypochondria with contracts.

The talk was of Vedanta, the metaphysics of the hippocamp; everyone had been very rude; he himself was nearly trampled on by 'primitive mammoth women'. Did we know that Grosz wore a corset, Stimmer had his pipes frozen for three months last spring? No, the Director admitted, we did not. We too would have been frightened of being trampled on: we would have forgotten names and faces, as if everyone was a monarch on a coin. We would not have enjoyed seeing the worn books open, and miniature figures stagger out, like clumsily pressed flowers, introducing themselves as famous abstract men. Most disquieting, thought the Director: the Christmas party in the department was bad enough, with all the staff waiting for him to drop unconscious, or vomit on the floor.

The boatload neared the Palazzo Tarrault: it really was a magnificent specimen of nothing in particular. Its shape, so familiar: intricate yet impregnable as a glass paperweight. The Director wanted to have this palace, then to throw a dull party at which people would be forced to talk about the new palazzo, lonely, yet luxuriating, in the official black velvet setting. A party with no excuses, none of the ghastly lycanthropy which was supposed to be the sign of success: just dull people, famous bores, in the presence of this violated palazzo, whose confident ugliness would shame anyone present.

The boat was moving too fast: Torgano's poles, rotten and

waterlogged, snapped and wallowed, while the steersman played through them as if they were skittles. In a destructive arc the boat lashed round, the landing stage barely obeyed the suction of the anchoring mud. There were cries, the inspectors began writing, 'Six mooring poles, rotten, the landing stage, disturbed.' At last, the boat landed its passengers, went away, leaving the Director and his companions on a platform just large enough and stable enough to permit one short, unemotional speech by one small, stable orator.

The Director looked in a file to verify Torgano's name, and his business. 'Synthetic parasitology,' sneered the Director for no reason, to himself. He rang the bell: the town clock struck eight. He rang again, a deep-throated bell with a euphonium timbre and unconvincing attack, summoned a vegetable man. Wizened and ill-nourished, a tuber left for years in the ground, forgotten by the forces of nature, the man made the usual sounds of noncommittal welcome.

'Please call your mistress,' the Director said. 'We have come to take the palazzo for the nation. Any claim will be considered against its merits.'

The servant obviously had no claim: the nation had wanted the palazzo so often, he and his ancestors had long ago begun to regard rights as frivolous excuses to give men-at-arms time to string their bows. Pierrina came, expecting a suicidal Torgano: rising straight from sleep, she looked rather hideous in the storm light. The old woman was grinning and beckoning even now: behind the soft hands, the moist head, could be sensed a sleepy, masculine old hag. She asked the Director in, the inspectors sidled up, umbrellas were sheathed and cleaned, the invaders, as it were, took off their bulletproof waistcoats. At once, the dwarf was running about the great stone hall, prying into chests, even trying the wood of the doors with his knife. The Director smiled, paternal, tense:

'We have come to take over the palazzo, as part of the heritage for which I am personally responsible. You will be compensated, and of course, we shall not be opening the building to the public for a week, or even a fortnight. It seems that you cannot afford to maintain the building; we really must not allow commercial interest to control the exhibition of our history. I am sure you will agree. We hope you will not let slip the chance we are offering you, of releasing yourself from the burden of what is, after all, a national responsibility. We do not wish to delay: the parapets are unsafe; these eccentric crenellations must be protected. Madam, we beg you to cooperate with us: you need our help.'

'We may have surprised you,' the assistant said. 'We apologise, but we do want to help the palazzo. We will buy it, for a time you may live in it at our expense: with our permission, you may even remove certain articles of historical interest. A lithograph, a chair or two: and do remember that it is, and has been, the nation which suffers from your poverty.'

The Director, surprised, thought 'sadist'; but he went on: 'You see, we feel that for you to come and see us, enjoyable experience though it was for me, showed how anxious you were for the palace. We want you to know that we too are no less anxious for your property. The purchase order, Paslik: here, in any currency, certified by the government.'

Pierrina looked at the documents: like inflated banknotes they were: chaste women, bundles of vegetables, thunderbolts marked 'social security', 'health', 'peace', a few anonymous animals made into thrones. They were fine forms: Pierrina admired them: she almost thought they were as desirable as the palazzo itself. 'But lawyers, my friends, my stone animals ...' she began.

'I am so sorry: we thought we might take it that you would be more grateful than to appeal, especially as you did not seem to be able to afford it. We have, of course, additional powers, which we seldom use: but I'm afraid the government are anxious education and government should not be held up by the odd exploiter. So what with the threat from the lost colonies, this state of perpetual emergency must be encouraged by every means. Give up your home gracefully; we have so many palaces, we well know how to look after them. Your palazzo will feel at home with us.'

Pierrina was about to reply when five or six men came in from the rear of the palace: they were grinning, glad to be part of a joke they did not understand, but for which they were being paid. They carried spades, ornamented troughs, surveying toys. The Director said, mechanically and dully, 'There must be some mistake: perhaps the dates were mixed because of the carnival. These men were not to come until you had agreed to the purchase.'

The man paused, confused, even angry; they put down their mixing bowls, like children whose excursion to the beach is prevented by rain. Indeed, the men were noticing the rain they had previously ignored; the water ran from them and, as if it had been hot wax, seemed to congeal in the dust on the floor. They shuffled and grumbled, with large boots, they joined lakes and ponds of rainwater to make a vast blotchy sea.

The Director pretended to despise his brilliant helpers: 'Madam, if you will agree to these men carrying out some preliminary work, we would be most grateful: there must have been some mistake by someone.'

The assistant prepared to be a mock martyr for the Director, but Pierrina was too awed and depressed even to start having reactions. She agreed. The men rushed through the palace, shouting and tumbling, the Director said, 'You see, my men see beautiful things so seldom, they are as happy here as in some grove where there are known to be punctual nymphs, and resinous liqueurs born to them in long reeds.'

Leaving Pierrina, he went upstairs; opening a shy door, standing concealed behind an undistinguished clock, he came into a long room. At one end, a broken pipe gargled and spat on the leaden windows. The Director went to a desk where there stood a small typewriter; he saw in the machine: 'He puts on a gramophone record'; beside it, in pencil, 'Torgano and me'. Without even pausing to say, 'It is my duty to read this,' the Director read it:

```
This is called Mladi, youth
Really?
Yes (bitterly)
I don't think I like it.
I'm damn sure I don't.
If you weren't always trying to be clever and
bitter,
people would respect you.
Can I sleep with respect?
Have you ever read a good novel?
I don't quote the good ones, and I only live the
bad ones.
That's a bad principle.
Your bad doesn't mean anything to me.
All right, say goodbye like a swine, it doesn't
matter to me.
Nothing matters to anyone if we're going to say
goodbye.
Don't be so dramatic.
I'm sorry, a big dog once bit me.
I hope you do got to be a lousy success, then you
won't have anything to talk about.
Look, can't we patch this up, thunder-child?
Why, you feel ill, want a shoulder to die on?
If you leave me, I shall cry till they send for
you.
Don't cry, love: I really don't want to see you
again.
```

The Director wondered if women he had known constructed libellous and unlikely conversations with him. It seemed to him unfair of Pierrina to explode Torgano's imaginary epigrams before he had thought of them. Anyway, Torgano did not look quite so ignorant as that dialogue had made him appear to be. The Director felt protective, or superior, towards Pierrina; he felt the concern of a foreman felt for a fine pick buried again and again in yielding rock. Perhaps the girl would wear out her sharpness on this man who was as tiresome and strongly resilient as tungsten steel.

The Director looked from the window, like a solid pane of water, at the nondescript landscape, smeared and featureless. The water was coming more slowly now, the building opposite was still as blotched and primitive as a child's watercolour. Impatiently, the Director waited for the rain to stop, for his new view to define itself. On the roof, the workmen seemed to be playing football; the dwarf had nearly pulled a cabinet over himself; he had picked up a pretentious red cat and was stroking it angrily to relieve his feelings. The cat's eyes seemed about to be pulled out of its head by the fierce caresses, but it did not look round. The unconcern of the palazzo and the temper of the Director were soon tried by the animal's uncertain electric purr.

The inspectors moved about; making lists they talked lovingly of the obnoxious families they had fathered, and which they avoided as much as their lives would let them. The Director's assistant was still looking for somewhere to put his superior's umbrella. Pierrina wished it had not been raining when all this happened; she despised herself for having promised to consider Torgano's arrangement. With a cursory pat for all the alabaster scavengers which preyed, in unhappy stilted postures, on their careless, tiny alabaster victims on the staircase, Pierrina went upstairs.

'Would you advise me not to appeal,' she asked the Director, 'speaking as a friend?'

'I never want to speak as anything but a friend – I have my orders, unpleasant orders. I believe in them, of course, but I am your friend at the same time. You will gain nothing from an appeal: if the government offers more after an appeal, you will have found nowhere to live, briefly, you will have your lithograph, your chair or two, and nothing. You must not be bitter: as a woman, you have lost a place; as a citizen, you have gained one.'

Would Torgano help? He had lost her home for her; he would leap about, he would fight a workman, and be impaled on some fake specimen, or crunch into an oubliette, forty feet and those weak eyes still slightly surprised, and no skull solid behind them. Pierrina was disgusted by this thought: that was exactly what the Director did not want; how right he was.

'I shall have to see if the price is reasonable,' she said.

'Why, of course,' shouted the Director. 'Take as long as you like: take a couple of days if you like – no hurry. My men will be around, they won't disturb you, they won't work on all the rooms at any one time: you'll always have somewhere to sit.'

Pierrina thought, yes, she could put up with some discomfort: she would show Torgano she was not immature, she would suffer discomfort while forceful men and ideas stole her palace.

Torgano was eating fossil-like rolls, obscure, amoebic shapes: he was happy, he put the rolls in his coffee until the bread resembled fat, nicotined fingers. He thought of the girl he was to meet next day: he could be brilliant and gemlike if he tried, practice would do him good. Pierrina would appreciate a man made fresh and attentive by guilt. Deliberately and carefully, he thought of her. She was a habit, a habit like breathing: he had broken himself of it, no more pain, no more sensation. And he was still as far from throwing her back to the pool of clotted marble, as if she had been a princess fish of solid metal.

What would she be doing now? Half past eight: eating the rolls, brothers, comrades to his own: that was as near as you seemed to be able to get to people. Either you ate the same food, and laughed about it, and women thought you confident and loving, and never spoke to you. Or else you told them the truth: you told them about yourself, you hid nothing of your fears and love, and they shrank away in disgust, as if you were insisting on showing your football scars at the opening of a session of parliament. The problems to be solved before you even reached the problems of actual communication, that is, the communication between sympathetic intelligent individuals not just people you were trying to turn into individuals by friendly revelation, those problems were huge and destructive.

Life does not seem real at 8.30, when you have to go to a café for breakfast. Torgano smiled benevolently at his neighbours, still spiced with sleep: but no one ever asked him how was his business: this hurt him. Today, he would sell his entire stock: perhaps some extravagant Armenian American would press bundles of foreign notes on him, would cram the tables, the monumental vases, the pictures with the mud trees, the aristocratic shopkeepers subtle and piquant in the hideous frames, into his monstrous car. Surely someone would be impressed by his collection of ancestral ugliness. He sat and did not think: pigeons and waiters reminded him that they wanted to clear away the remains of his meal. He hugged his coat round his ears, against the rain, and ran awkwardly like a woman to his shop.

In the palaces, the sound of busy men was distinct: the ceilings bulged with dampness and plaster seascapes: the Director was angry that the rooms should still seem oppressive. Pierrina wandered about, to talk to the inspectors would be collaboration. The Director remembered: 'Of course, there is no garden, there are no flowers.' Perhaps Pierrina grumbled at the flowers till they shut their faces to her, thought the Director unjustly. He sat down and began to write: it came easily, his staff admired his facility.

'We took over the palace in the rain: there was no opposition. We shall continue to do the usual things at the usual intervals. Our workmen are breaking down the roof, preparatory to repairing it. We did not require the services of the police, who were detailed to come, if notified, armed and truculent, "believing", as I put it, "that violence was being done by Pierrina Tarrault to officers of this department". We shall stay here all the morning, partly because it has not stopped raining, because I am lazy and because I think Pierrina Tarrault must dislike me intensely, and I want to leave her no cause for changing that view.'

He knew his notes were handed round before cabinet meetings: after that, they admired him. They were like sensitive children, the ministers, who had kissed a play princess in the mirror, and felt the touch returned. When they read the Director's notes, they were reassured as if by someone who agreed with them that nothing could be real. They asked him riddles on national history, and he replied very seriously and sincerely: told them politely who was doing research on the period, and made them uncomfortable and humiliated. His friends saw him as dangerous and an omen corrupt and twisted as an entrail: at the thought of this, he laughed.

He strode about, as if he were some noble in skins, with blundered copies of imperial insignia around, barbarian flattery to a savage lord. He would have liked to call Pierrina, commanding her all manner of quaint things. Instead, he looked at the pictures: they were good forgeries, or perhaps they were originals. They were a part, their intrinsic beauty only figured in the price; they were not history. Let no one ask what was good art: if you were a historian you knew the answers to things like that. But you did not tell them to clumsy dwarfs, angrily muttered the Director, as the small man clambered over the wooden model horses which were proudly and timelessly displaying recherché horse armour. He had the palace, what did you do in these circumstances? You had a revenge, and then an amnesty: was Torgano his revenge, Pierrina his amnesty?

You had the trial here, in this room; you sat on this chair, you ordered that window to be opened, you told that workman to fetch the prisoner. You asked him, such and such: you played with him a little; you shouted at him, you tossed him, for his life or yours. And you won. And you asked that workman to tie a sack round his retching face, that workman to secure the twitching feet. The rope brought, you yourself pushed the hooded penitent off the balcony over there, and saw him strain the cord, till it snapped back like elastic. And, after three days,

days in which you slept in the next room, hearing at night at night the rope rubbing and groaning in the weight and the wind, you gave the order for the corpse to be cut down into the water, by that workman who was even now asking some pointless question.

'Yes, what now?' asked the Director.

'We have found two statues on the roof,' and, as the Director made to go up there, added reassuringly. 'I wouldn't go, if I were you – they are not very suitable, nor beautiful.'

And indeed, as the Director found, they were not. One was of a man being strangled from behind, by a pair of stone hands, whose nails were orientally diabolic, the fingers apparently frail and arthritic. The man knew he was being strangled, more than that could not be interpreted. But his hands were clenched by his sides, as if the pain were almost self-imposed, a spiritual masochism. The flesh of his neck was squeezed into great folds above the grip of the hands: he had bared his teeth in an effort to brace the muscles of his neck, his nose was splayed and arched with strength and fear. The eyes were understanding, the brow fantastically pitted and eroded with strain and concentration.

The other statue was of a man eating a rat. He was a reflective bourgeois, he had pulled the animal's limbs off, and gently held the soft body in one hand, while he swallowed the previous mouthful. He looked unconcerned; it seemed that he was used to this diet, he showed neither interest nor disgust. He was not old, a family man, respectable, you would say well-nourished. Then you looked closer at this imperturbable rodent-eater: you looked into his eyes and you saw that he had none. The stone had been carefully ruffled and furrowed to show the ridges of flesh where the eyes should have been. There was no further indication of the circumstances of this philosopher.

'Charming,' the Director said with fascinated speculation in his voice. 'Just the thing for the children.'

The workmen smiled nervously: they were not quite sure what he meant. They had seen for themselves the macabre intelligence which had inspired the sculptor; they recognised the inspiration and attraction of the subject. But they did not understand the minds which had put these statues on the roof. Nor yet those who had broken them off the masonry and covered them with rubble and sacks in an obscure corner.

'Take them away, and eventually we can put them in an exhibition.'

'Or in the cemetery,' muttered someone.

Work began again. Pierrina went through her cupboards; she too found things which were frightening and evocative. She was reminded of Christmas: by then probably Torgano would have said goodbye, wished her a good life. Now, she thought that would be for the best, but at Christmas she would miss him: the men still happy from the summer matings. The women holding bright catty parties, inviting all the wrong men. And Pierrina missing all the childhood humiliations, all the disappointments, missing Torgano.

There would be long dances in the shrubberies of suburban houses: men and women would couple in the streets; the churches would ring and resound as they did in cartoon films. Pierrina remembered how you had to shout at parties, how she wished there was a church service for agnostics, full of scientific sentiment. She recalled the deserted streets, just a few drunken cats loitering and embracing in doorways; snow falling into the water, Torgano even seeming happy for once, though not for long. The bands on the wireless, playing Respighi; the bands in the streets, musicians playing clarinets, zithers, trombones, playing carols, the Internationale, and no one objecting to either.

Where, anyway, would she be living at the end of the year? A minute lazy flat which had climbed very awkwardly to the top of some building, lain down in the sun and gone to sleep? It seemed the only responsibility: and, she thought gladly, I shall not have to think of Torgano, for we surely will not know one another then. It had stopped raining: a limited everything lay before her, and she was reasonably happy.

The Director felt old and stale: the palazzo was not exciting: he wanted the next one already. He had finished playing with Pierrina; he had opened the doll's house; he had found dream corpses there. He went to a café: he had to go past the backs of the palaces; there was no boat at the front. He walked along a mud path: had rats or humans thrown those punctured eggs carelessly under the bushes? What chaotic women had pulled their clothes to pieces in what strange orgies by the dustbins? The clothes had been delicate and cultured; were there thin, mute sexless bodies lying under the slit mattresses over there? Were those tins full of blood, or rust or ketchup? The Director hurried past: the day had been good; now it was becoming most unsatisfactory. He had two brandies with his coffee, and a cake.

Torgano sat sadly: the rain had brought out the tourists; it brought them to the shop but gave them no ideas of spending money. They came with their children: impeccably polite, in their blond wigs, long white stockings, and the usual children's uniforms; they gaped with guileless eyes and evil mouths, fingering and smashing with their long, supple fingers. Torgano tried to jump about expertly on the furniture, slap a few prying savages. But the furniture was unsure: fathers looked at him for a long time, as if he were a woman from their past, then silently led their children away from the shop. This did not please the owner.

Other women came in: they were not mothers, they were those whose employers or other male acquaintances could not be persuaded to take them on holiday. They were of course unmarried: they came with other families: they pretended to culture; culture was religious lithographs, china kittens called Verona, Salzburg and Prague. They spoiled the children, they spoiled the holiday; they came to Torgano: they thought, 'What an ugly young romantic man.' They pestered him: they never had the money to pay for things, though, as they explained, they were passionately interested.

They explained in dumb show that 'The customs, you understand?' and 'Alas, I never married,' but Torgano knew

they were really china kitten women. He politely directed them
to a shop where they sold real kittens: the women were too
charmed by the animals to be angry. Torgano sold nothing:
people would burst in, talking together; they would scuffle
through piles of worthless prints; then they would see Torgano,
sitting like a beggar beside them. Surprised and pitying, before
they went out, they would come near to pressing a coin or note
into his hand.

Torgano liked these best but still thought them scarcely
worth his time. He knew he could sell anything, if only people
wanted to buy: he had stock for the connoisseur. He had sets of
novels by all the best known dictators and revolutionaries: he
had walking sticks presented to nineteenth-century popes; he
had glass worlds full of anaemic flights of birds, birds of
washed pink and a distant kingfisher blue. Surely people would
want these antique marvels?

At the palace, the workmen were beginning to forget their
breakfast; they thought of marine foods, cheese confections in
rough porcelain crab shells. They imagined the insect lobsters,
strong, plated, guarding their strange flesh with careful claws.
Idly, the men gnawed sandwiches. they spat into the water;
motorboats full of challenging girls went past, the men waved
lazily. The inspectors came up to the roof: they were tired of
keeping up a flow of tired conversation with one another; they
prepared to be natural and pleasant.

All felt the time for lunch could be invoked now. Many of
the workmen could afford no lunch; still, it was a convention
that they should talk of it, and take time off for it. They enjoyed
working in palaces; it gave them a chance to see degraded
nobles, it amused them to arrange bricks in the form of slogans
and initials, only to be realised as such from the air. They
laughed sometimes to think that the Director was like them,
communist or socialist. But they were not quite sure why they
laughed, even as they did so. And on such days, those who had
lunches resolved not to eat them, out of sympathy with those
who had not, they attempted to produce material benefits with

their vehement, masonic gestures.

Pierrina had not breakfasted: she wondered if she should go to Torgano. It was awkward when the only person who might help her was the one she despised for her self-pity and infectious and irrational unhappiness. Torgano enjoyed his lunch, he always dithered before going to a restaurant: he would resent it if she came to tell him her palazzo had gone. Again, if she went to see him, he would assume she needed him: he could not divorce business from private unhappiness, and she could not write a note to say who was coming on business. She would have to let him know his antique shop could not be put in the palazzo, but later; besides, to watch Torgano pulling desolated faces while he ate the little animals cooked in those intriguing brown vases; no, that could not be endured.

She began to wonder if she could exist on the government's money: since the sixteenth century no Tarrault had lived in a flat – no legitimate Tarrault, that was. She imagined that the illegitimate Tarraults grew rich by confidence tricks in London; certainly even they would not live in a flat. It meant she would have to create, once more, a Tarrault empire. A challenge, a responsibility, a tiresome burden.

She wondered even if she should write a novel: she had heard of many who would say, 'I cannot stay up late. I am writing my novel' or 'When I want to write about my characters, I find they have gone for a walk, or are playing cards like idle stage-hands in some inaccessible part of my mind.'

But then, no one had decided what novels were: and bad novels did not pay. Politics? Her greengrocer was a new fascist: when she asked for minute phosphorescent foreign fruits, he scowled, and gnawed his fingers. She did not think people would want to hear about her vague passions; her agents, with their hard, ebony hats, their noses veined with alcohol, these men would frighten her. Should she play with her divining cards? Should she reassure herself with the messages of these pasteboards envoys from the courts of disillusioned chance? They seemed now no longer a facile amusement but a pack of furtive associations and memories.

She could sense the sawdust and poverty of the fortune houses. Gross women, swollen and distended as if they were one huge gland, fingering the cards: the smell of paraffin, mangled grass and nausea which hangs round fairs. The stately, deceiving voice, the balding scalp bandaged with rabbit skins. And in the yellow, chemical light, the cards showing their meaningless wooden faces for an instant, the heavy sleeves obscuring them, and the voice of the monotonous woman droning on about the destiny in the arrangement of the clumsily shuffled pack. Pierrina saw there was nothing to do, and prepared gracefully to do it.

The Director had missed the palazzo as he sat in the café: he walked back, along the gipsy slaughterhouse in the lane, went through the palace courtyard: he was pleased, and disappointed. Were these weeds or shrubs, pushing their great medicinal leaves around the knees of naked stone women? There were memorial plaques on the walls: 'To Arabella: God rest her, the best of cats', and indeed, there was Arabella, in marble, sleeping with her face on her tail, an impossible tail. The Director was not amused: the floor of the courtyard, where it was exposed to the weather, was cracked and furrowed: it looked as if geese had been living there until a short time previously.

There was a fountain: it threw a nervous jet of crystal high in the air, catching it as it fell back, but unsurely: it recalled a man balancing a long pole on his chin for the first time, yet it was attractive. The Director knew this courtyard could be improved: soap and geraniums would remedy much. Perhaps they could have concerts here; the horns would sit in the corner and bounce their precise notes round the walls. Men could do much with a palace: a fashion parade, perhaps, the sadistic applause of an epicene audience; or a conference, with delicate old statesmen sitting in rugs with revolver holsters sewn in them, and reporters afraid of asking too few questions. The Director went to see Pierrina, unexpectedly asking her to lunch.

They went off together; work in the palace stopped.

There was a conventional meal: they sat with a tall, decaying man who was playing politics with small pieces of bread. The tablecloth was brown and smudged as a map of mountains: the man seemed to know every metre of the terrain; he moved his agents from valley to valley with lunatic precision. The Director frowned: usually such men who pretended to think while eating were clumsy and pretentious. The place to think was in offices: elsewhere, you considered the passers-by, you were frightened of waiters, you looked at the tourists, and wondered why they had come here. The Director and Pierrina frowned at the man who, looking up as a persecuted Napoleon, quickly relaxed.

'I apologise,' he said. 'I am a schoolmaster and I grow careless about things.'

'Evidently.'

'You must understand that I live in a pygmy world: I am an example to my people. With my charges, I must be a leader. When I was young, they came to me, asking about their girls, my opinions, what was expected of them. Now, they sit like empty blackboards while I write my wisdom over their unflinching faces. Yes, it is a fine calling.'

'And apparently a deceptive one,' thought the Director, who remembered how teachers betrayed confidences and scholarship in the pseudonym of discipline and academic ethics. But he encouraged the man, who continued, 'Consider how frightening: these little men before you, swearing like men, cheating, lying, lechering, to escape from the pursuits for which you stood. They have an odour of confinement about them: they stink of iron and wet wool. Their games are fantasies so complete, especially their organised exercise, it takes a strong man to refuse to believe in the relevance of their application.

'There you are, standing before them: you wrinkle your dainty nose, you think what to say. And that feeling continues: you adopt poses, only to abandon them after years. What can you say to them? I know these things, and these, you may attain this and this in such a way, can you say this sincerely? You need to be a king even to pretend that you can: a god to believe in it all.

'Do you wonder that I am confused, when I come among you? Imagine – I never talk to my pupils as I would a man. Insults, sarcasm, force, and irrational prohibitions – that is my life, it is also theirs. I do not want to destroy them: some are intelligent, some refined: but I have to make them do the same things. I cannot say to Panelli, 'You have a fine manner, and a pleasant grasp of the ridiculous. If I had your gifts, I should become the lover of numbers of rich vapid women.'

'No, instead I must say to him, as to all of them, the heroes, the poets, he braggarts, the perverted, 'You must go to a university if you can: you may do what you like in your spare time, provided it does not destroy the myths of the school, in your work you have great licence, of course, but you must do the subjects set and decided for you.'

'I do not say we destroy them entirely: rather, they destroy us: I do not say we should have no discipline, but this refusal to recognise individual values, or talents, the hypocrisy of the teachers, all this is evil.'

'Why, then, do you not leave your job,' asked Pierrina. 'Surely, in discovering all this, you must have communicated much of your disappointment to the children you should love? You do not seem to have attempted to present your view to them.' The Director thought how dutifully Pierrina would love children: an unkind thought amused him.

The man answered, 'But do you see, under the system, the boys are there: I can do nothing about that. They sit and watch: they can tell if my hand shakes: they know if my shoes are clean, they can tell if my wife has given me a clean handkerchief that morning. They draw me: they spend hours fixing every detail of me; they know what annoys me, better than any meticulous lover they know me. And I know them: I have to know if a cough is a cough, or if it hides a laugh: I have to know their writing, their style, if they have parents, or any other abnormalities which may account for something in their work. And it does not matter that one of us knows all these things about the other: there is never a stalemate. It is most frustrating.

'Inevitably, we distrust one another: the best loved masters are the dashing generals, the steel-plated soldiers who have major campaigns each week. On Monday, the new plays begin: there is mobilisation, trenches are dug. Tuesday, punitive measures, light cavalry attacks beaten off. Wednesday, the camp is sacked: women abducted, old men butchered, the standards taken. Thursday, the boys counterattack: they say they do not regret the loss of their ideals; they say they set no store by liberty. What must the teacher do but accept their terms? And on Friday, both sides are so affectionate: envoys are sent out, and spat upon in secret; the banners are furled, the soft attentions of the weekend comfort the wounded.

'That is the same for generations of these short-lived animals: I am the government, they the agitators. That is the only way I can think of them. That is why I devise these schemes for their destruction. I was reminding myself where they sat: if I break up their alliances and their coalitions regularly, by moving the intelligent ones around, I may manage to get the stupid conformists to betray their more adventurous comrades. I am beginning to agree there is an ideal boy, towards whom it is my duty to aim: we must teach these unhygienic scholars that there is a model boy, that they will have failed if they are not like him.'

The master did not seem to want to add to this dull exposition. Pierrina thought that schools were a good reason for not having children. The Director suggested they return to the palazzo: a wicked smile was beginning to turn the teacher's lips in a crazy spiral. The others guessed that his punitive measures would incorporate the taking and torture of hostages.

The Director felt unwell, as if he had idly watched light playing over a leaf by his head, and become aware that the movement was in fact that of small omnivorous vermin.

Children were so strange: they were not small adults, but another species which were slowly turned by suggestion and propaganda into imitations of their fathers. Men who controlled them were like lion tamers: brave, accomplished, but on an inhuman level. In the streets, families of trams squealed and grunted: the traffic went round like an electric model, the trams struck tiny blue flames from the steel.

There were cars: priests smoking cigars rode like devils on motor scooters. There were infants in cars: they looked proud, they wore silks called 'fine rain' on their fist-like feet; they wore white gloves. The women manoeuvred their compass legs to the best advantage: watching them from roadside burrows were plump men. Somewhere a bell rang: without metre or purpose, the single stroke rambled on: it was a bell talking to no one in particular, in a dialect as individual as that of a shamisen or Breton bagpipe. The Director felt unwell: he leaned against a wall, and for the third time, told himself he felt unwell.

On the wall were posters: '120 clowns', 'Typhus protection', 'Young men of the class March to June 1941', 'THESE are your enemies', 'Freedom and self-expression'. You might choose which you preferred: the last was the motto of a delightful man who ran a society of theoretical assassins. The wall and the posters were close: feebly, he put out a hand to the 'class of '41' for support, but withdrew it when he recognised the significance of his gesture. Having shown weakness, he felt better.

Pierrina stopped cursing him for being a decrepit old nuisance, and prepared to enliven his convalescence. They reached the palazzo: the Director laid himself into a chair carefully; Pierrina went off looking suitably disturbed. The Director awaited some pleasant infusion of herbs, some lucent drink pounded from cool plants. But Pierrina did not reappear; he had to feel better by himself. He was in the library: it was a summer library, the leather bindings were green, you could imagine that small learned beetles had been crushed to death in many a picnic, and brought back here for storage. All the great bores are here, of course, thought the Director. With pleasure he saw that indeed the shelves were labelled in insect leg script: 'Great bores', 'Lesser bores', 'Dull maniacs', 'Interesting maniacs'.

It was good to see a man being honest: the Director thumbed through some of the interesting maniacs: Plato, lives of Mazzini and Azev, the Tsarist policeman, Ciano's diaries. There were ladders, in the corners of the room ghosts of subdued antique conversations had been imprisoned by the silence for sacrilege. The Director felt drowsy with the boredom left there by generations of conscientious August readers. He closed his eyes: abandoning himself to vertigo, he rush to sleep.

*

Pierrina was reading the newspapers: they had names such as you would find in novels; mixtures of all the 'Posts', 'Mails', 'Dailies', journalists could devise. Editors were saying that palaces were sordid places: the nation should be burdened with them, leaving their owners to go off and be poor in comfort elsewhere. Pierrina sighed: so much for the opinion of any jury, if she appealed.

*

Torgano was displeased: aristocratic dogs had snuffed at the furniture, children had stuck their wax sweets to the pictures like seals. Adults had fought over the piles of rubbish towards Torgano to ask if he could mend suitcases, cure traumas, or recommend an hotel near the station. With relief, he saw that that a man had come in who might buy something; he was dry and cunning, his veins protruded like tasselled cords. A book bound in enamelled paper was under his arm; by twisting his head, Torgano saw it was called *Bronze Monsters: Twenty Years' Experience in the Cinema*. He must be very stupid or very famous to walk around with a book like that, thought Torgano.

The man said, 'I have a niece, you understand: I first met her when she was one of the models of Jacques Vertu.' The man paused, seeming to find the name as unlikely as anyone. 'She used then to enjoy the company of woollen pigs: I myself gave her several hundred. But they got burnt at a party, and now she is more sophisticated. I do not mean she is a film star for culture, but like me she just loves beautiful things.'

'What a nice man, or is he?' thought Torgano hurriedly.

'You see, I am not wealthy: this little girl is lonely, she needs decorations for her flat: she has many friends who are interested too in beauty; they were most upset when the pigs were burnt. I tell you this because I see you are a generous man; a man of generous spirit, a man, if you don't mind me saying so, who has obviously had all the advantages to make a success in whatever career. I want something cheap, I admit: but lovely. Have you one of those shell mirrors perhaps, or an Alsatian dog to stand on her mantelpiece? Any old glass paperweight, or a first edition of some quaint work, Nostradamus, Shakespeare, any old foreign writers, must be old for my little girl to have it. No? Well, I couldn't expect it really.'

'I'll let you have this case of birds for 17.50. See, all different colours. All delightful bird shades. You can almost hear their muted pastel cries and calls: those little birds will call of love to your niece, I'm sure – 16.50 then.'

The niece won her birds at 10.50: the uncle was ready then to talk.

'Talking of art, I see that you, a gentlemen of education, must know all the great men.'

Silently Torgano wrapped the awkward glass case, spurts and trickles of decay came from the rotten birds.

'I too know them, you know: I go to schools where they are lecturing; they let me read their manuscripts, correct their proofs, as they call them.'

Torgano wondered why the man took so much trouble to lie

about something which was of no interest to either of them.

'Would you care to see something else, sir?' he asked.

The other made the expected remarks, and left: Torgano was glad to have sold the birds to such a shrewd customer: they had cost him what he had been paid for them.

He curled himself into daydream once more: a bold pigeon stole grains of sawdust some uncooperative manufacturer had left on his antiques. Torgano thought of the guilty girl he was to see the next day: certainly she, or he himself, would not go, he lied to his panic-stricken conscience. There could be no meeting: it only remained for him to comfort and convince reluctant moral parts of his mind, that he excuse to himself were credible. It was a challenge to explain and lie to different parts of yourself, to coordinate the little pockets of conscientious secession into one happy conformist agreement. It was not hypocrisy: it was an exercise in tolerance, one to be practised on all occasions: Torgano closed his eyes to concentrate, and dozed.

*

The girl Torgano had met at the carnival worked in an office: she did not know what she did, she was a link in a chain which let itself down a featureless wall to swing fathoms deep in cold, fishy water. There were bright cards to be sorted: someone had punched jagged holes in them; often she punched more, for amusement. It was scarcely possible to make a mistake: when she had finished with the cards, they put them away in caskets which lay like bodies in the catacombs beneath the building.

Her work gave her an impression of flurried nothing: men would come in, ask her for figures: she would draw graphs in delightful inks, optimistic, comely curves rising and falling with her own imaginative salesmanship. She enjoyed the cedar smell of pencils, the sweetness of the red inks, the tart flavour of the blue; her rulers were tall and jaundiced as Slavonic kings. She even designed booklets, folding whimsies which made sentimental tycoons laugh in a forgiving manner.

It was a life, like any other. Her superiors did not know what she did: she was usually out when they came to see her: they would sit and wait, playing with rubbers, bouncing the green shapes like crickets across the desks. And they too would say, 'Yes, it is a life like any other.' Their parents and friends had always said this, they took a pride in covering up for the indolent and intelligent, who do no work. The girl herself spent hours looking out of the windows: she would say to herself, 'Today, I must only look out for two hours, then I must work.'

She knew they would not miss her the next morning when she went to the clock tower: often she went to a cinema in the afternoons, came back to the office purblind and refreshed at half past four. She had friends, of a kind: they asked her to terrifying parties, which were always worse than she could have imagined. The men fought, the women laughed and laughed like neurotic terriers: jealousy, cigar smoke which smelt of cider and perspiration, that was a party. She would not have missed one for anything. As she looked out of the window now, she imagined herself as the target, shaped like the eye on a peacock's tail-feather, at which aimed the sporting Tibetan cavalry.

That was a party: troops of interesting Mongoloid faces riding up to some inaccessible target and prodding with their ungainly lances, or shooting with their ram's horn bows. And afterwards, you would see squat unhealthy-looking men riding off on their imaginary horses, accompanied by their unfortunate polyandrous wives. It was all degrading, and satisfying. It would not occur to her that men who claimed to dislike the company of such oriental party warriors might be sincere.

She believed there was a basic similarity in men, which went deeper than preferences for certain foods, or lies about certain schoolmasters. Knowing older man described her as old-fashioned, but trusting: this was the most comforting, and comfortable, thing they could say about her. She was the sort of battered pretty creature men liked to collect, and put with the transfixed butterflies and St Sebastian beetles which they kept in neat cork cases. Her life was not an enquiry, or a cross-examination: it was not even a refuse collection. Rather, it was an emptying and sorting of waste-paper baskets: her sharp-filed fingers would spike through crumpled doodles and sweet-papers in vain efforts to find a pure copy of a managing director's signatures, or some similar saleable toy. She sat down to play with irregular bundles of spent tickets.

*

At the palazzo, Pierrina had decided to write to Torgano after all: she explained to herself that she could not break her word and see him, but she was bound to tell him the nation would be sleeping with her in the palace for three days or so. She wrote:

> *Today, the man I saw yesterday, Director of Public Monuments,*
> *took over my palazzo. This may be a surprise, it is always*
> *unusual when a casual acquaintance, director or nation, takes*
> *your home. I fear any arrangements you have made will have been*
> *quite useless, but you are never good at arranging things anyway,*
> *so I trust this finds you well and not at all disappointed. No*
> *doubt I shall see you when this week is over: perhaps you can*
> *wave to me as you pass in a motor boat. If I have found a flat in*
> *the meantime, you could enquire at the post office, in case I do not*
> *have time to let you know the address. I am well. I have no doubt*
> *the Director would send his regards, if he knew I was writing this.*

She posted the letter; she prided herself that a formal friendship avoided all wickedness and informal demands.

*

The Director was walking among pictures: the frames were heavy with coiled sealing wax: like huge heavy parcels, enclosing all the best addresses with their wrappings. Without curiosity, the official looked at portraits of antique bureaucrats; they stood proudly with their files, their sand, their ink and pointed feathers. They rested their hands on their desks as if they were immortal, at the very least. Yet they were kind men: they had birds and mistresses; some of them had small portraits of their wives beside them on the desk. There were pictures of parks with uncouth boys pointing at synthetic ruins: towns smoked like stew-pots in the background of tall daubed woods.

There were still-lifes: twisted in death, their plodding feet curling in agony, heads shattered and distorted by the impact of the shot, birds were dead. Scabby fruit lay inedible, a squat fly sucked the sweet blood with his long greedy nose. In the background, young ladies could be heard saying, 'How sweet – especially the fly.' There were musicians: plump, epicene and unworthy, they posed and strummed. An oaf with a red face sang a wordless song to lovesick greyhounds and a fat girl who could not have been more than thirteen.

The Director moved to a battle scene: rainbow galleys circled one another like violent water boatmen. Oil burnt on the water, oars interlocked like fingers. On the poops were engineers, poets, with bear's heads threatening on their soup-plate shields. Men struggled in the water, but it was painted a warm, sustaining watercolour. No one was actually being physically hurt, but there was much tension, much fighting had presumably taken place. Flights of arrows rolled in mid-air, like divers or fish showing off: in the distance, two galleys had rammed one another.

Captains ran about awkwardly, as if to say, 'What next?' They were obviously reluctant to board their opponent with their exquisite knights. They would eventually unchain the slaves at the oars, standing discreetly aside whilst the servile mobs slaughtered one another. Far away, there was a walled town; the battlements shone like sugar, brocade banners and helmet plumes nodded with the calm approval of the lazy veteran.

'Yes, I suppose it does look rather overdone, when you see

a picture of your patriotic theories,' said the Director ruefully. On the other wall was a land battle. 'No one seems to have thought of infantry firing a volley as an instructive study: all those minute rodent movements, the suspense, the slow manoeuvring, the race in slow time, the irresistible attraction of croquet. Such a pity.'

The Director considered the cavalry: statuesque in their loud uniforms, a faint surprise came into their well-bred eyes as sabres rattled, and lances drove up through their horses into their courageous stomachs. They were different colours: that was the time when paintings became useful, when you could distinguish between Europeans by the colour of their uniforms. Before, a war might be a sordid feud: but give a man a uniform and he also acquires a cause. The Director went downstairs, looking back to see if a man rolled on by a spitted horse, and with his own arm sliced off at the shoulder, should really look so scrupulously clean.

On the roof, the last two workmen were arguing: the rest had said the height affected them. On being questioned, one said the height more than affected them, it disaffected them. In fact, they were bored: and boredom is a gift which a lifetime of oppression and jibes cannot take away. Tired of seeing the Director feel ill and work behind closed eyelids so often, his men decided also to be ill. Two, however, had stayed to talk.

One said: 'I call you comrade, I ask if you are a slave, I address you in a Romance dialect. Do I speak to three problems, or one? I say, you pauper of a prose poet, do you still live on scraps of galantine and lark, which charitable extortioners give you when they feel like it? I say, the nation or Europe, you compulsorily fascist democrat? How many problems? How many problems? How many confusions? Am I indeed as out of date as you believe? One solution, or many, one generation, or a thousand? Whatever you answer, you will mean "I do not know".'

The other replied, 'I cannot accept that anyone tries to solve each problem by a random solution. Every party has a complex of policies which may or may not arise from a logical theory. Having made their generalisations about man and the state, they apply their schemes to each individual problem. It would not be possible to formulate one comprehensive solution which did not also include methods of solving and reforming the paradoxes and archaisms you mention. No government or party can say it has no attitude to some aspect of life: it will have positive or negative attitudes, but they can never be unprejudiced or unbiased.'

'Then you think a piecemeal reform is impossible?'

'I find it a contradiction in terms: any change implies an attitude in a government, an attitude implies a state of mind, an outlook. Even if you believe government can restrict the sphere of its influence, that the state legislature cannot meddle in certain things, you will find that this reservation will eventually have to be applied to other branches of government: it will have to be treated, if not followed, as a principle. In a dictatorship, too, the theory may not be legally logical, but it had behind it the logic of a human being. And of course, in any legal state, the judicial and legislative arms must eventually come to terms, law and government must be allied, usually the legislature wins. There are only different speeds and degrees of reforms: I cannot agree that there can be such a differentiation as you see, between doctrinaire and humane reform.'

The Director was confused: he could hear the men thinking, shuffling their rubber boots on the tiles. All his men talked like that; it humiliated him: and he noticed that he could hear clearly conversations on the roof, when he was in the hall. At night, he reflected, the palace must sway and rub itself together, like an ancient barque made of phosphorescent spiced wood, breathing deeply on urgent tides.

The inspectors came and stood in the hall: they had covered much paper with prosaic descriptions of unusual objects, they felt slightly sick, their inquisitive index fingers were covered with ink and rust. The dwarf still pried: the cat ran after him with angry, demanding endearments. It was the sort of cat that followed men like fate until they turned round and kicked it, whereupon they would observe with shame that it was indeed a real, unhappy animal. The dwarf could not push the cat away: he stroked his small reticent beard, and the cat shouted and flourished itself jealously.

*

Pierrina was looking out over the water, polluted and congested as soup, it was. She was looking too at the cool sunshine which lay pale on the window sills, and climbed slowly over, and off, the palace façade. A few more days, and she would have left this ramshackle paradise: that was what she always called it. A childish tune, a quartz charm which had hung for years on an underdeveloped chest: that was all her home was. She repeated all the evocative epithets and superstitious admonitions of embalmed aunts, but did not manage to be sad as she felt she ought.

In the sky were whipped shapes of clouds: they moved jerkily across the anaemic lyrical blue. 'Clouds do not really mean anything, except as guarantees of more weather,' remarked Pierrina. Indeed, there was nothing more she could say. She was mildly sad: there seemed little point in calling clouds under a sub poena to testify to their sympathy and reciprocated emotion. Perhaps she should stand like a goddess or a sacrifice on the balcony, commend herself to the sun, and drown herself. Or persuade her domestic assistants to bury her alive in the courtyard, under the lilies which always reminded her of mandrake and funerals.

But the Director would be dismayed if she showed such desperation: part of his plan of annihilation was that everything would be offhanded: she would hurt him, if she had a ritual suicide. The only death which would appeal to him would be if she fell down the back staircase, the one made of brick loaves: she would lie on the red bread, with blood and hair indistinguishable in the moonlight. Ever after, the Director

would talk of the glorious myth of bread and blood, his
abbreviated fingers clasped, his voice excited and
unconvincing. She went indoors, and began to pack.

*

The Director's assistant crept around the darkening rooms: an
echo of dusk, as it were rang over the capital, making haggard
shadows and blue-rimmed streets. Later, the real evening would
come, strict and unsubtle. The assistant knew that in a year,
even a generation he would be Director himself. He could wait,
he had trained himself only to wait: he effaced himself, he
erased himself in the crushing task of waiting. He hated the
Director as he would have hated the slowness of an executioner,
or a sentencing judge. Had he not been so intent on bitter
anticipation of office, he might have plotted against his
superior. Yet, he was half afraid of responsibility: he was afraid
that by thinking of his future duties, he would make himself
unfit for them.

Waiting was the test: it was even easier to wait than to
struggle, once you had given yourself up to love and abasement.
The assistant thought the present Director ineffective and
vulgar: in the department, he used to ask his colleagues if they
did not agree with this view. All assented: all told the Director.
Consequently, the Director flicked once or twice at the irritating
parasite, but gave him little thought. The Director did not want
to notice the self-torment of the assistant: he let him fetch
umbrellas and run ignominious errands, but never gave him the
satisfaction of appearing to remark on these wifely attentions.

No one could have called them friends. Somehow, men
seemed to guess at the conflict, and say, 'Yes, that assistant of
his is a hard man, he will make a fine Director when the time
comes.' In reality, of course, the assistant was as soft as a baby
squirrel, but men in offices seldom like to admit that their next
leader is selfish or neurotic. Certainly, in this government,
inferiors carefully respected their superiors, saying that all high

appointments were political, therefore unable to be judged by bureaucratic standards.

There was not much for an assistant to do: it was an ambiguous position: it turned him into a grey, shiny envelope of ambition. He admired no one, would admit no merit but his own: yet this was not so much self-satisfaction as selfless devotion to an arid cause. He could no longer distinguish colours or textures: everything was the colour of trees and thin laughter in lonely parks. All objects had the rough smoothness of orange peel: when he touched someone's skin, even his wife's, he did so with an abstracted amazement, that something living should feel so thick and unresponsive.

It was the end of a day: in the wings, moon and stars were being gilded for yet another popular appearance. In the restaurants small boys gripped bloody sacks, squeezed the fish tails in the grubby fabric. Then, they beat the uncomprehending heads on a stone, rhythmic, delighted. Women with bone-deep sores on their stained fingers scraped earth and stones from expensive vegetables. In the slaughterhouses, woolly legs kicked on the low tables: the bullocks squirmed uncomfortably after their heads had been removed. Capable, pitying men stopped whistling for a moment, as they killed horses; the thud of the killing machine, the legs jerked out sadly, like a stockbroker having his reflexes tested.

Then an urgent, swarthy man, bending over the nervous body, as if to catch the last words, preserve the last breath: like a lover, he bends, leans against the chest. Then, he moves back: the steel finger has pried, the heart beats out its blood, a long sucking stream. It seems there could be no more blood, anywhere: the corpse is picked up, still there is more blood. And the cows: soft, feminine, anxious to appear unruffled. The poleaxe: busy men, they strike kindly: one has lost a leg, he gashed himself as he was dismembering an animal; somehow, it does not seem to matter.

The cows die with patience, as it were impersonally. A pause to light a cigarette, then the brown beasts are crucified:

fiendish doctors with knives begin their delicate experiments. The skin is clean, it comes away like mink; there are ridges where the knife has gone, the carcase is soft as molten wood. The inside of ruminants is packed with many strange and useful things: you come to handle bodies like suitcases; you look on entrails and blood as string and wrapping paper. You hose away reluctant rivers of offal, and tourists think happily of dinner.

No brother has embraced the veal, the mutton did not die secure in the knowledge of patriotic values; no priest mumbled as the horses fell without time to shut their eyes. When municipal officials went round the buildings, they thought, 'We cannot be surprised at anything men may do, or may become used to, so long as we have slaughterhouses.'

But they still enjoyed meat: a trace of regret crossed their faces as they munched, the food became even more enjoyable. In the hotels, chefs of all sized and qualities prodded the subhuman shapes as they swung forlorn and comically naked in the boisterous kitchens. The town prepared to eat.

*

Torgano shuttered his shop: there were leaves in the chairs; leaves had fallen to dust on the tables. He powdered the brown crispnesses in his fingers: these came from last year. He thought of Pierrina, and of his other girl, and regretted both. Opposite, the shopkeepers were calling to one another as they ran feebly into their shops with galvanised iron shapes in their arms. Quickly, they locked the buildings: Torgano watched them go and wondered how it was that he had come to be so unlike them, yet, like them, a dealer.

*

In her office, the girl, she called herself Gallista, was colouring herself. She was older than you would expect: she was an excellent portrait painter. Most women paint the same face on themselves for years, expect their patrons to subscribe to the same unimaginative features for ever-increasing sums.

Gallista, however, had pride and she made subtle variations on herself every day. She would strip her face to the bones, and build there an effeminate old man, an eleven-year-old girl, a medieval snake woman, or some anonymous spinster who might have a small reputation as a political reactionary with a consequent vested interest in charity. Those who recognised the forgeries she used to make of herself were frightened by the thought of the possibilities of such debasement of official facial currency. They would go home, looking suspiciously at their wives, who usually seemed to be guilty of something as an occupational hazard.

*

The Director waited impatiently for the boat to take them back to the department: he did not know what more he could do with the palace, he wanted to leave it to allow his anticipation to increase once more. He called to Pierrina to expect men tomorrow: or perhaps not. Now that the palace was theirs, they need not pretend that work there was urgent. The door was opened: flies lay like currants on the warm wood of the landing stage. Perhaps they *were* currants?

The Director put his foot near one and it walked away contemptuously: the platform lurched and subsided; no one said anything. In the distance a displeasing mechanical purr could be heard. It reminded the Director of all the girls who had laughed with him, snapping their wedge-shaped teeth, thin tongues hovering on the verge of bubbles, the long simian lips arched and coy. They had not meant anything, they had understood nothing: like unpunctual hired motor boats they had made sounds of friendship, their internal clockwork running smoothly and inevitably. The boat arrived: steering it still was the decrepit Napoleonic official, all enthusiasm and sabre. The officials made thrilling gangster leaps onto the deck; they looked for Pierrina, but she did not appear. Someone had nailed a government plaque to the palace: the door swung open, the flower-faced cat looked out, wrapped itself in its tail. The boat moved off.

The officials were interested by the crowds: it was as if the hives were emptying; climbing over one another the healthy golden neuters went in search of cheap-smelling flowers. Now, there were grey ships invisible between the sweet heaps of cells: all knew that that evening, mariners in mutton pie caps would fall on the capital, drunk, smelling of sawdust and sea loneliness. Who could tell what damage could be done, how many respected women seized by these respectable pirates? The Director knew of diplomats who left the town when one of their nation's ships put in at the port. They had no wish to be awakened by rags soaked in petrol flaming through the windows, youths climbing lamp-posts to hang nooses from them in protest at the sailors' behaviour. Now, the vessels were solid, brooding: they seemed phenomena which had drifted in during the afternoon, calm Mediterranean icebergs.

The boat came between granaries which seemed to stand back to back: trickles of alcohol dropped into the water, cranes dropped their fists over nothing. The buildings leaned together: the boat's wake rebounded in the channel, making diagonal patterns of inconsequential wave forces. There were foreign churches; broad flights of chipped steps led down to litters of drums of tar, empty champagne bottles, and oil-soaked cork rings. All this the officials saw, trying not to appear excited; they read the tin advertisements, the familiar names were more attractive on warehouses where picturesque children dabbled pieces of bread and butter on lines, in attempts to catch fish.

Then there were parks for foreigners, car cemeteries, model flats which had been displayed like doll's houses, the fronts removed, replaced by areas of glass. The ride was over. The boat was back with its owners: in the morning, for convenience, it had come to meet the officials: this evening, time was unimportant. Gratefully the men showed their strength and experience by scorning help in disembarking; instead they leapt onto the mud and cobbles; tramping on fruit and mineral refuse, they slid vigorously, balancing themselves with violent arms.

They went away, some to look up the lists they had made, others to pursue their offensive second lives. The Director walked to his office: the rooms were disinfected, scooped out: a pleasant anaesthetic smell lingered in the building. The occupants had gone, leaving a few books, wastepaper baskets full of mottled blotting paper: the air was soft and tinted, as if women had been drawn lightly through it.

The Director paused and sniffed: it was delightful; he had often thought of the variety of sensitive deceptions a playful mind might devise and exaggerate for itself. The Director walked upstairs; he imagined himself growing smaller in the eye of the camera. At the top of the stairs, the man turned for the fadeout: with a reticent gesture, he motioned to the sky, the architecture, the scurrying women with pails. Then, shyly, he whisked round a corner, lost himself.

Chapter 3

AFTER THE NIGHT, the colours were changing: in the barracks and all the other prisons of the town, soldiers, children, and men woke to hear the more free, working and shouting. They saw too the luxurious world which was so near, of which they were a cold and uncomfortable reflection. In the schools, girls wistfully gave themselves to disdainful milkmen: boys would sometimes kill themselves, jumping from the windows, small and terrible against the sky, onlookers would shrink from the avenging leaps and the suicidal concussion of the landings.

In the gaols, men and women longed for each other: they looked at the sky, but some divine vandal had drawn stripes, narrow, metallic, through the clouds, even through the ominous birds which hovered over the quicklimed prison cemetery. Few thought of these people, they had been locked up, the only concern was that they should not break loose. The soldiers comforted themselves with uniforms: they cleaned themselves like women; their officers were plump and foolish.

When the army marched through the streets, few were impressed by its obvious gentle inefficiency: the confined, thwarted faces of these broken conscripts were proof that such frustrated citizens would not hesitate to attack parents and neighbours. When morning came, men laughed to see tin buglers blundering their themes, but the shattered notes roused the camps, as if they were muscles tensed by nervous impulses. From all these proud institutions came brief cries of pain, and reluctant obedience: summoned to eat and watch by bells and whistles, the experimental animals obeyed the simple signals without enjoyment. Those outside thought, 'And how else to order their lives?' but did not attempt to answer themselves.

Torgano found Pierrina's letter: he read it, careful to

91

remember that it surely said many things which did not appear at first sight. He recalled the meeting he was to have with Gallista: a wretched morning. He went to the clock tower: he thought of the palazzo. He was used to disappointment, though he could not yet disregard it: he would have to see the Director. With disarming duplicity he resolved to put his scheme for the shop before the department of public monuments. Perhaps they would appreciate the services of an expert in the marketing and sorting of antique rubbish. They could only laugh at him, it was no more irrational or unreasonable an idea than hundreds on which he acted every day.

In the cafés, the orchestras played to dispirited tourists: waiters performed simple acrobatics to simple Delibes and Chabrier. The tourists smiled; military veterans frowned when others talked: they stirred their cups of purple chocolate in time to the music; they grinned condescendingly to withered, beaked women. Torgano hoped he would recognise Gallista: often he found he was confused by slight changed in conventional disguise. The violinists marked his impatience with inaudible irritations of their instruments: brittle music made itself into sweet biscuits, sickly circles of mid-morning confectionery.

Gallista came. Torgano had reached no decisions about her; he looked to her for conversation.

'Braided soldiers were blocking the streets with pines as I came here,' she said.

Foolishly Torgano said, 'How do you mean, braided? Perhaps it is an exercise.'

'They have black hair tied like tails under their caps,' Gallista replied. 'They are also iced and piped with sugar ropes; their clothes are a mess of metal tags and artificial colours. They are struggling with rough logs: the cars can still go past; they have nearly blocked some finger-thin alleys leading to the centre. And yes, certainly, it is an exercise. They are singing sentimental Christmas songs such as you hear on the radio: I do not know why.

'A water main has burst: water is pouring down like ice;

there is a lake with birds and week-ending cats playing and sporting in the new water. There are transports in the lanes, testudinal creatures, steady, short-legged and cautious. What do you suppose all this is illustrating? In the government alarming us, or our visitors? Are they our soldiers? How can we find out? Should we start demonstrations outside some palace? If so, what must we shout?'

Torgano was not impressed by her enthusiasm, but he could pretend that he was.

'I wonder if the lost colonies have reclaimed their fatherland? When I was a soldier, you must understand that we talked of nothing but brandy and retrenchment. I remember we had a general who would ride his horse for our amusement. A fine rubber horse, it was: and strong! It would knock a man down and trample him, as if he had been a penny bun: and eat! It would knock eat three or four pounds of potatoes at a sitting, a great worm-eaten stinking brute, it was. We called it "Gipsy chrysanthemum", why, I can't recall. We had some fine fellows in our company: three of them found some peasant stealing bones from the refuse bins: they pinned him on the commander's table with bayonets. Rough justice but grand soldiers.'

The girl sneered at Torgano, who was wondering if he had exaggerated too blatantly.

'Shall we go and supervise these wreckers?' he asked.

'That would be most stimulating: I like to see men working.'

Torgano decided with this to see her never again. To admit she enjoyed seeing these effeminate warriors working was the worst lechery he or Pierrina could have imagined for her. Pierrina had a privilege court in which she tried and condemned those who demonstrated dull fantasies, or kissed other men's fiancées though themselves engaged. Just minor signs of deep inner corruption and mortification. Gallista was evidently gangrenous: Torgano began to treat her as if she were critically but pleasantly ill.

'Yes,' he said, 'there may be a seat where we can rest, or some shop where we can buy chocolate and stimulant drugs. Over there will be the easiest way up, though it is longer.' They set off, Gallista infuriated, Torgano pitying and afraid, as he had feared heavy drinkers and the immaculate rich. They came to the military preparations. It was impressive, and Gallista forgave Torgano for his extravagant impoliteness.

Torgano was lonely with the girl: he could have wept with the dry loneliness he felt. Often when he was with Pierrina, he had desired her, so that she was alarmed by the slight uncontrollable spasm which marked emotions she preferred not to recognise. But that passed: that loneliness might be forgotten. Even by calling it 'loneliness' when it was years older than that, made it seem bearable and transitory. But now, there was no desire and no longing: he was alone with a girl. She felt nothing for him: worse, he could feel nothing for her. He despised himself for this, as all the best and most worthy people would have advised him to do, but it did not help.

He felt like a man, slightly drunk, might feel on Christmas Eve, leaving his girl, going out, going home in a world of determined happiness, Christianity in the windows and sensible women drunk and promiscuous on the buses. All the properties and enjoyments of a world which separated him from his clinging night girl, but would only console him if he paid with his mind. It was all confusing: the immaturity of being 'one of the boys' was seen as even praiseworthy: the immaturity of growing into a forsaken wrecked old man was considered a defect of upbringing and character. Torgano gazed at the unusual soldiers without excitement: Gallista would undoubtedly ask an officer what they were doing; soon all would know, they would be called martyrs, peacemakers, or inquisitive – it mattered little.

The soldiers curled their arms round the rough wood: the spidery, thinned limbs clutched with blind precision at the dead thick-skinned trunks. They were swinging them monotonously, their officers strutting, giving the time like conductors. Behind the road-blocks cars and small boys piled up in eager and frustrated confusion. Donkeys came, meek and compromised; they drew carts on which were machine guns. Old civilians led the animals; they made courageous sounds to drive the hooves to excited syncopations. More soldiers bundled in felt hunched over engines: they lay in the carts, impersonal shouts, smoke, a crackle of blank cartridges or the breaking of wooden sticks.

The crowds scattered: a gun had jammed; the soldiers smiled; officers reassured soldiers and the children who had feigned death in the doorway of the sweetshop. There were mechanics, they dismantled the guns, laughed with a pretty dialect; shrugging their shoulders, they laughed at their officers with the impunity of those well aware of their own indispensability. Orders, and the donkeys trotted away; the soldiers sat on the barricades, then deceitfully exploded into unexpected commands. The soldiers began to dismantle the piles of logs: a lorry was shouted up to take the shattered conifers away. Torgano and the girl were puzzled; they walked with self-consciously unmilitary steps. They went to eat buns and cakes at a café; they discussed the soldiers.

Torgano said, 'There are always incoherent activities pursued with tidy ritual for the entertainment of onlookers and leaders. It means little: certainly here the nationality of the soldiers is immaterial. These things happen, you understand: it is at military-masonic gatherings like this, that lovers find themselves and are lost. You will understand perhaps, when you yourself have become warm and dependent. It does not matter that the army should not accomplish anything: you should not look deeply for symbolism in the army. It is full enough already of sadistic lyric poets, who see divine retribution in every petty excess. You must read nothing into these illogical exercises. We have watched the soldiers, we have felt important, we have made stimulating errors in our appraisal of these no doubt charming serfs. That is sufficient.'

And Gallista, who was finding Torgano a pretentious nuisance, said, 'We must surely practise our reactions. One day, the soldiers who climb and exercise on the dunes over at the golf club, they really will be the fine raiders who will seize me and take me off to happiness in a tent with mothers and goats for my family. Or one day, the car which coughs and reverses under your window will contain sparkling animals, rank farmyard women, the beauties of your childhood extravagances. You know your fantasies best: you know the secret loves you think you hear, making apologetic whisperings and rustlings in old houses.

'We must consider every chance that these exotic creatures will appear, have appeared. That is why I watch men: some of them must be the heraldic beasts who paw and threaten their coy prey. Some time I will meet these mythical lovers; they will carry me off, of that I am sure. One day, the obvious things will happen; there will be the revolution, the disaster, the annihilation which alone would fulfil and explode our childish epics. That is why I go everywhere I can, talk to everyone, run for months trying to catch up with new experiences. And because I follow experience, all experience must fit into a complex pattern, but I do have to believe that the pattern exists, that it is an end in itself.

'I have to convince myself that novelty alone, the accumulation of personal explorations, can trace the themes and motifs of the meaningless life pattern. When I am seventy, and people remember reluctantly, but with forgiveness, that in my youth I was a woman warrior, a wrecker of all men, then I shall tell my philosophy. It does not matter what I say: philosophies of experience are all happily sententious, all true and useless. "I believe life is love and to laugh at chance," that is what you say when you mean you have lived by adultery and gambling; and of course, both are true, you are happy, and you make yourself even happier by pretending to principles which, despite your own example, you continue to believe are necessary and desirable.'

Torgano thought of Pierrina, thought of the palace abducted by stern, respectable men whose dreadful efficiency surpassed the hunnish robbers of Gallista's imagination. He wondered how he would fare with the Director: he knew he would believe anything he was told, yet he still feared the deceptions of the Director. What could he do with Pierrina? That was a question not to be faced when awake and active; only elementary decisions about elementary people like Gallista could be taken in daylight, the open public light which was as vulgar and intrusive as breath. Torgano did not enjoy daytime, nor summer: it was difficult for him to handle his life in the open; he needed the odourless dark, the antiseptic cold, the night breathing inoffensively through its pores, before he could happily make necessary decisions.

He walked with Gallista to the centre of the town. Women who had spent many generations living in one room, fading into the wallpaper, growing mute and meaningless as furniture, had come out for provisions. They talked as if they had forgotten how: they carried baskets full of the groceries of eighty years previous: the shopkeepers cheated them, but they did not mind. They had been turned into advertisements for boredom and suffocation. They were the women men did not notice: they seldom penetrated to the glass and metal framed shops in the arcades. Gallista was worried by these sour, hidden faces: she suggested coffee, they sat at sticky tables, covered with savaged buns and sugar defiled, clumsily torn from the neat wrappings.

Torgano drank, and a world swung up as he inverted the transparent cup over his mouth. He remembered what his parents had said, when they drank coffee; his father said, when the coffee was badly infused: 'Grounds for divorce.' And his mother would laughingly agree, saying, 'The colonel walked for hours in his extensive grounds.' And now, that was how Torgano recalled his parents, by puns in restaurants, and he regretted that they would not have been proud that he should remember them by the easy privacy of their ritual laughter. Gallista studied the machines round the walls: she slipped a coin into an electronic musical instrument.

The interlocked sounds arranged themselves: it was music

like an aluminium puzzle; you seized a metal member, slipped
and twisted the smooth shapes, and all the metal components
fell lifeless in your palm. That was what she could do to
Torgano, if she could bother; if she sufficiently degraded
herself, she could make him do many nauseating things for her.
But it was scarcely worth it: of course, you could dismantle a
man as small as Torgano in a short time: a few weeks, you
would have run through his emotions, his resistance, and built
up his future, But that was not completely satisfying. You had
to choose someone rather more complicated: it was not by age
or sensibility that you chose those you wanted to dissect, to
understand, but by the hardness of their shell.

When you had pinned out the brain of some thick skull,
when you knew someone by his intimate, subcutaneous organs,
that was success. You picked your knife carefully: the specimen
was ready, you cut deep into the living, cowardly tissue. The
colours ran, the red smeared into the green and the grey; you
diverted the purple rivers, the heavy brown streams; hurriedly
you dammed the swift chemical floods. You picked out
thoughts with tweezers; you isolated areas of guilt and deceit,
dropping disinfectant on the porous masses. Then you sewed
the bulge of brain back in its container. Then you were a brain
specialist, not merely a sensual surgeon, who burrowed and
exclaimed in any part of a stranger's body.

Yes, that was the true reward: to fight to the brain, and to
choose the thick skull. Her mother had laughed at her, saying
that the brains of old man would surely smell, if not quite
putrid, at least musty to a young girl. And Gallista could never
explain that age bought not attraction and charm, but resistance.
She did not want to find someone soft with age and decay: a
young athlete might be ideal. But he must be slow, slow to yield
to her, coming to her without explanations and medical
certificates. She wanted to explain the illogicalities of her
friends without having them disagree, or quote a second
opinion. She wanted to say, 'Djinnic, you love me passionately
because you live on a farm and have been brought up to believe

in eugenics. you have no idea of the powerful use of lovers' anti-climaxes.'

And she wanted to be certain that stupid Djinnic would admire her for her perception, and not call her ignorant and conceited, nor yet weep or put his hands feebly round her throat, murmuring, 'If I were to press, little puss ...'

He must not be tiresome: he must be brutish and passive, interesting and elemental. The two sat quietly: the music stopped, girls with newspaper cones of juniper and rowan came round the tables. They chanted despondently, they had been whipped, they had pushed their thin legs through heather fields, looking for obscure pearls and berries. Their flesh was full of sores; they held out the beautiful vegetation like a reproach. They sold little because of their involvement. In the background was their father: tourists saw him, thought he was exploiting his daughter, and refused to give money. The father carried synthetic leather work, covered with empty wallets he swayed and smiled, not knowing how to approach his audience. Torgano and Gallista were sympathetic, for the most diverse reasons.

Aimlessly, the couple wandered down the lanes of stalls: it was a nursery town of dwarf shops. Rejected goods filled the shallow trays, flies walked between rows of sweets, staring up at the high sugar walls. The stallholders were plump with hunger: at night they slept under their burrows, the rotten wood soft and crusted with fruit and old syrup. The cobbles were silted with dust: there was purple fruit-packing and pear cores flushed with furry active wasps in the gutters.

Torgano knew that nothing could be said to advantage: there would be no climax of revelation: he had deluded the girl; he had made her think he was worthwhile, a new, clean human, ready to receive all her judgements and endearments. He had spoken to her in a dream: he was still in the dream; now he wanted to escape, wanted to return to the old unhappiness, the old reality. He no longer enjoyed a world without an edge: he did not need a blurred outline to everything he saw. Only in some pictures did a drunken outline imply happiness; he longed to feel again the precision of nervous senses, slaving and self-critical.

Here was a bridge: it was clean, the sky too seemed to have been recently scoured over the bridge and the water. Fat golden boys with wings curled themselves scroll-like on the braced fingers of the bridge. Where the fingers broadened into forearm, where the strong hands left the banks, and harder muscles carried the structure, silver pets were built into the iron and wooden drapery. There were men to walk up the semitic planks; there were men to lean over the parapet, stylised Persians they were, wickedly lovesick. This was an oriental set piece, erected for contrast.

'Well, I doubt if we shall see one another again,' Torgano said. 'This is a fine place to part: it has no context; people who walk on this bridge are changed into air nobles as long as they are suspended on these engineered arms. If you stand on the bridge, you will be transformed as in all the best stories and the worst novels, to a thoroughbred creature, fit to be presented to emperors and magnates of all kinds. Perhaps I shall believe that with you I have lost something valuable; perhaps I shall look on you afterwards as the last chewed toy incinerated by self-conscious parents. Go up on the bridge, say goodbye, and let us regret one another.'

He was pleased with himself for having devised an inoffensively sentimental expression of his dislike for Gallista; he smiled at her.

Gallista was prepared to be deceived by the strength of the truly weak: she did not understand the power of the feeble and the insincere to use vivid lies and emotional confections to avoid unpleasant commitments. She was nearly touched by the beaten poet who gestured and acted before her. He must be far gone in sensibility and depression to give such an artificial description of an artificial bridge. Torgano saw maliciously that his talented failure had made an impression. His illogical faithlessness had been terminated, leaving him free to concentrate on the one central unhappiness to which he had devoted his life.

He was an expert in a narrow life, anything which did not come within the slim intestinal artery which alone prolonged his existence was regarded as possibly a disease, an illogical germ. He no longer could manage parts of his life which came outside the shop and Pierrina: he applied with insincerity the principles which underlay his attitude to Pierrina when he dealt with other women.

This impression of emotion was most convincing, and Gallista said kindly, 'You must not mind that chemical metaphors could not effect a literary fusion of our affections, let alone encourage us to kiss with our long noble lips. It remains for you to dream only of saying to me, as you sink into the kaleidoscope of a drunken party, 'Kiss me.' You will draw out the imagined syllables, perhaps you will catch sight of your heavy lids and sunset eyes imagining these foolish delights as you stare into some mirror. I shall be for you an imaginary girl. I shall feel myself important to comfort you when you are sleepy or maudlin. I shall not regret you, I want you to believe that for you to be in my memory, that too is important.'

Torgano was not impressed: soon there would be a day when he could no longer accept the existence of minds outside his own, and Gallista would not be important to him then. Abruptly he left her: there she went, someone else to be avoided in a small town. In ninety years there would be so many unpleasant centenarians pushed by grim children through the streets; he would never be able to go out in case he met one of them with all the consequent reminiscences and embarrassments. He walked back to the shop: what would Pierrina be doing now?

*

At the palace, Pierrina decided to live with acquaintances until she could force herself to look for rooms. It was tedious, her new room would be incongruous and disturbing. All her friends, if they did really deserve that name, furnished guest rooms with the wreckage from a hundred fires and auctioned castles. There were usually three beds sleeping against a wall, some helmets and a crutch in a corner, no cupboards or chairs. Visitors felt after two days that the furniture carried some violent significance. Writers of short stories in particular constructed lazy plots round the three beds: birds would rehearse at hours normally extra-musical; there would be vicious cats calling suggestively from among the stiff shrubs, and the privets cut into poisonous birds.

But the palace was finished: she had gone round that morning prising off memorials from the walls, removing miniatures, birds' wing on crystal, dismissing a few servants who had lingered on in the kitchens, forsaken and useless as shaven brooms. She had said goodbye to them with the usual feelings: it had upset her, even; she lay down, listening to the unhappy silences of her resident unemployed. She could hear the self-pitying inflections of one man, his words slipped through the floor of her room, small shavings of desperation chinking up from the hall.

'I have often thought of this: the wings of imperial birds furled over our homes, the sneaky leopards on guard outside the homes of the rich and the intelligent. It is our law that suffers, our law which is fired by eager functionaries in pyrotechnic arcs over the happy yawn of crowds. It is always us, the servants of the wealthy, the retainers of foreigners and shabby spies, who lose by radical politics. We are not many, but we keep suffering; we have never known luxury. We have not been the ones to toss cut-glass containers at friends in galleys heaving round the canals. We have always been those who sat up all night with jaundiced fox-hounds, or cleaned the walls of the ballroom, sponging off cake and the refuse of aristocratic partymakers.

'Do not misunderstood me: I have always served the Tarraults with a reformer's hatred and love. Hatred for the principle, love for a generous opponent, whom one is pledged to trample into the ground. But we will be unfortunate now: we will be distrusted; men will say of us, "They are no doubt worthy reactionaries who believe in God, fear vaccination and a Mongolian revival," when in fact we do none of these things. I do not even quarrel with this: I know I have myself chosen to consider myself a political man.

'But I wish that a regime would not further its cause, however just and noble, by making a popular explosion with its principles. They proclaimed that law should rule their state: and here, it is evident that it does not. It was perhaps merely an extension of initiative, by some official, the action of one accustomed to praise for his needy actions. But it is dangerous, it is indefensible.'

Pierrina felt sorry for these men, this man. It seemed that a general situation was being applied at least to her palazzo, and she, the least aristocratic of enervated gentility, was causing many difficulties for men she had always regarded as superiors. She sighed: it would be a luxury to be languid; swept onwards by unmannerly tides, she would finally have to stop being languid and realise that she was merely lazy.

At times like that, she knew she was unfit for any employment, however limpid and functional she might picture herself. She remembered the Mozart song about birds having to follow the spring to fulfil their destiny as eternal lovemakers. She tried to hum it, but she felt too exhausted even to fulfil her destiny: certainly it made her tired to think of chasing the sun to inflame the dying red foliage of an autumn passion. She confused her seasons: thinking of the mechanisms which inspired birds, she dozed.

*

Torgano went to the Director: like Pierrina, he had nothing to say, but relied on some administrative mind to discover something which would need saying and explaining. On the steps of the building sat an old beggar, knotted into crude ugliness by simulated diseases. Torgano knew a man who ran a school for beggars: he could turn an army deserter into an oval of boiled white sinews, in a week. He would, for a fee, turn youth into a nightmare of oiled wrinkles, a faceless dream-monster who dragged a shapeless body to a favourite church, or industrial concern.

The theory was that an incredible face or body could not wholly destroy the charm of a young man. The elder destitutes he cleaned and straightened; he thought true misery depressed charity, making the wealthy unlikely to anticipate the thrill of giving, if the beggar was repulsive and needful of more comfort than casual alms.

The graduates of the schools were successful: though some complained that after a year or two, it grew difficult to stand straight in the evenings, and take their place in respectable suburban society. It seemed that the school was growing into a laboratory for the manufacture of genuine Southern Spanish spells for the artificial ageing of frustrated princes. Torgano thought that men who would tie themselves into such ungainly bundles deserved recognition; he gave the man a pious coin, which was accepted with a saintly frown.

The Director listened to Torgano fumbling into his reasons. He understood half of what was said: by gross over-simplification, he explained inaccurately to a grateful Torgano what should have been said. Torgano wanted a shop in the palazzo now that it belonged to the government, he did not want Pierrina to know yet that he had spoken to the Director; he wondered if the decision on the palace was irrevocable. Torgano nodded at each point: if you left out every qualification, things did indeed become simple.

The Director talked on: Torgano thought, 'This is truth, it does not need explanation or qualification. If I let my attention wander, the truth will continue, and he will eventually condense all he had said into easily assimilable directions and elementary slogans.'

Coloured sounds came through the window: opposite, men on a scaffolding played hangmen with buckets and steel tubes. Their lazy shouts hung over the streets: below, their comrades semaphored in the heat, welcoming the containers full of rubble. Torgano watched, and it seemed to him as if the sticky air were water, that the men in the street used the careful, restricted movements of creatures far below the sea surface. The lowered buckets were like sticks or stones thrust into a mass of lobsters. In the restaurants, and in the shops, women were having things bought for them: they would sit in the springy steel chairs, and convulsively cross their legs. Then they looked round proud and nervous, and all the time you could hear pretty movements of the pointed feet of chairs.

The polite scrapings, and the anxious compliments and reassurances, these floated up so slowly: Torgano could just see into a jeweller's cave. There, the women sat down carefully, as if the chair was all part of the ritual and the service: he could imagine the slow, smug voice of the man.

'I want something pleasant for this, for this lady. A rope of black opal and rhinestones, perhaps?'

And the jeweller would nod and smile, and show off his exquisitely cut head, and keep one finger lightly on the alarm bell until they had left. He would bring out the imprisoned minerals, some of them with dead smoke and flowers enclosed by the sharp walls. And the women would imagine themselves half dressed and intoxicated wholly at the government's parties, the pure fire of this jewel or that curled line like a unicorn round their throats. The man and the woman would pause before the chemical colours, and think that one was the exact shade of some sentimental abstract.

And the jeweller would feel into a drawer, cock his revolver, feel happy and brave. He could imagine his manager, saying, 'Yes, Tonio, it is a pity that such men should die for our jewels: but you are faithful, and you are a good shot; for your courage, you may take an extra twelve fifty a week.'

'Thank you sir: I would shoot anyone if it were in the firm's interests.'

And the woman would come to him, breathing of relief and salvation. But he knew he would never shoot anyone, and often this thought was comforting.

Torgano heard too the street quarrels: men pushed through plate glass, slowly relaxing in shattered displays in the shop windows, wet with blood and anger. The crowds formed, the police threatened, moved the crowds back a few paces. The comedian or pickpocket in the midst of the tourists dispelled their fear, turning it to disgust and ruthlessness. The onlookers began to be objective about the sanded blood on the pavement. And the Director talked on, knowing nothing of the adventures below. He was feeling old, he felt he was pouring the mature old wine which was himself, in long conscientious glottal measures.

He wanted to say to Torgano, 'I do my job so well, there is no satisfaction in it if you leave me as soon as your case is finished. I do not wish to gloat, but I would enjoy seeing my clients; like the magistrate after the flogging has been carried out, I would like to talk to my victims, be pardoned by them, tell them what fine types they are. If I turn Torgano down, I shall never see him again, and there will be no pleasure in being grim and just, when I never know the reactions of those with whom I deal.'

Torgano looked past him steadily and receptively: a knock on the door disturbed them. It was a woman, tall and uncomfortable; she was wearing the clothes of a lady; they scarcely seemed to belong on her. She had been a legend: you could see that from the way she dressed herself, like a Norwegian tree. She had covered herself with Celtic silver, tweed scarves; you noticed her boots, fine and decorated as cheap lace. She was not impressive, her voice was worn and rusty; it seemed that some spring deep in her impeccable interior had been corroded, and was in danger of snapping.

She ignored Torgano, vaguely included him in an apologetic request for an audience. An apology in form, the

Director could only welcome her, agree to all she asked; he did not seem to know her. She settled herself, am unyielding geometrical shape, she tried to indent the chair to accommodate her stiff body. In the street, someone was repeating a curse, taunting and charming, the voice recited its anger, breaking now and then, as if the repetition had robbed the word of meaning, and the tongue of the power to launch words it did not understand. No one spoke: the desperation in the street become first embarrassing, then obsessive. The voice stopped: the obscene echoes flew round outside the windows for a time: the woman slipped sentences through the silence.

'You will not remember me, because you never remember anyone. I was small when you saw me last. I was three feet high with experience. I fought at dances and feared them more than anything. I was young: you could have seen that I was minutes to your years. I was small and perishable: I was not the sort of girl you could have sent by post, or embraced in a taxi; I have come back to see you, to see if you are interested in what you may be said to have ceased. My life may interest you?'

'Certainly, certainly. I am always pleased to see my old, er ...'

The Director wondered what was happening. Would she fling him back through the window on the point of her sword-umbrella, would she claim he had fathered some angled brat of hers? What might she not say, or threaten? She continued; she had the obvious gifts of suspense of a fourth-rate actress. She described herself at twenty:

'... I was a pad of foam beached on a fingernail of sand. Men would run up to me, prod me with their bare feet, and run off to their picnics. And I would lie, very beautiful, very useless. Then there would come young creatures, they might be horses, they might be children, I could never distinguish. They would breathe over me, they stayed with me till the tides came in, and I was left once more to dance and lurch on the rocks yards from shore. Then, you came to us: we lived in a house unfortunately old. You wanted our house: we did not very much mind that you should have it. You did not mind that you might do a small injustice: you looked at me, you saw a conventional bundle of post-adolescent woman.

'I doubt if I looked at you: I did not look at men until I was past thirty. We left our house, we lived here and there, we had nothing to do, we did not know what we had to do to live. Then, I was alone: I gave you my life, though you did not know it. I thought of you, there was no one else. I grew with you, I grew into you. I fastened on you like a squashy amorphous worm; clutched at you with blunt, rudimentary fingers. I did not marry, I never blamed you. But you must see that you, and your department, they were my life, they moved me and shaped me. I wanted to tell you this: you might forget that you are powerful, that I owe my life and development to you.'

The woman stopped, she thought she was being significant, even tragic: she did not tell her story well; she grew uncomfortable; her eyes seemed about to melt. The Director relaxed: he was glad he had fostered an anti-climax, he would have despised her if she had been merely strong, bitter and ugly. He told her that of course he knew he was powerful; that he could not be responsible for the lives of those affected by his duty, that he was flattered by her anonymous love for him. He smiled and stared to annoy her, but he did not feel intelligent, or any of the usual things he felt when people sat before him not knowing what to say: had he been smoking, he would have drawn a picture with his fiery comforter, and passed his hand through it, to mark and beautify a pause.

'It would be simple if you were not human,' she went on, 'if you rode over people, a centaur, an unpredictable lycanthropist, then I could consult you freely. But you are so obviously a compromise, I feel I cannot blame you for my own failures. But your injustice altered everything for me: because it was subtle, because you slipped in your sting while I was admiring your beautiful wings, and the nervous splendour of your wing-cases, I cannot forgive you. There is nothing to forgive, because there is everything to forgive.

'You were not a director then, you were young: I suppose it takes a special course to learn how to take palaces. There was a different regime, even. But we both know you abused your powers: even if you merely used them, you knew by the avowed principles of your superiors that you were deceiving yourself and many others.'

'I do my job,' the Director said. 'I would be a fool if I did not make the most of it: ideally, it is not an immoral job. It can be made oppressive, it is not tyrannical, even by the most exacting European or oriental standards. I would agree that that does not mean much: but I am bound to get the bargain for my masters as long as I do not warp my conscience. And you are my masters: you, by giving me your house, became my master. Politically, I have given you the best deal I could, we could, find. I am sorry, that is what happens: you cannot anyway expect me to agree with what you say.'

He thought of the trick he had perfected to win his monuments: he began to hate the squandering, cloying, shabby lover opposite. He imagined himself at a mass: a Slavonic mass, the true golden virgins rising in banks like candles, the topmost blonde heads fusing into the ikons with their broken crosses, the lame explanatory characters set lopsided in the crumbling mosaics.

He felt himself into the middle of this vast pagan sentiment: the Glagolitic sounds twisting and slipping from wriggling girl-mouths. He always imagined in this luscious cathedral when illogical avengers were attempting to make him feel awkward; sometimes he was the young patriarch whose beauty dissolved the scene into orgy; sometimes he was an insignificant dignitary, obedient and small, pressed against the legs of the front row of singing girls. It was pleasant, its imaginative details and unlikeliness amused him so that he smiled at angry opponents without thinking. This woman was not satisfactory: she was one of those who leave scent on the hands and lapels of their men, and paragraphs of spiteful words in their ears.

Torgano sighed: she was the sort of fencing woman who

was drawn to you by the vortices of a petty, mechanical world which condemned you to fifty years in love with her. She was like Pierrina, unsure and fascinating. He was sorry for the Director: poor, very small man. He was quite exhausted for a minute, sitting there in his desk, blinking and imaginative.

'Consider if you had been my love years ago,' the woman said, 'and had left me without a word. Suppose I became ill, and screamed at flowers, seeing nostalgic butterflies in the bottom of teacups. Suppose I collected our favourite walks into one great sentimental garden, our slinking jokes into one jabber of private nonsense. You would have become me, I would contain you, all you said and thought: you would think nothing of me, but I should have stolen you, taken you to slave for me and love me in my paradise of delicious fears. I might be in your life, just a tradesman: you might know me as a superior kind of baker, one who calls with ear-shaped buns and a flow of technical queries. But I would see myself as your deep lover, life-deep, so close and important. How ironical: that is how you were to me. How can I complain?'

'How indeed?' the Director arched himself in the chair; he flicked at a sunbeam which prowled among ominous doodles on the pastel blotting paper. 'How indeed?'

The three of them needed little to repeat the words until they lost meaning and became a faith. He went on, 'Yes, indeed, like a blind jaguar, an event thrusts its thin claws into the dust, springs, pounces, in the permanent dark it prepared its leap. I cannot say I regret what has happened, and still be sincere. If you have finished, you should leave: I am not responsible for your exaggerations.'

The woman left: she had been humiliated, she had been shaken into weak imitation by the Director. She had not allowed herself one blasphemous snarl of anger at the men: as fury had clamped her lips in a maniac ellipse. When she got outside, she cursed politely: she would have liked to beat her forehead just once, fairly lightly on some wall softly papered. She resisted herself: that was a pity, for she would genuinely have enjoyed making a silent private scene.

Torgano asked the Director, after a resentful pause, as if he were waiting for the woman's pale lavender ectoplasm to settle and evaporate:

'What do you think of my scheme? It would be a useful experiment, we would all amuse ourselves. Perhaps,' he said for an accusing joke, unsuccessful of course, 'when Pierrina Tarrault has not eaten for a month, she will be glad to marry me, her spiritual banquet.'

The Director laughed, a cool deliberate laugh, as if he had put a bronze paperweight on a pile of troublesome and frivolous documents. 'I think I should like discreetly to telephone the palazzo, to see how she feels, you understand. I shall conceal your presence.'

Torgano hid himself nervously while the other phoned: he made sure Pierrina would not hear his familiar breath as the base to the Director's hurried monologue.

'Yes, you are well. And the palace? Another animal? Perhaps the air affects them. Could we dredge for them? What's that? Something about fruit? Oh yes; the rotten fruit will sink and bury them, of course. I'll send divers down with spades to exhume them. No, not a pleasant job, but necessary: the department does not keep a large stock of unicorns and so forth.

'Yes, we have made inventories: you may decide what you want to keep: we shall not be difficult about small things; anything unusual will be deducted from the final price of course. Yes indeed, we do apologise for the hurry, but, as you see, the parapets and the roof are not safe. How heavy are those animals? Well, if they weigh as much as a small man, we don't want the police jumping in to rescue them at night, do we? No, of course not: I knew you would agree. Well, I won't keep you.'

The Director sank away into his chair as he retreated, a suitful of mystery, at last: 'Look here, Torgano: there might conceivably be a job for you, to supply the government with antiques. And if you do, they must be good: don't even get genuine ones if they look like fakes. This isn't a definite offer:

everything depends, that is what I have learnt from life, everything depends. And here, everything depends on me.'

He laughed with insincere self-depreciation. Torgano was prepared to laugh at anything now: he was used to feeling the marginal happiness of undiscriminating laughter. It was an emotion he knew well and distrusted. He realised the Director had made a vague suggestion: he had no reason for unthinking relaxation. But he wanted to be an official, wanted to sit with the other confused officials, to be ordered by these polished unmilitary gentlemen.

He suddenly longed to participate in conferences, where coffee was brought to tired, irresponsible comedians by cultured women, who were scented with square, difficult concepts, who wore administrative complexities like chaste, stiff skirts. There would be a life, a career; yet, apathetic, he made little noise and delight for the Director. It was so hard to be interested in things unemotional: Torgano had come to ignore events which did not shatter or transfigure him.

The buckets on the scaffolding rose and fell, like a game started, abandoned, still obeying the childish details of mechanics which errant owners had ignored. The listless men worked on, their ears cocked towards a summer andante of trombone fanfares: the heavy chocolate music was hypnotic and boring. Work flitted through a routine, a routine of sly evasion, of wistful guitarists playing reluctantly in out-of-season rivieras. The supervisors tilted wine from leather: they played with the warm liquids, throwing them greedily down their throats from a distance.

They laughed monstrously; they roared in mock beastliness to old schoolboys, who had been drinking all the afternoon in restrained, muted beer cellars. Everything was a joke to cry about: the girls, they were funny, but they were tragic, so the supervisors, inflated with obscure lusts, jumped round them, with great laughs, tears, accusing curses. It was an amusing pantomime, this pageant of the incomprehensible: the bottles of strong honey were passed round. The other workmen looked down incuriously: no resentment, no laughter; no anger; no work. Torgano dreamed himself Director, watching the idle lines of the picture flow and gurgle with alcoholic suavity. The silent orgies ebbed to repletion.

Another interruption: the Director suddenly whimsical, Torgano aroused and apparently intelligent. A man, firm, respectful, full of misconceptions and conceit, he came in, horribly hot. His face should have run away to its bone, streams of hot fat and exhausted blood ran from his cheeks over a once-silk shirt. He was obviously a carnivore, probably nourished on small boys and squirrels, from his colouring. He was offensively hot; he made others guilty because they did not feel the heat with such sensitivity. The Director fussed with the window: hot draughts thumbed through papers, smoothed ties with soft, feminine fingers.

'Yes, it is hot,' said the Director. 'Perhaps you should try to extinguish yourself. Or let us roll you in mud; I feel sure we should bake you in clay, like some hedgerow animal, through your own internal combustion.'

The Director could be impolite, obviously; the man smiled: he did not understand. He was stupid enough to exhaust anyone's sense of humour. He spoke, and the words came oiled and lucent:

'I was a policeman day before yesterday; a fine officer I was. Admired, loved, especially by the children, as I fished in the carnival waters with the classical piece of string on a truncheon.'

'Ah yes, I see: harbour police.'

'Not quite: carnival policemen: otherwise unemployed. I came down in the world, I give you that. But I'm not proud now: give me a job, Director, and I'll show you what a private education can do for you. Did you see me yesterday? No? You missed a little gem of an actor then. Modest I am, but I can tell you, there wasn't one who saw me who didn't say just that. A little gem, that play with the truncheon: the hat raised, you might say taken off, my *papier mâché* head! a rare sight!'

'It must have been one to make children grow a decade in a day: I wish our treasurer had been there; it might have given him ideas for a national theatre. Now, useless funny man: what can your ordinary playful Director do for you? What, though, did you do yesterday, that you did not come to me at once, after your successful appearance?'

'Sir, I have a temperament: I am delicate, nervous, I confess. I did not wake up yesterday. My friends had offered me brandy, in case I was too frightened to give of my best. You must understand,' aggressive, the carnival breath feeling its age, making its age felt in the still room, 'you must understand that I am no ordinary clown. I despised the other unemployed, I hated them because their children dressed so badly. I called them "state brat", "Aryan hybrid", to their faces. They had a dialect: why, when I was ten, I had mine painlessly removed. I am not like them, the poor, who talk wrongly, who get drunk, who cannot afford to dress themselves decently.

'Yes indeed, poverty is a disgrace to the poor: no government is any good which allows these degenerates to flaunt their incompetence before honest, intellectual folk like myself. I admit, I am not high in my profession: even as mock policemen go, I may not have international standing: but I am good. Give me just any job: preferably on the administrative side. I can do most things, you see: I was well taught – and faithful. At the open prison, I said to the guards, "Here I am, here I stay: I keep faith." And do you know, funny I said that, the very next week, three prisoners shot while escaping. Funny, really: here I am, here I stay; and them all fingering their submachine guns; they couldn't do anything about me, you see, for I keep faith. They were just waiting for me to walk out of the door, but no, not me.'

The Director, waiting for him to walk out of the door, rolled him through it: though he was standing, the movement was that of a man-sized barrel. Outside, the hot man was saying, 'I am lonely, fetch me my wife.' He tried to stand, pushing himself up from the floor where had subsided with bowed, unreliable frog's legs. He splayed himself over the corridor: he lost himself and scrabbled on the walls like a fly on glass. Torgano would not have been surprised to see him reel over the ceiling and sit disorientated on a wall. The Director was smiling: why? He himself did not know.

'Ah well,' he said, 'I suppose it is natural for some of the carnival jokers to hang fire for a day or two. He wasn't sober, you realise; you looked shocked when I staggered him out.'

'Why, yes, I soon spotted that he was drunk.'

The easy lie came pure and free as a bubble: all his training had taught Torgano to lie: lie about books and people, 'Life', to falsify even optical delusions. Usually. it was not just conceit and laziness which made him do this, but occasionally it helped to have perfected a shameless technique. The Director said goodbye to Torgano, with many sleek kindnesses; he pushed him past the hilarious offices where respectful men made love to fantastic secretaries, stalking them on hands and knees.

Down the stairs, where sad men and women went for their private conversations, across the hall, where the government had placed statues of porters and automatic assistants who were operated by bribes or gentle pressure. The doors, bronze with allegories, the glass soiled with fingers wet and squalid from the street, or women, or other alien institutions.

Torgano did not try to digest his interview: he watched for a few minutes activities in the shops and buildings. But it was not real: it was jerky, the actors shouted across one another, they did not have the measured realism and timing of the accomplished creatures Torgano had watched from the Director's office. There were no fanfares, just women throwing their hips to the saxophones and play horns of the invisible impresarios.

Somewhere a child was singing his sins, 'The blue horses, *qu'est-ce qu'ils font*? Snagged whips, they leap slowly over my new trousers. And now quickly, horse ladies, in the clothes just as you are in the enamel books: quickly, Lord Carol, my rabbit sweetheart, with your exciting wings and wet ears. Quickly –

basta! Es is genüg. There are ghosts in love at the head of the stair. It's just five o'clock, *et j'ai tué mon père.*'

'Really,' thought Torgano, 'some of these old songs are quite primitive: they must stem from the Thirty Years War, I suppose, I don't really think they need to be taught in folklore classes though. They leave a taste in the mouth, like a mosquito quickly and unthinkingly nibbled. Now, let me think of something unpleasant: pain. The idea and images of pain: that would be a purifying subject for contemplation. A man twisted like a doorknob on a clean wooden bed: the face crumpled by emotion and thrown into the fire like a piece of despised paper.'

Then he thought of Pierrina, and the man in the straps, the man bearing down on the methodically adjusted thongs was himself. What was Pierrina saying to him? Did she really write those letters, or was it all his imagination, all a romantic game to make himself unhappy by demanding impossible emotions from Pierrina? Was not their relationship hindered by himself alone with his ridiculous tantrums? He could only guess; and it was a theme which recurred and puzzled him for the rest of the week.

*

Pierrina went to her solicitor: she expected nothing, but she began again to feel greedy for the money she was to receive. She came into the office: sporting monks stopped illuminating divorce reports with pictograms, politely stuffed their unholy laughter in their cheeks while they motioned her into the inner cell. When she was inside, she could still hear plainly the oblique comments and the artistic games of the obscene seminarists.

She wondered why the solicitor did not object to this. He was more than old: he was of an age to be transfigured: he was the incredible saint who had lived for many centuries for his piety to be recognised, for the divine transport to taxi him alive to heaven. His natural functions had obviously ceased to have relevance long before: undoubtedly he neither ate nor breathed, heard nor saw. Life had no more tricks and indications of extreme age to produce and apply to him. He had outlived natural resourcefulness.

Pierrina was surprised that he should need a window in his office: she thought light and birds and rain would confuse and destroy him. She explained all things to him. He made careful, precarious movements of his rotted disgusting neck in professional answer to her indignation. Pierrina went slowly on: she felt like a revolutionary explaining kindly and patiently to the idiot uncle of some reactionary king, that his nephew had been chopped up and fed to swans, and that he too must shortly be painlessly dismembered over the dark lake.

She felt she needed to explain things like care and love and war to him. This was how Torgano should be: ever listening, courtly and decayed, without pretension or extravagant secrets. She would never feel bewildered by the strange passions of this ruin; she would never be made unhappy, as Torgano made her, by the sophisticated reason of this unlikely survivor. She mouthed across the piles of lives which separated them:

'This Torgano, you see, well, I do not get on well with him always; he demands too much illogical passion. He even frightens me, I do not know what he wants me to do for him; he always seems angry and aloof. But it is not true, I have to consider the proposal he made: he must at least be considered, though we may discount his loverly qualifications. Can you say what must be done? Can you perhaps tell me if this is what a palace is worth?'

The old man came cautiously out of his shell: the crinkled arms and legs were driven out, as it were by hydraulic engines, then the bashed face, brown and blighted, pushed timidly into the green light.

'Yes,' he said, 'I see I see I see. Strange: well, there's nothing we can do, you know. What? Yes, the Director's quite right: the price will be quite fair, and you would be foolish to fight him. Of course, I have seen everything like this: I am not going to remember it all, because you are not listening, and all my clerks are. But, believe me, and I speak as one who remembers everything, jazz, the Turks, *anéantissement*, the Kaiser's troublesome duodenum – you escape lightly.

'You never know how fast you may find yourself betrayed by the ideals you followed in your youth: you should be glad that there are no metaphysical surprises for you in your disillusion. You might so easily have found yourself washed up and pounded, unable to float high on your beliefs, over the roofs and the bunches of poisonous tentacles.

'Now, I was not so fortunate: my ideal was youth: I did all my parents told me. When I was small, I was a legendary conformist. I was the boy who never bit his swinish comrades to the bone: I never went out in the evenings when I could work; I never stayed in, when I could play some fierce game in rank autumn mud. My morals were nondescript: I was all my family could wish.

'As I grew older, I was never found jolly with gin among the doorstep milk bottles in the morning. I always took my girls to hotels, never to their homes, or mine. My morals grew still more nondescript: I was popular, I fitted into any system or society like a piston. How proud I was! One year I wore my collar tight as heraldic coronets, the next, soft and bosomy; never did I imitate the pathic Bohemian and wear none. I went into the law, and the girls became women, and more discreet. And I gently drank myself to sleep, and each morning I pinched my sick fingers round the syringe and woke myself to rectitude and an awareness of all that was beautiful and meaningful.

'I prospered, of course. I have no ties, men and women fluttered round me; I was the most opaque and fascinating flame in my suburb. Yes, I was a success – then, disaster! To a man in my position, a public figure, imagine the consequences of a shift in the conception of what was required of a successful man. Of course, much remained: the training of the young did not change.

'But it was no longer enough to be as elegant and accomplished as a fine chauffeur: men were required to be inefficient and noisy. They had to be found out, they had to be attacked and insulted in public. At parties they had to throw bottles, not accurately, as I did, but foolishly, splintering the heads of visiting old women. They cheated clumsily at cards, they hit their superiors, instead of the promising youngster, as I always used to.

'They insulted men who carried coshes and could garrotte superbly with their wives' nylon stockings: they were hammered like loose floorboards with heavy shoes by the women they approached. They got drunk until they could not see which women were attractive, and which disastrously and thoroughly married. They ran into endless trouble: they had breakdowns of all kinds. They went shoplifting; they refused to profiteer during wars. They stubbed out their reefers in the ashtrays of sensitive policemen.

'Yet they were successful: I was outmoded. I had not, as they had, friends, carried to success by similar orthodoxies. They took pity on one another for their dangerous mistakes; they squared coroners; they swore that the wives of ministers had led them on with promises of office and Afghan hounds. All this they did for one another: they perpetuated themselves. And they had the nerve to call me a gentleman, but too gentle! The first time I heard these gentle maniacs call me that, it stopped me drinking, I grew healthy, even more out-of-date.

'Ah love: I wanted love. I wanted to sink deep in the feather beds of the passionate bourgeois. But these piggy men had changed the women. Women wanted a hard time. They grew used to carrying sotted men to cars: they were accustomed to seeing their husbands prowling vicious parks like public health department employees. They knew what it was like to be humiliated or assaulted every time they went out with their little men, and yet they enjoyed it. How could they? I was not asked what I thought of life, or the latest opera, on which I always held an opinion, though I never actually went to them.

'No, women asked me who was living with whom: I felt like a hotel receptionist questioned by the house detective. I was humiliated: I could touch no one without a hundred eager mother-women saying how good it was for me at last, and would we like to spend a weekend at their empty flat if that wasn't too inconvenient. Times changed, you see. Now, all I have to talk about is my unnatural age: my housekeepers look on me as a delightful rich child: horrible old reptiles they are too. The thought of their great nursemaid paws putting me to bed, smoothing the pillows, it all revolts me. You had better see my partner: he is a new man. He is concealed in the gloom. Perhaps you had not noticed him. But first, guess my age. An old man's whim: do not hesitate.'

Pierrina impatiently thought: does an old fool want to be thought an even older one? Does he want to blame his belated and adolescent sexuality on some nightmare vision of senility? Aloud: 90, or 120? The delighted neigh, the yellow coral gums uncovered, then the realisation of some callous insult.

'Madam, I am 73, I always understood it was a well-preserved 73.'

Pierrina went thankfully to his partner. He reassured her, trying to make a pure but interesting impression.

'I fear my friend has suffered unduly from his illusions. But there is no reason why we should not find some method of preserving yours, is there, my dear?'

The partner was apparently 35, his acting the habitual father must surely be bogus. She did not like this man, uncomplicated by asperities or roughness physical or mental. He too said the government would have quoted a good price: the palace went. He did suggest that Torgano and Pierrina should go together to see the Director: Pierrina felt this showed a romantic belief in nothing; she did not protest, she resolved to contact Torgano soon. The younger man seemed glad to have finished his business: he had many wisdoms to bore women with, he spared few.

'You know, you have an opportunity to make yourself a life of normal felicity. No palace or other archaic responsibilities. I am married, I have a spaniel and a wife, I am happy. You might be like me: I can do all I want, games and amusements of all kinds. One day I may romp in the snow with what they used to call a pug-deb: you know, those society men or women who brawl and prance in endless epicene adventure through the jealous imagination of ambiguous wives. My wife does not control me, she does not mind about me: sometimes I train as a military officer, ah, comrades, that is what I ask of everyone: *Kamaradschaft*, comradeship. You will find one day, that is all that matters: to be able to talk to anyone about nothing. That is my definition of the gentleman.

'Yes, you are right, I have made a study, one afternoon, it was, actually, of European art of this century, also by accident a copy of New York Dada I found in the library. I got much pleasure from such research: it all started when my wife brought home a cast iron lampshade. Ever so Twenties it was: or 'Teens or Thirties; anyway, ever so almost old, if you understand. I am interested in delicate things, beautiful things. I love the unusual, the strange, and oh, yes, I am so very strange a man myself. Yes, I am a scholar, of a kind. But I do so believe in liberal scholarship, don't you: the superficiality of the liberal mind?'

'Not entirely.'

'Oh come – you're not an academic?'

'Only when people like you argue with me.'

'Haha, haha! I see you are a very delicate thing. You know,' he moved in for a flattering close-up. 'I could be fond of you: I'm not really married, not properly, you know. It needn't matter, if we want to go for a meal, or a walk by the long sea. Nothing need ever matter.'

Pierrina thought how the films and novels, from which she hoped he was consciously quoting, continued. They would say: 'She held an umbrella over herself like a tree. She knew she had never looked more beautiful; an ant ran over her head, and he crushed it between his strong fingers, and once more she marvelled at his wonderful masculine strength. That strength that was so Masculine, impressing because she was so Feminine. They stood up, and he carried her over the marsh and the frogs and the sea unicorns which had swum up to admire her, until they came to the trees and the banks of pansies in the moss, where medieval portable organs were trilling sexless invitations on their straight girlish pipes.'

And so on. Horribly, she was not sure that he was joking: she thought with pity, how unlucky she always was. No one was pleasant and interesting. Except the Director, but from him she was cut off; they would never know one another well enough to omit the things from conversation they felt both necessary and hurtful. She left the office, she felt dusty and contaminated. She would not have been surprised if her skin had been veined with black, like the curious face of a servant, interrupting as Luther, for the hundredth time, repeated his diseased trick with the inkpot. She felt ashamed and angry. She walked by the canals, which were tossing and slopping like a huge tureen, and longed slightly for Torgano.

*

Torgano was attempting to create in himself an unusual despair: he walked in the parks, where sailors were throwing tin souvenir knives at the trees. In endless games of violence, children were accustoming themselves to death: they irritated the rationality without reason of their governments and parents. They were having conferences to decide whether to use as weapons the crude flints lining the flowerbeds: their reasons were exquisite, soon Torgano was attempting to avoid stones. The trees were black: men had written on them; cats and cashmere squirrels disputed in the branches. Torgano composed many wearisome arguments:

'So we have no values: that is evidently good, since we have the best reasons for our rejection of standards. There is left to us, for me, in a world where all the nicest people have always abdicated responsibility, only the last heroic gesture, the act of inspiration or madness which may cut through prejudice and argument to reach the truth, but which is essentially the romantic renunciation of a dying man.

'The act is against government, reason, even liberty; it is a sign of the end of a world, however fine its results, it is irrational and dangerous. The act of a man committed to nothing, it may be to disarm, to give a tithe of the nation's jewels to schools of bayonet fencing, or even to climb into gold-plated cars and be fired to the end of the world. We are children who see our fathers coming to close the sandpit, who work feverishly either to build tiny palaces on wet sand mountains, or to collect sand to throw at the inevitable and decrepit old gentlemen,

'Perhaps one day I shall hurl my life and my love in two trickling handfuls at the sagging engineers who come to collect me: but that will never happen so long as I know Pierrina, for I could never leave her.'

And at times Torgano thought how dreadful if bombs should knock the heads of those immutable trees, and flake their bark; and at other times he thought how wicked if all we erratic and heedless people should not be punished by the powerful chemicals of our elites. He had all the questions, none of the answers; he sighed, and somewhere in his chest, a door creaked open.

He breathed deeply; there was the rasp of oxidised leaves deep inside him; he laughed at himself for imagining illnesses, then coughed furtively into his handkerchief. He sat in the park; all this ugliness was quite beautiful; someone had stuck cotton-wool plumes on the bald heads of factory chimneys; the slums had never looked so picturesque, with the old men stacked on the balconies, waiting to die.

Birds flew swiftly over the heaps of brick, as if afraid they would be paralysed by the fumes of beautiful weeds; the tenements were so full of life, so organic, that animals scuttled through the courtyards, afraid that buttresses would lean down and snatch them up. Torgano imagined the elder, more pessimistic rats wondering how long it could all last, the cheerful youngsters and economists assuring them that there were no signs of these decaying skyscrapers ever subsiding. Torgano knew the foundations were firm: as the old slums collapsed, new were built on the ruins, so that now thousands of stinking homes lay beneath the narrow shoulders of this new world. In the waste ground nearby, boys were burning worn tyres and rubbing mud into deep wounds to cure them.

'This is the spirit of my country,' thought Torgano. As long as there were slums, there would be men to be liberal about them; and what women, what men the slums produced. Of course, the women were nothing to look at when they were over twenty, and the men were only fit to be soldiers when they were over thirty.

'I must be grateful that chance gave me these things objectively.'

Enlightened though Torgano often was, he would have admitted himself, that he was not really sure of how to assume a radical attitude: people were born conservative, and if something unpleasant and traumatic happened to them they became interested in truth for its own sake. Nothing had ever happened to him; all the more reason for remaining conservative; meanwhile, he might allow himself the occasional burst of indignations, so as not to feel more than just a few centuries out of date.

Dogs walked about fastidiously: careful, sensitive, they inspected their park, the easily offended housewifely noses running over every inch of the seats and the lower parts of the tree trunks. They would come over to Torgano and breathe lightly on him, till they were called away. And Torgano was embarrassed by this interest; he wished Pierrina had been there to make precious jokes about the dogs, to clothe them, like joints of meat, in captivating paper ruffles. They would wrap themselves in private illusions and allusions like invalids in rugs; they would drink each other's nonsense like cocktail drinkers in advertisements. They would be as far apart as ever, but to be able to laugh about how incongruous they both were; that was surely the first step to a lasting and quite juvenile partnership.

Torgano watched the flowers intently, they did not move, did not wander about aimlessly, fidget, or scratch themselves: he felt like a sentimental statesman who blows up a world because he has seen the flowers, eternal and silent, and has drawn all manner of inhuman and far-fetched analogies from their supreme indifference and insensibility. Overhead, there were swans; they flopped along, fully extended and breathless, their wings groaning, their heavy bodies defenceless in flight, not a little unnatural. They ploughed on through the sky, never calling encouragement or friendly ridicule to their fellows: their beaks were jammed shut with effort.

'I should not like to be a swan,' thought Torgano. It was the most original thing, though not the most profound, he had said that day; it cheered him slightly.

He wandered through the people who snorted and trampled past him: here were hordes of horses, and their leaders too were horses. Yet Torgano was comforted by the pressure of the hairy bodies, the play of the hooves, scented with crushed herbs and nettles. He heard the men saying, 'Are you going to the match between Youth and Beauty in the Pallana stadium tonight? Youth has a good dirty team, I hear Ballanin came out of hospital yesterday, but I don't think the forwards gouge as well as Beauty's: they don't use their knees and elbows either, as I like to see it done. Get scared as soon as the blood flows, and the reserves just sit in the dressing rooms sucking aspirin when the doctors are called onto the pitch. And of course the Minister of Sport is coming, and we all know he is a great fan of Beauty.'

Everywhere there were dejected little men agreeing, their huge comrades went through the motions of crippling someone, and laughed without malice. And the women said, 'Well, I knew he was coming round to me that evening, so of course I went out to watch the goldfish, if you know what I mean. And when I came back, about two, that was: well, there he was laying on the sofa, with some socialist newspaper over his face, and a great tabby cat licking up a puddle of gin in a corner. He looked so sweet, but I knew it couldn't last.'

'And what about the cat?' asked uncomprehending women; and the reply. 'Oh yes, the cat,' did not satisfy them.

*

Gallista found some battlements: flung on a hill, they were baked and crinkled, lizards ran among crumbs of masonry: purple and gold, the lichens mocked imperial pretensions. Men and women looked down at the houses below, the buildings which had fallen from the sky, splitting with the impact like soft rocks, scattering rubble and clothes over the toy gardens, Gallista felt enormous: to move her feet would be to kick against the pleated tinfoil of the sea; she moved to the stone blocks behind her, composed herself against their curious stained surfaces, their patches of butterflies and rain patterns.

A rock, a girl, some dragons; and indeed miniature dragons with sun-heavy lids peeped from their comfortable homes and declined the challenge. Inscrutable insects ran across a slab, gesticulating with blind feelers at insects marching in the opposite direction. Gallista could feel her heart synchronising itself with the waves of transparent smoke which beat slowly upwards from the stone.

Soon she was keeping the same lazy time as the day: abandoned to the surefire clichés of nature, she felt no restraints; she thought, 'I am so near the heart of things, I might even take off my shoes, or swing inviting filigree traps for butterflies,' but it was too hot to be immodest.

She laughed and said to herself, 'In all the best operas, after a climax, all the singers should fall back into armchairs and cough, even weep, like bears trying to climb out of a pit.'

And she smiled when she saw a man struggling up the slope, slowly as if the sunshine were treacle, and the rocks heaps of sulphur. It was the Director: the coincidence which curls furry and taut beneath every conspiracy, every novel, to be released like a feline spring to make people laugh, and children cry. The Director said accusingly to Gallista, hating her as if she had been one of the Fates: 'It's hot.' He spoke in neat blocks of meticulously punctuated sound: like a mechanical author, he composed small beauties and comprehensive slogans with compulsive monotony.

Gallista agreed with all he said so eagerly, that it seemed to the Director obvious that she was thinking of something else, or possibly nothing at all; with his long and powerful wedge-shaped tongue, he attempted to rouse her, insolent and insistent, he was politely rude. She was thrilled, pretended not to notice.

'This hill jumps up like a tall star,' he said. 'I see from your white emotive eyes that that is what you were thinking, always think. I knew someone who used to say how people like you, receptive and soggy, were "adept at separating the chaff from the chaff", but he said this just once too often, and then we all knew it meant nothing. Down in the city, thousands of men even now are loading wagon loads of girls exactly like you, chaining the lathe-turned limbs together, exporting the mundane beasts to all parts of Europe. But you escaped to this hill: you live, queen rat, under a limestone cube, and when dogs come and push their noses at you, you bribe them with pawfuls of unripe corn mixed with sand.'

Gallista thought, what a fine Spanish gallant is imprisoned in this obscure old man, who I hope I dislike; and aloud, 'As you say, the view is pleasant; but why think I live here? It is a public monument.'

Delicious and respectable child, secretly smirked the Director; let us, having climbed this volcanic monster, take advantage of our height to enjoy a breathtaking metaphorical leap with this girl, who had such a regard for public monuments, and doubtless, for public institutions like me.

Amused and foolish, the couple played with obsolete words, even threw fir cones at one another in lazy half enjoyment. Gallista said to herself that here was at last a man who did not care for anything, one whom she could explore and crack open like a set of interlocking eggshell caves.

They walked together down towards the town: on the way they passed processions among the copper bushes, the shattered lumps of stone honeycomb which made the artificial landscape. There were priests, swaying along like elephants in their gorgeous sacks: youths carried poles on which symbols had been mounted: old men mumbled cheerfully, the priests intoned without moving their lips. It was a festival, animals were being taken to be buried; the beasts lay on biers, their legs pinned prayerfully together, the unfriendly paws open towards the sky, like tables they were carried to graves by sad small boys. Here and there you could see a stiff snout, the drooped mouth and pathetic ears of some failed beast.

Behind the animals came confused women, who did not really feel like laughing; children, immaculate and scourged, leaping ahead of their avenging mothers, wailed to go home, or be buried. In the road came three happy men, tiny in their unsuitable suits, they staggered with wreaths; they were hot, they draped the laurel and the lilies of lacquered brass round their necks like lifebelts. Solemnly, they answered the priest's ritual questions, then turned to laugh wet and golden at one another, ecstatic and speechless. Quivering with tears and laughter the cortege ambled to the sandy pits, where the animals were tipped from their lace paper coffins to thud unpoetically into the rubble.

'That was so unlikely,' the Director, 'the blessing of dead animals must certainly represent a truth: a truth, or an observation of what is necessary, And for the priests in their big silken boots to walk all in this way, that too is faith. And those children who did not want to come, it really gives meaning to sin and discipline.'

Gallista smiled; really it was impossible to penetrate this plated bore: she only hoped he did not mind her keeping silent when he sparkled with thick-skinned platitudes. She put a hand in her necklace, and let it swing in synthetic rustic abandon for a few seconds; as time went on, she saw it as the best answer to most of the Director's questions, to set her mushroom-shaded fingers on the crystal and resin beads, and to smile like one who had been preserved in aromatic disinfectants and tobacco for some centuries, the archetypal smile which exists only on the fingertips of the embalmer. Gallista thought of it to herself as a venerable smile, disdainful but lively, as captivating and disquieting as a caterpillar making of itself a cynical moustache on a sleeping face.

Gallista and the Director thought themselves very wise: a careful look might have shown that the Director regarded the girl with the fear and pride a schoolman felt when, to bolster an argument, he could produce one of the rarer, pocket-sized demons. And Gallista, winding her life down a spiral, thinking the inevitable changes of direction had no natural motivation, had only the ideas about the Director she had about everyone else. In being wrong, she was not even inventive. For the wrong reasons, they were quite happy.

Into the town they came, from their hunting trip: amused they chattered about the allegory of the town's illuminated crest, a centaur carrying a dead man across his back, they made the usual tiresome remarks about it. And the Director felt happy, that he had so many palaces to share with such an obvious collector as Gallista.

'Funny old man,' thought Gallista, for the moment unsophisticated; she thought of the men who had trotted along with her, men who lived in worlds so full of overtones that it was like living in a bell. Men who would go to concerts, see animals' eyes in the gold wallpaper, and produce from their pockets kittens, presents for her, while the music ground on self-consciously. Now, the Director was too artificial to be insincere; surely no one could be so patriotic and so cynical?

Surely here was a hero, the man who goes away for fifty years to fight dragons, women, his own moral mediocrity, knowing that when he returns to his ravaged and scolding wife – or was she his sister? it was all so long ago – there will be dragons curled in baskets on the hearth, women locked in trees whispering to be loved, and all the doubts of his own existence. He was the defeated general going home to revolution: he was a legendary man, who saw to the end of his fable, but being a hero through and through, resisted the temptation to act to change the ending.

Gallista prepared her little emotional deceits, the sentimental ligatures with which she bound her men; when they had been trussed in a chair, she could ask them many intelligent questions on the great absolutes, and the lesser; did they admire Delphi, steel, adolescence, vertigo, all the repetitious riddles of the truly inquisitive. And the Director walked along in a small transparent envelope he had quickly constructed, made of that exquisite fabric, self-pity shot with conceit. Majestically he moved, tossing people aside to make way for his girl, like a capacious and competent agricultural machine, he pushed Gallista through a market, stumbled her through roots and edible flowers.

He knew that if he said one wrong word Gallista would leave him, would not provide for him the compensations for a life of dull theft. He thought of a man he knew once who had gone to Japan saying, 'Of course, one must appreciate things in comic terms,' whose only accomplishment had been to play dice in numerous chipped brown interiors, to live in miniature landscapes in cardboard boxes.

The Director had been a useful animal, every part of him had gone to be sustaining and uninviting food for people who would never thank him: and now, after years of a fierce enjoyment, of being devoured, he was lonely: gently he would rest his head on cushions and curtains, whisper into the ever-ready ears, that he was lonely, that he wanted to be prime minister or something similarly comforting and emotive. And the Director would imagine the well-filled textiles whispering back the replies he wanted to hear.

But now, through the squares, where policemen in feather hats drew along traffic with strings and intimate pipings, soon Gallista would arrive at his office. He concentrated on developing his nervousness into a charming hysterical lunacy.

*

In the prisons, after a few seconds of daylight, warders were putting the sun away in the broom cupboard: thousands of prisoners listened for the whispered coaxings, before the lights went out. In the schools, children made poems with spilled ink, and like convicts, sweated out their sins. Communications were primitive: once more words had to be distilled from identical sounds; prisoners, as they tapped the necessary formal introduction, longed for the cheap words which flowed through wirelesses. The students and the religious locked themselves in their stone worlds, and swore that, if they were ever released, they would make every word meaningful, the slow dissipation of a hoard of repressions. Cats wondered why it had gone dark in those large, uncomplicated buildings where the rats always seemed too busy and preoccupied to be caught and eaten.

They resolved to penetrate the locked courtyards, where rank rhubarb poked its head over the wall, standing no doubt in some bizarre, horticultural nastiness. Sometimes a child would fling a ball, like a parody of a hydrogen mass, over the wall, and it would seem to be about to bounce through the bars. But the children cried to lose a toy, and sentimental prisoners were, with justice, beaten up by their more realistic fellows for encouraging in themselves many fantastic and unwholesome daydreams. And the soldiers took off their splendid sashes and ornaments: sometimes an officer would look in, to tell them what values they could dream of defending that night; and he would leave part of his uniform to be cleaned.

In the political prisons, where sometimes, joked the governor, 'democracy is being protected at the expense of law, sometimes law at the expense of democracy', men thought of their wives and their judges.

'Odd, that to a judge, the idea of death is more familiar and respectable than that of imprisonment. He would have liked to make me a martyr, for he knows what that would be like: he hesitates to put me in prison, for that has nothing to do with any life he knows.'

The prisoners thought of this for hours, then, with eloquent taps and one painful word they painted a picture of themselves for their neighbour. Hunched like insects in a schoolboy's matchbox, they crept to the corners of their cells; and listened for the noises only they could make. Then, after an hour of thought, they hammered out 'Comrade', to the man in the next cell, perhaps, after all, one day they might discover who he was: perhaps he was only a criminal, or a tourist who had lost his passport, or photographed a policeman.

Another hour: outside, the cats played at tigers under the smelly bushes. And, from the next cell came back, as it were whispered, 'Comrade?' and both would call back and think of crying, because, either way, comrade or not, it hardly mattered; but a small part of them knew that it mattered very much. And they could do no more; and each night meant the end of some more wearisome time, but also the beginning of a new darkness.

Chapter 4

A RETURN FROM DEATH: the dark coins are taken off the eyes of those who sleep: the curious birds which have hung all night over the linen cemeteries turn out to have been seagulls after all. A sleepy world rolls over, and chases darkness and shadows over its plump back. In the exhausted air of a thousand bedrooms comes a little bright life, sufficient to wake the sleepers whose mouths are full of bitter herbs and stale marigolds. Piles of abandoned belongings on the floor are no longer the ritual sweetmeats and dead slaves for some king demanding even in death; only the night workers know that in the night no soft plague has taken away the quiet lives.

All night, locomotives have moaned like nightwatchmen, their crews have creaked to the line on bicycles to speed the destitutes, the rich, the homeless and the soldiers through the bewildering anaesthetic of a numb night. The steelworkers have prodded their crimson ovens: with long, fizzing needles they have tested the embryo objects, the tanks and the chairs scarcely organic in the hot lap of sparking fires. Then with their spoons they have politely and with exquisite anticipation lifted the soupy ore into cool blue lips.

The men make a mist of sparks when they touch something: in here, even the day is a troubled vision of an endless tormenting night. In the town, the citizens adjust themselves to their context. Before stepping out into their daily stories: before work, an unreal world, of journalism, blood on the pavements under the broken lampposts, the cats coming home guilty and strained after a night of song, and murder. In the all-night entertainments men and women switch themselves off, like lamps in their transparent containers they have glowed all night, now they are dead; food and paper hats are smoothed out, put away for use the next evening.

With infinite wisdom, the policeman shuffles his feet: like a prayer repeated to scare off sin, he moves his feet in unexacting spiritual exercise. In the offices, the early typists uncover the creative machines they will never appreciate, on the calendar they cross off today before they have had it.

A minor official says to another, 'Did I tell you that thirty per cent of my bulbs never appear in the spring? I used to dig for them in the hope that I could steam open their white eyes; or boil them for the children. Do your children ever tell you they like tulip bulbs? To eat? I worry about mine, I wonder if they dispose of that percentage I mentioned. And the things they draw, too: most disquieting: old men eating their hands; eagles with briefcases in the buses; I feel sure it is our maid who tells them troublesome things. These Slavs, you understand.'

The officials laughed knowingly together; the other said, 'I hardly think we need worry: I read that mental disease is so prevalent, especially among those in positions of authority, that doctors are thinking of selecting men for higher education if they are sufficiently unstable. I myself always said we need men who can dedicate themselves to their job; so I suppose the logical conclusion is to accept a thorough fantasy, even in politics. Anyway, we all know that the commands of madmen are petty things compared with those of the rational amoralist: as for the rational madman, we survived him in the army. And whatever anyone says, this cannot be a bad life, for we survive.'

'I had never looked at it that way.'

They were still laughing when the cage in which they were riding stopped; they got out, the battered machine jerked downwards; the officials fought paper battles with one another all morning.

*

In the palace, Pierrina prepared to meet Torgano; they were to go to the Director to discuss many unfamiliar concepts, to be gently angry, till they had argued themselves into logic, and out of the understandable and reasonable positions on which they had taken their stand. With the Director, the retreat to the logical conclusion, the fatherly virtues of repression and oppression, duty, defence and patriotism, would be swift. Pierrina would unwillingly come to the motherly principles, liberty, intolerance, wilful misunderstanding, defence and anarchic violence.

Taking their stand on the logical application of irrational and mutually contradictory tenets, they would reach a conclusion. And, afterwards, they would walk separately by the canals, and think all the usual thoughts about water, and be comforted by an immense and mystical ignorance of such natural curiosities as where the water came from; did it thin, or just lie and stare at the sky, growing more and more vapid and frivolous?

And after a quarter of an hour's musing on these eternal and soluble problems, reality would seem sufficiently far removed to cure the loss of the most intimate and personal palace. In the courtyard, a dog or two stirred; the fountain flung its thread into the air with more restraint than usual; a bird began to wash in the marble basin amidst the stares of copper lion masks. Singing slightly, it flung some gentle diamonds over its crabbed body, then was overawed and lonely. A servant poured a smell of coffee into the noses of the inbred dogs: a lunatic shouted; after a long pause, he answered himself, in a different voice. The palace hung between relevance and whimsy, between minute and meaningful observation and chance.

Pierrina, with irritating slowness and poverty of imagination, said one did not think 'that flower is a bird, perhaps', nor 'that legless man on the trolley is not a cripple on other days'. But there was a state of being not quite awake when the soul asked the body the most delicious and stimulating questions, demanded that the body prove its assumptions. And because the body was tired, and the soul was wide awake after a night dreaming of sin, the body could not be bothered to argue: and rejected most of what it heard as, if not actually a cosmic conspiracy and deceit, at least a pleasant municipal joke, some irrelevant but friendly art-form.

Pierrina had little hope that the Director and Torgano could be dispelled with a light laugh, or a quick twist of a ring: but it was pleasant to believe that a formula could be found to make them charming and even valuable ornaments. Even, she timidly embraced Torgano, in some shrubbery of the mind they had a breath of circumstantial happiness together. She went to meet Torgano, feeling self-sacrificing but not committed; she would not have been surprised if unknowingly she had started the wood and glass machinery of a minor tragedy by the tiny admission of strength and weakness; strength to admit to a forbidden emotion, weakness in having it.

But Torgano, whatever Pierrina felt or did not, was lost: he was sacrificed to suspicion and a bitter sense of all the unhappiness which had ever affected anyone. He was bound for emotional martyrdom, was pledged to a policy of polite but final despair. If an angel had come to tell him that all was well, he would have turned the tall, white gentleman round, and sent him away, to prove that the wings bulging under the correct suiting, really functioned. Torgano had renounced hope in return for a certainty of unpleasantness: he could devote himself to a life which ambled downwards, with psalmists reciting in the most classical measures his inevitable self-destruction, or self-attrition.

Still not awake, Pierrina had given Torgano the gods' embrace: she had slipped a reprieve into his hand as the official paraphernalia of an execution was lugged onto the stage, but he was praying, or weeping or waving to the crowd, or writing a speech, and had not bothered even to read it. All he knew was that the execution must go on: everything, the people, the governor in the uniform which did not quite fit, and might have been borrowed from the real governor, all this was purpose and reason in itself. It all led up to something once one had decided it all led to disaster, one had to be consistent, even a little stubborn, in persuading others not to interrupt when the doomed hero was cursing his judges, or giving his body to medical research.

So, Pierrina went to meet Torgano; like apricot juice, the sun ran down the walls and into the road; the palazzo was in places chilly with the blue in its brick, elsewhere the immature shapes of the stone confectionery were made proud with lukewarm light. A child fished: the vicious bullet-head, the close-cropped ears, irritated Pierrina, as they thrust themselves into view of the canal. He was fishing with maggots which were apparently suffering unspeakable torments on the eve of their execution, but the girl wished they would contemplate death with composure; regard it as an exercise in archery or poker, as something to be conquered by philosophy and produced for a joke at parties.

In the churches, the sun came round to shine in the unashamed eyes of saints: old women fastened together with string and feathers swept up mock cornices which fell with the dew and the damp. The wind blew through cracks in the split studded leather of the huge doors; something in the organ stirred and croaked; some prodigy levered himself onto the instrument's saddle, and sat, with his legs dangling as he rode the musical horse through a prelude: then he walked about on the pedals – a heavy barbarian on a loose grille in hell, till the women screamed and shook their ugly bodies at the noise.

And some official grabbed the boy and showed him with great courtesy the plaster which had fallen while he had played, cursed him, and threw him out; and neither minded greatly. And Pierrina grew slightly excited, just enough not to notice that the church she had just passed had roared with wind and the grossly magnified tread of brass boots. And if she had seen the boy come out, undoubtedly she would have rejected the shabby and inappropriate symbolism. So, at least, she would have hoped.

*

Torgano walked slowly, eloquently pretending small gestures of despair, though he kept his hands in his pockets. In the shops, small and useless articles swam like well-groomed and refrigerated fish behind the thick windows. He felt that, if someone dug a pick though the glass, enough to splinter a hand-sized hole, to send ice patterns over the immaculate surface of the aquarium wall, water would spout onto the pavement, the display would be but a few scraps of coloured flesh twitching on the floor.

This made him nervous, he was coming to believe that one day, to prove his fantasies, he would swing the axe at the cases of luxuries, of necessities so packaged that they too appeared to be luxuries. He would smash his world for the reasonable, even religious, pleasure and experiment of testing his illusions; just as the democratic general may attempt to prove that out of force can come a respect for its absence, a cogent belief in non-violence, so Torgano was ready to sacrifice himself and the property of others in his abandonment to the attraction of destruction by the haphazard, the petty, or the irrational.

Standing before a shop window were two women; they smelt expensively of much dust bound with a little perfume; their cosmetics had not penetrated into the dried up channels of the peat streams which drained the disgruntled features. They wore vague clothes, clothes selected from the exactly correct sections of the most sympathetic magazines. Hung with transparent rags, pierced with pins with bulging heads, they looked smudged and inhuman, like all the best advertisements. They peeped confidently at a selection of peasant pottery; posing in a paper kitchen, the gross gluttonous shapes looked blank under their patchy glaze, Stupid faces had been painted on them, mousy claws were clasped on the bulge of the coarse jugs, And the women talked about them with all the extravagance of an effulgent critical vocabulary.

'I always feel that the tactile quality of this particular ware, so redolent, don't you feel, of horribly old donkeys and perverted women, is prejudiced by the facile personalisation of the comic faces? I mean, even bodies are only shapes, a loosely coordinated ramble of angles and provocative perspectives; you can't begin to pass a moral judgement on a shape, even if it is a body, by giving it a face, or a smell. A shape is a shape, I do so hate, don't you, having faces put on everything. I mean, it's bad enough having to care about people's manners, without having to consider their characters and qualities, and when I am asked to make a moral judgement on a jug, surely that is asking too much of the aesthetic accident.'

Torgano sneered to himself that it was a pretty idea to make parthenogenesis a part of the life cycle of a work of art. The other woman agreed with the first, without enthusiasm; obviously, her companion had voiced a truism, a slogan of some elite, hidden and powerful in the town.

The women were part of a self-perpetuating myth: they bore children who took up these illusions and elaborated them, until the only real thing about their life was the warped and unreal view of the original myth. The belief that they served an old, lost truth was necessary and natural to these women: this was fair enough, but in fact, they could never define this truth, they had not so much an attitude to things, as a way of deceiving themselves till they thought their reactions were positive attitudes.

Most things bored them. The second woman asked, 'Did you read that Bulgarian transports have been seen off the coast, that submarines are refuelled from tanks our fifth column maintain in the countryside? I am told that people in the country are not like us, that all those animals and wrinkled fields induce claustrophobia, socialism and *Schadenfreude*. They think nothing of accepting Orthodox missionaries into their homes, I believe.'

Without emotion, she communicated the ironical lies of perverse newspapermen as truths. Her companion accepted them without great interest. Unconsciously, she prepared herself to repeat a version of these to friends and social enemies: 'Bulgarian missionaries making raids in submarines to kidnap isolated country analysts, perhaps,' searching for an opportunity to corrupt completely, these people had no thought that perhaps they were debasing their own illusory superiority. Indeed, their position depended to an extent on an acceptance of the uselessness of their contribution to everything; and yet, and yet.

Torgano was staring at them rudely, embarrassed they moved the painful jelly bones in the ragged necks; they turned their heads to Torgano, they had the shocked, foolishly proud look of bees about to be crushed. He condemned them without pity or anger: two elaborate phenomena, it was as if different centuries could exist together, as if a few conquistadors and their women could be preserved as curiosities to amuse the intellectuals.

Torgano walked on; the women were still peering at the bloated clay men. He walked across a bridge: 'like a god between earth and heaven', he remembered, with a smug, mocking smile. With a mental invitation to his unseen audiences, he presented himself as a modest smudge on the end of the long light-fingers of searchlights; he told them, 'Yes, I am my own recurrent dilemma: I am only happy when I offend my sensitive sense of sin. I am the most tiresome ancient adolescent, nostalgic for the disappointments of a well-documented childhood, but a measure of my being tiresome is that I know how foolish I am. Will you not love me, turn me into a success, exploit me, despise me until I have found myself? Humiliate me, till one morning I wake and find my shadow, censorious spirit, adding up the marks I have scored that day, for and against myself.

'Then what? You must tell me, my friends. I think I should lock myself in some medicinal island, some soothing gelatinous alp, some mountain sanatorium: twice daily, I shall take my temperature, play with a blue bottle, containing water, which I shall pretend is curing my diseases. I shall be free, I shall devote my life to curing what does not exist: I shall expectorate into basins, I shall wind myself in sheets and croak for my nurses. I will be hypocritical, but not hypochondriac; I shall save myself in pampered societies; I shall preserve all my social conceits, until the time comes when you, you the audience, the reflected light strained over the white pimples I presume are your heads, till you ask me to return, to save you, to throw myself away, spend myself to buy you the treat for which you always whine.'

And for a moment Torgano sickened himself with this Teutonic imagination; he shuddered at this play vision of being locked in a hospital, which was somehow not a hospital, because it was an institution to preserve the well, not cure the diseased. For a moment, the Mediterranean wore thin, and what had started as a parody of the less fashionable American sentimentalists became real; and he remembered someone saying that it is not the intention alone which can induce men to desperate and destructive actions, but a mental training, a predisposition to think in terms of violence and failure which may create intention through a habit of thought.

Really, it was not conducive to a thoughtful existence, if every time he thought, out came slope-shouldered patterns of folk culture, the sick hero trained hard and narrowly to save his country and die. How unpleasant. How unsuitable, when he was about to meet Pierrina; why, here was sun, the streets had been disinfected with chemicals which smelt of musty roses and filed oily steel. The leaves – which year could they have belonged to? – the leaves were making shadows of men, whirled into human-shaped pyramids, for a few yards the vertical creations staggered, then fell apart. Surely all was well, only one had to think back, decide where the dangerous and provocative thought had crept in, excise the nasty idea behind it, and continue from there. Torgano nearly walked into Pierrina, as he tried to dissect his consumptive oddities.

They were together again, said their polite physical reactions; and Pierrina saw that he had longed for her, and he only saw that she knew how exhausted and fractured he was. He wondered, should he explain about Gallista? No, it did not really prove anything: besides, at the time it had been meaningless; now, it was almost forgotten. And if he dared think again, he had little money; his shop was full of chairs and tall spinster lamps, which daily became more convinced of their own inadequacy and uselessness.

After years spent with furniture in transit between death or bankruptcy, and the happiness of new owners, Torgano had become most receptive to the moods of furnishings of all classes and degrees of integrity. It was like keeping an animal shop; to come down every morning and see the contemptuous woolly playthings despairing of being sold; this would have been only slightly worse than the reproachful asceticism of chairs which have become resigned to never again being sat in. They discussed everything: an exchange of symptoms was how Pierrina unfortunately put it. And Torgano found all this infinitely refreshing, for a while. They walked together: once more, all was romantically Ruritanian.

All that was unpleasant seemed introduced to make an artistic contrast: knotted beggars were fun-loving extras from some musical play, the women who squabbled over refuse in courtyards where soot fell hot and greasy were no doubt bogus, but useful for persuading Americans to spend freely, and work off their extra-European consciences. These oyster shells and those flies trapped on them by their greed, and fishy feet, had been arranged by painters; the sweet purple flies walking heavily over the mauve and green, nausea colours of the shell, this was an attractive conceit for amateur artists.

The water sucked gently at the shore; the clear lips pressed absent-mindedly against the congested pebbles. Pierrina remembered that nearer the sea, there were practice waves, a few inches high, which dragged away the stones like the bones in a marine churchyard; she thought of the water rotting away the palace, an old undermined tooth packed with rusty metal, the nerve curling back on itself while the acid saliva nibbled at its root. She wanted to finish with the palace, go and live in a greenhouse on the top of a mountain of people, the stratification of a thousand families must support her, as it had her ancestors. Only now, she would merely live above them, in   their apartments, they would not think of the lofty aristocrat who lived far above in a mess of glass and introspection.

She asked Torgano, 'If we are to see the Director, we must decide on the principle on which we stand. Shall we say that we agree to the nation, as a rule, taking over her leased resources when they have been abused, but point out that I have not exploited my palace; it is a burden I, as a woman almost wealthy and completely infatuated with the illusion of the wealth I hold in trust and the position it might give me, were I ill-bred enough to demand it ... Yes, I had better start again: Torgano, you must prompt me if my sentences are too long.

'Again, in a system of priorities the palace cannot be important. I do not exploit it; I do not let it spoil me; I have a tentative partner, the palazzo is not beautiful, people can see it now, without having it bought for them. And to intend to use it as a patriotic anaesthetic, letting the public gape at blood while their lives and wills and heads are amputated, that is, er, immoral. You agree?'

And Torgano agreed. He did not think Pierrina was intelligent though. He said, 'Can we have a coffee before we go in?'

Pierrina hoped for a cup of nigrescent nastiness in the office, the official-tasting horror which stimulated the crawling brains of the makers of decisions, coffee with a base of purple bitterness. But she went with Torgano.

'I wonder who will make bizarre conversation for us today, to conceal our own lack of ideas?' asked Torgano, with the voice of one who has lived through the Arabian nights and found them 'somehow, alien – if you understand me'.

Nearby, a policeman rode up to the railings on his bicycle; he undid a briefcase on the crossbar, and handcuffed his machine to the metal fence. With a sick effort to wring some metaphysical wisecrack from this situation, Torgano saw the shapes of cathedral windows in the ogival hoops to which the bicycle was chained; but his observations were trite. Men touched women lightly with their eyes, hummed songs which squeezed out the essence of 'love', 'heat', 'retribution'.

Torgano did not understand why these men, and indeed he himself should be tied to the neurotic debris of a religious attitude with whose essentials they had no sympathy. He thought of the Director, a man who did not feel that to requisition property was theft, as some might come to believe it, but merely dull: it was the insatiable appetite of a young man which in time leads to ulcers, discomfort and alcoholic self-pity.

It would be wrong to look at this as a perversion of a political attitude, it was a man growing old with a habit, resenting it, unable to break it, longing to have a life outside it. And Pierrina, what could she do to such a man? The Director might use the wrong arguments to reach the wrong conclusions: but all accepted that some time, perhaps thirty years ago, his motives were pungent and clean.

'Nothing is very beautiful here today,' said Pierrina. 'Perhaps it is the climate which frightens off our ecstasies? I always think, don't you, of ecstasy as being some prickly African thing, you know, an Eland or something. Some sophisticated antelope in a short skirt, laughing and smoking with an aluminium holder while men pour gin over her hooves. I don't know why I think that.'

And Torgana thought, 'I fear her conversation is far from hack exercise: it requires an unwarrantable intellectual patience and faith to follow the darling through her word-tortures.'

Before he had to answer, a conversation was started nearby; the two of them were able to forget that they found each other superficial, in laughing at the chinoiseries of others. There were two men, perhaps they were   postmen. Their clothes were covered with whispers of braid; their faces were stained with hours of waiting for nothing in brown paper offices where only a pot of paste and a cat were useful and comfortable. Their lives had run with a desire to sum everything up in one epigram, tragic, powerful, enigmatic, like the Bible, they might have put it. They were not the men to run from their wives, buy apples and a tin of meat and live for a week in a hotel in desperate squalor.

One said, 'What a time, this morning! As you know I like to say I do my job; well then, I was pasting up yesterday's results in the far corner away from the girls, you know; and this new chap, Anton something, came in, and started asking me what a moving picture was, did I know? Well, I said yes, so he started telling me, his way, you know.

'He said, "You have one eye that matters, and everyone gathers round it to look in. And all they see is their own eye, or perhaps a spring of brain snapped off and rolled to a corner. And the light – like needles – and the women, yes, they're like needles too."

'Well, I felt sorry for him, being new to the department and not able to console himself as a gentleman should, I said, "Let's act this out, if you don't mind, sir: you just sit in that chair for a few hours; you be the director, and tell me what you see in the eye when I come back later."

'Well, he called me a good chap, in between times, as they usually do, and in the end, I had to strap him in the chair. And there he is now, so I'll go back soon if you don't mind.'

The other obviously approved of his friend's handling of Anton. 'I hear he is something of a genius,' he said. 'One who thinks nothing of having a fine joke, at a party being carried in on a stretcher slung between four black horses. I believe he was educated in England; ah well, suppose we are bound to be deferential to our superiors so long as they amuse us, and insult each other.'

The two jade philosophers inverted the lotus cups, their eyes showed that they drank. Pierrina and Torgano prepared to leave, their morning so far had been a time of comedy and doubt. They did not spare themselves; emotional exhaustion was thought no more terrible than a physical exercise, which could be repaired by half an hour in the embrace of a large chair. They walked through a square; foreign buses were stacked like sausages in a corner; everywhere there were priests with comforting cigars; religious youth organisations singing hymns, carrying furled fascist banners importantly, as if they were sunshades.

A thousand people were being told that here was a real Habsburg square, built by one – the '*lapsus mundi*', a Habsburg freak he had been, in a family turning by way of an exclusive and ingrowing system of marriages based on madness and coercion back into anthropoids. A face so refined that it was no longer human, so arrogant that it was not animal sat on a little body stuck on a bronze horse; the horse was surprised to find itself thus humiliated; bowed its head and metaphorically crossed its legs.

In niches, like the chorus in some statuesque production, stood other statues; some were eating pineapples, and what appeared to be wrinkled tomatoes of doubtful significance. Others were supported by women or tree trunks: all were parodies of types of humans who posed perpetually to be turned to stone by the flattering monsters two centuries ago. They had the look of those who have sneaked a look round the back of venerable Western institutions and peepshows, like war and duty and self-determination and progress, and found that there were a few laths holding everything up.

They all wore their hair crinkled and imperially fey. The deceptive curls were brushed upwards like the hair of coconuts; the air was intended to convey red-faced tyrants, whose grey hairs marked them as possessors of divine right; an amusing and quite in-keeping idea, thought Torgano, that the touch of God takes the colour out of things. Some of the statues carried microscopes, dead birds or fawnlike children; or perhaps they were fawns? Or an idea that the children of peasants, picked up for propaganda, should look like fawns?

The characterisation seemed so arbitrary, that quite probably the properties, children and all, had been taken from the sculptor's basket, and handed round indiscriminately. At least the council had been politic: they had built a platform at one end of the square, and charged photographers a fee to use it;

consequently, few pictures were taken of individual statues and the illusion of beauty and proportion was preserved. The photographers had sat in coaches all day: they had tolerated the incipient claustrophobia and extreme frustration of sitting in a mobile tube whilst acres of pearly toothed mountain were drawn briskly past the windows. They had stood the smell of overheated women and oranges opened up with toy penknives; and now, they wanted to be among other photographers, to justify their claim to be experts by taking the official photograph, and paying to do so.

A band marched in jerkily: the band disliked playing on the march; they walked gingerly, lest they jerk the instruments into their lips; the tourists looked round, a class of children interrupted by the entry of the contents of a bestiary during a Latin lesson. The leaders of the band looked round; perhaps they had expected an audience to step from the sea-shelled niches, courteously applauding maestros resurrected by ill-blown military marches. They thumped and squeaked for a time more, but they were no better exorcists than the policeman who was trying to catch criminals while pretending to be a plain-clothes detective in the bar across the road.

The leaders conferred; the band was manoeuvred, it wheeled, the inside man stepping short to make it look like a caterpillar; soon it boomed off. The leaders said, as they passed Torgano, 'Wrong square: these signs, so misleading.' The neat themes receded; second- and third-hand versions of the music began to blur the outlines as the notes were passed round forests of stiff-leaved columns.

Torgano went with Pierrina once more towards the Director: they passed through a number of antique stalls. Old women imperfectly packed into men's raincoats stopped time and cleaned their noses with newspaper; men sat looking at their boots, occasionally they would buy something from a colleague's stall. When customers came round, they would shuffle their wares casually; the antiques fascinated Torgano; no one ever brought such things to him.

They were not so much antiques, as wreckage: when the
ship of a decade floundered, a few drowning holidaymakers
might throw overboard sentimental curiosities, some dolls from
Bali, say; an old jar someone used to saw was Persian; the
spoons which were never quite good enough to use, but were
always going to be given to some alcoholic uncle only he died –
you remember. But mostly, the stuff was genuine arbitrary
wreckage, as it were, the faulty lifejackets, the cane chairs, the
captain's stuffed horse.

And here it all was, in a competitive museum: refugee
robbers, the stallholders lived with all that was insignificant
about other people's lives. Their faces showed that they knew
this: Torgano would have stayed, but Pierrina thought they had
seen enough of the old and the failed that morning. She did not
want to find that all that was left for her was to be put in a niche
with a stone pineapple for generations. Palace or no palace, she
was not going to be pickled by the Director and stopped up in
an ornamental jar at the foot of a staircase. So she was not
pleased when Torgano said:

'Have you played with your Tarot pack lately?'

'I find it rather disgusting, you know, I only use it because
you bought it for me, because of my name. And do stop looking
hurt, I told you when you gave it to me, that it was a reasonable
joke, but not a thing I want to elevate into a habit.'

But Torgano was disappointed. Squinting crossly at him,
Pierrina began to despise, and like him, more. Silently, they
clambered up the inside of the Director's office block; they felt
dirty and impure against the metal friezes and the uniformed
grandfathers who trotted with trays and packets through the stiff
intestines of the department.

'Fanfares of flunkeys,' thought Torgano. Softly, he sang:

'My love is a rat in a cage:
I have fed her with honey.
Perhaps I'll cut her throat.
Tirralee.'

It was a folk song which had become popular after an arrangement of it had been made for clarinet and piano, where the piano made fretted wire barriers and the clarinet ran up and down inside, trying to get out. Torgano despised people who thought of such songs, but he enjoyed singing it; Pierrina frowned at him.

But, mild and smug, Torgano walked on, into the Director's office; as he said afterwards to himself, 'The irony seems to have entered my soul.' Gallista was there as evidence or decoration. He knew that if no one said anything, he would be safe and unembarrassed, but he dared not hope that all four would converse by smiles and sympathy. He prepared to be uncomfortable: outside, an argument was starting, the voices reared up and gesticulated just below the Director's windowsill.

A fishmonger and a taxi driver were shouting: safe behind the cold battalions of his wall-eyed captives, the fishmonger was laughing scornfully at every rush of tepid comment from the other. Angry but with a quick flick of laughter he went about his business, opening the mouth of a cod so that children might admire the wisps of teeth, and women pity it for the dead pink of the scooped throat, the implicit fatalism of the eyes.

The fishmonger had a child's view of his public; he thought he could arrange the oysters with their wavy hair and tall heads, the flat fish with their cynical smirks, so that they appealed to buyers as edible pets: 'Take a fish home with you,' said an advertisement in shrimps. The little boiled question marks with the currant eyes spelled out the romantic invitation. Fish with bodies like blue cucumbers stuffed their tails in their mouths to hide their boredom; for the shop was prosperous, all day boxes of twisted fish and tanks of moribund fish stew were sent off to the hotels and villas.

The taxi driver shouted across the road; he drove his imitation leather office a hundred miles a day, he had an impression of motion, of being an acolyte in a dangerous and demanding religion. He knew that at any moment someone could scoop him into a ditch and use his car to bury him; he was aware that he was entitled to attitudes and eccentricities because of this. But all he could say to the fishmonger was that he sold fish; that dead fish look slightly less intelligent than live ones. And, by definition, almost, a dead fishmonger could look little different from this live one. Eventually, the taxi driver too began to laugh; fascinated by the two-part invention for nondescript voices, the four in the office above paused. The Director claimed the silence as his own policy, by first breaking it.

'You will have come, together, thinking my heart is an altogether more superior device than it really is, able to be worked by anyone. You think "Sentimental organ it undoubtedly is, that heart: we will charm it by stroking our golden palms over it, we will blow it gently till like a hedgehog it moves off where we want it to, blurred and rough, but amenable to bread and milk." And you will have said, that I will give back the palazzo, because I am old and lonely, because I think I am perhaps a cruel man.' He waited.

Pierrina said, 'If we had thought you cruel, we should have exposed you to the newspapers and crushed you with narrow columns.'

The Director smiled gratefully. 'Just what I would have said in your position; and of course quite wrong. Do you not think the newspaper editors would rather I took the palazzo for their readers, or for them? I'm afraid you can't appeal to people's kindness now; you are part of history. You may not agree with *my* motives, but you must agree with the national motives. I am not who you should see; I am merely the nasty man; the archetype who stands beneath every tragedy and sticks awls in the actors' feet.

'You must see the nation, if you do not like me – my motives; your motives do not matter; the state has concentrated in me the essence of the wills of thousands of individuals. I acted on my interpretation of that will; if you now wish to be treated as individuals, and I never looked on you as such, charming people no doubt, but not individuals, then you must appeal to those I represent, as individuals. We had dealings as two machines: you the aristocratic bourgeois; I the Director. You don't want to be a machine; nor do I. But I am paid to be a machine, your business lies with the thousands who are only paid to serve the machines like me.

'Your palazzo is no longer a home; it is an expression of will. The original owners of that expression are dead, dead for the state; they died for the nation, give that palazzo the same peace; let it lie with the dead builders, the architects who long ago dropped to mould. I weep for your tragedy; see, I would drop a tear, a token for display and reference only, in this cupboard with all my other official regrets and suffering.'

Pierrina looked at the Director as if, in a tapestry called Autumn, a distant embroidered peasant had swiped at the amber corn with a scythe.

'But I could not stop my ancestors dying as they wished,' she said.

'Ah no, I fear they had their fun, and left you to pay for it; to call it poetic justice would be amusing, but not fair: poetic injustice. The mortified priest inheriting the diseases of his alcoholic father; we can't make the priest live; you cannot be allowed to survive in the palazzo. You must imagine yourself no more betrayed by the accident of your birth, than those who will come to see the palace; we must share round the inadequacies of our parents, who failed to provide us with palaces.'

The Director sat back: Gallista watched two men in the street struggling to load packing cases on a lorry. The men waltzed round underneath the musical cubes; on the sides were stencilled stylised workers carefully demonstrating how to lift formal packages. Gallista was more prepared to admire effort for its own sake; satisfied, she saw the men leap like huge cats as the cases swung to smash on the pavements.

Torgano asked the Director, 'Could we be kept on as employees, as you er, suggested?'

And the Director laughed. 'Well, now! How impolitic you are; I hadn't really thought about that job. Surely there is no hurry.'

Pierrina said, 'Surely, if you are a socialist you are at least a heretic, if not a schismatic?'

Again and again the Director laughed. 'You young people may think me a cynic; you see, I have been here so long, I am no longer a socialist, I am an administrator. Like the senile bishop, I can forget religion, and live for being a bishop. I merely apply theories; I no longer question facts. Fifty years ago, my theory was settled; all that is left is ruthlessly to apply it. And does principle or politics enter here? I think not, only for the moralists; one has responsibilities as an administrator which do not occur to one as a man of mere conscience.'

The incredible friar has taken our nickel counters; he had taken us right up to the lantern, where a few rarefied cherubs flutter round the daylight on indistinct painted wings. We have peered under his cowl to see if he is death, the spirit of the constitution, or someone we knew at school. We have followed him all over the cathedral-shaped institution, we have heard his faith, we have seen the bones in their cardboard boxes, the ugly paintings turning black above the candles. We are aware that an epoch, or a holiday, has finished. We go out into the rain, and the guide peeps round the door for a moment, he pulls a grin on his skull for a second, and goes back to his accounts.

Pierrina and Torgano left the Director without respect or awe; they had a conviction that anything so venerable must be true and correct. They had talked to the official guide; all they could do now was to forget what they had heard.

When they had gone, the Director sighed, and turned to Gallista:

'Gallista, if I told you that after all, I was lonely, what would you think?'

'I should not believe you, thank God.'

'No, of course not: I knew you would say that. That is why I asked; there is scarcely a better reason for enquiring anything, especially for the man of unbounded conceit.'

For a few minutes he dazzled her with some samples of gemmiferous deposits collected from a lifetime of listening to drunken idealists, until she grew obviously bored.

'So soon, have we nothing more to say to one another? When the children's rocket has jumped with its one golden leg above most of the nearby houses, surely the cries and exaggerations should continue for a time? I do hope Gallista is not one of those tiresome girls who insists on ignoring father's beautiful and costly firework, and looks scornfully at the milk bottle full of smoke, and the dead matches which launched the sharp, sensitive tongue of gunpowder.'

But Gallista wanted just to wander through the Director, preferably when the guards were not looking. He was a bizarre suburban museum, well-stocked with leather dog-carts and nursemaid dolls with sick wax faces. She thought of Torgano, who looked always caught and confused in a spate of divine banter.

She said to herself expressively, 'I just don't care about more than one person at a time: and that, I think, is all that is left to us; the meticulous cultivation of the tiny talent, the isolation and staining of microcosms.'

The Director watched an insect which had dropped through the window on its lifeline, and now was tying up the desk with its silk with the precision of a magician. He did not want to talk to Gallista of the awkward movements of incoherent inconsolable emotions which prowled round his stomach; perhaps he was hungry, perhaps he was in love, perhaps the lining of his body was rotting.

He said, 'Shall we all four, that is, with Torgano and Pierrina, go say to a theatre tonight? It is quite in order, we can have photographers in the bar to flash their silver eyes at us when we look suitably Bacchic. It will be a part of the transaction; regard it not as sharing our evening, but watching a play with a palazzo by proxy.'

Gallista made the usual disgruntled face, secretly glad that the specimen she was working on should show some life, however spiteful or destructive.

'I shall send a messenger in a rowing boat to the palace, to invite them. There will almost certainly be some dramatic delicacy where we can show off our prisoners. Something, perhaps, with music, a few successfully articulated dancers thumping from the wings to the orchestra pit in an excess of art and skill. We shall see the reduced gestures in the distant rococo frame, the actors waving to us, trying to pull us down the vortex of smoke and coloured light, down to their emotional world on the stage. And how bravely will we resist: we will cling to our seats and hold hands to avoid being drawn into their tragedy, where everyone sings, and when people die, they are allowed to fall to pieces under the gallows. For an hour or two, of course.'

Gallista was not impressed by this brief quintessential criticism of the theatre. It did not excite her, it made her want to resist the attractions of the minute and no doubt immoral actors. She thought of the whole affair as something without meaning, a gigantic confidence trick, you resisted art as long as possible, then, with a last puritanical shudder, you joined the men who blew down long curly tubes and scratched away at pretty old woods. There was no meaning in it, it was a superior religion for frauds, somewhere in the middle there was an altar of solid gold from which the successful were allowed to cut slices.

But when you saw it all in terms of violence, all the yellow and red sandstone lusts of Spanish summers, then it became stimulating. Its application to life was direct: it was a fashionable swindle, which it was necessary to know about; often, it sounded quite nice, almost like conversation, or songs from radio advertisements; often, but not very often.

The Director closed the window, shutting off the complications of life; impatiently he brushed the insect into blood and suffering; cursed the trail it left of someone else.

While he waited for a messenger, he said, 'I hear the nationalists in the lost colonies are objecting to our offers to help them become free from foreign control if it means that we will incorporate them, and protect them again. I always tell people that there is really no quarrel, we are all nationalists, we all agree on essentials. We all know that in the last resort, no one else has the right, the ability, or the strength to govern themselves, except us. We can justify anything so long as we preserve an inflated view of the moral superiority which in theory justified our first campaign to win an empire.'

Gallista thought this merely cynical; she herself believed the government was run by elephants or electricity; something either so large or so elusive that human beings had no part to play in it all. So, of course, she supported the implicit right of her country to oppress others for the good of her soul. She had no time for cowards who did not relish shooting the unarmed; as her friends told her, hers was a charming feminine trait, her belief in the need to protect foreigners from their leaders and their own aspirations by making practical limitations for their freedoms and education.

Thus, one of a class proudly claiming it had no interest in politics, she gave politicians a constant and easily acceptable stimulus to act unpleasantly. Thousands like her said they did not care about politics or art; and so let reactionary policies and immature art proliferate.

The messenger arrived; his uniform made a well-aligned pattern against the door; the cuff buttons shone with the right degree of nonchalant official chic. His face had been well designed to fit on top of the uniform; he was a credit to his creator.

The Director said, 'You will go, please, by rowing boat, along to the Palazzo Tarrault; you will know it by its cat, a strawberry cat, quite young. By its landing stage, which we destroyed yesterday; by the department's plaque. Take this letter; deliver it to the young prince personally; the wicked pantomime uncle demands his presence at a fresh humiliation tonight.'

Laughing importantly, for the Director was famous as a character, the messenger went off. Soon, like an aquatic beetle, he was walking tediously on the oil-ringed canal to the palace. It was hot, the water smelt of broken promises and exploded dogs, the cranes held hands ostentatiously over heaps of grain and sawdust. The messenger pretended Greek fire and Turkish booms stretched across the water in front.

He found the palazzo; an old man fishing neurotically with a long piece of wire and half a sandwich shouted, 'Don't go in there – there's been a death.'

'A death?'

'*When the Palazzo Tarrault goes to the nation, Seventy dukes will face ruination*; that's the old saying, and a duke will die rather than be ruined; no Tarrault would surrender to government forces – so there's been a death.'

'But there are no more dukes.'

The messenger felt like the man who had just shot the last four hundred aristocrats.

'Aha, they may not call themselves dukes ...'

A pause. The old man splashed about with his wire to attract the attention of fish. Then:

'I saw them all go. Count Balchin: he rode single-handed out to sea in his galley, then split it apart and sank to an undersea city dry and lively as I am. We had the Aurora for weeks after that. Then Duke Argeste: he made his wife drive his coach everywhere he went; one day, he said, "Come on, woman, I'll make you drive till these horses drop dead."

'Fine horses they were: luminous too, but that came later. Well, first she shot him, then she whipped the horses into the canal: great pity. I always wear one of his teeth, because after a few months he came ashore round about where we are now. Quite a nice smile on his chops he still had too; well, anyway his tooth has kept me free from all manner of diseases; it's an ill wind.'

The messenger clambered into the palazzo; no comment seemed necessary. Pierrina was standing by the open mouths of packing cases; the lips were drawn well back to receive the scraps of food which she and Torgano desultorily threw to them. The pictures of battles, the Chinese porcelain animals, the staircases, the pillars – were they jade or old kissed marble? – the statues which were so useful for playing games with at parties, and holding overcoats, all these stood round bored and disillusioned.

Torgano would not let the servants help them, servants reminded him of uncles who boasted of their whippings, their life barefoot and in the snow, in order to justify corporal punishment or forced loans. Torgano knew he was more of a servant to Pierrina than a friend, or so he thought he knew; he could only look on them as rivals.

Pierrina too did not enjoy the help of her (as she called them) 'traditional employees', and she was sensitive about Torgano reminding her that his father had been a welder for a time. The messenger delivered his message:

'The existence of God might be deduced by some, seeing that this messenger has delivered this message: clear proof of a divinely ordered world, with a preordained social order, and lacquered angels to summon the tribes according to income and sex. Know then, that I summon you: Torgano and Pierrina. To an entertainment. This evening, God willing, and you yourselves being agreeable.'

A time and a place had been suggested: briefly amused the couple accepted, Torgano with a trace of embarrassment.

'Shall I throw in these little men?' Torgano asked when the messenger had gone. 'The china hunchbacks with which your ancestors beguiled their teatimes? Do you want to smuggle them away to your flat, or did the uxorious inspectors put them on their lists despite all that babble about the offices and the children?'

Pierrina looked across to the manikins Torgano was waving at her. The repulsive, crushed, nutlike faces showed that they were an Austrian's idea of orientals. The faces were ready to absorb any myth, invented to condone brutality, ignorance, fear, fatalism, the fatuous sterility of Zen, even, thought Pierrina, over-population.

'No, I think it is up to the nation's art censors to decide on the official attitude to the more monstrous monstrosities.'

Torgano put them aside; one of the palazzo's rough clay dogs sidled over to the dolls and licked at them.

'What are you going to do with these animals?' asked Torgano. 'They look so arrogantly artificial; perhaps if you pack them in straw, they will survive indefinitely in storage.'

'I shall take the cats, and sell the dogs; the dogs have certificates of birth, of quarantine, of parentage; they can look after themselves.'

Torgano thought of the cruel joy of the cats, as the dogs wept in the hampers and suitcases of their new owners. The cats would resent their new home, but when nostalgic, would think of the triumph over the dogs, complete because there was no violence, they themselves would not have been involved. Torgano wondered that Pierrina did not see that in spirit her cats were assassins; that the delicate sophistication, the raised paw, the look behind to the ill-mannered shout or the rustle of mouse with cramp, this was not a natural sensitiveness of cats, but guilt. It was the flannelled executive in the luxurious alleyways of commerce wincing and looking round at every imagined cry of 'thug', 'murderer'. The cats purred stiffly: lying down, they whirred like a summer field and kicked their russet fluff legs.

When the four met that evening, amateur sky painters had been busy. Before leaving work that evening, they had designed new colours and schemes for the sky: grapes – or was it wisteria? – hung as a squashy motif round the east. A brushful of green paint had been stuck in the sun's eye, blood and green tears were squeezed into horizontal strips: the whole sky had been swamped with the easy metaphors of a benign inspiration.

'Sunsets may not be vulgar, but they certainly bring out the vulgarity in those who praise or describe them,' said the Director, trying to ignore the feast spread out above him.

Gallista had, of course, coaxed her not unlovely body into its usual gilded cage. She was hooped like a barrel, in places she ran so straight and true, she must have been bolted to railway sleepers. It was proof indeed that 'all art is tension', the interplay of forces and feminine stresses made some of those who saw her feel some slight engineering challenge.

Pierrina had not been told what they were to see: she had compromised. She wore some exquisite imitation jewellery which had delighted her grandmother, it looked so false no one could believe it was not fabulous. If the jewels were for a play, her dress was for a bullfight. Red, cunning panels sliding aside to reveal leather lozenges, it had been gored and tossed by the most tenderly raging bulls in all the best salons. Scented matadors had been pelted with roses for saving it as bulls menaced; it was not suitable for evenings indoors, without animals and blood.

Torgano tried to look as much like the Director as possible, but he found it difficult not to look like his son. And he had to avoid Gallista; he was not enjoying himself. Indeed, he was becoming for everyone an anxiety object: precariously balanced within the party, he seemed about to fling himself under someone's feet, but politely.

Pierrina asked, 'Is it a play, a musical play?' and 'Not exactly,' replied the others.

They were moving now towards the theatre; in the twenties, they would have been wearing camouflage jackets and short wings, and qualified for similes about moths and dramatic flames. Now, they merely chattered as business acquaintances do so charmingly, till they almost forget that they were rivals, that they hated one another, ethically but with a strong economic motivation. They passed a newspaper stall. The owner thought they were tourists.

John Fraser

'Magazines to impress your London friends? Shock your English acquaintances with photographs they are never allowed to see. Read about our national heroes; the flameproof detectives, the railroad wreckers, the class-conscious rippers, the lady-heroes eager to love; see, I read from a magazine advertisement. Things of the mind, sir? A review? This one will keep the communists at bay, sir. Refugees, lives of the great contemporary mass aesthetes; poets, poems by the editors and friends of the editors. A fine treat for the weary intellect, sir.'

They passed him by; he did not seem surprised: men who sold books had to be used to the defences of guilt and carelessness built up in the half-educated and the half-illiterate. Past the food stalls, with storm lanterns swinging shadows over the spiced saucers, the idle snouts of rolls and sausages; past the amusements, where a coin brought canned laughter, or the future. Sententiously, they passed the shooting machines, the trials of strength, the Hercules blind and bald offering to fight everyone, talking of his classical labours, his former Aegean physique.

Gallista ran back to the arcades: to show that she too was young and pliable, Pierrina followed her. They were irritated by the Director, with his patronising disapproval, the revelation that possibly behind him sat an anxious, mean prude, jerking the big, bland puppet's wires. At last, there was the theatre. Generals leapt to the doors of taxis; and bent commissionaires fished people out of the expensive cars, proudly.

'Architecture: opera with gilt buttons. Service: epic with nigger minstrels' swagger canes,' said Gallista, with an accomplishment rather too calculated. The women peacocked up the stairs: princesses do not need tickets. They sat high above the stage; it was like looking down into a kaleidoscope, and before the curtain rose the audience in the stalls whirled, confused, a handful of confetti dropped prematurely. Then, an overture: horns and trombones driving in their phrases like studs into a boot.

The conductor fanning the orchestra into life, the vague life apparently about to take shape in the swelling curtain; to see on the stage, the audience seemed to sleep, insulated against all attempts to connect on the stage a reality more humanly applicable than life itself. The frightened men and women were afraid that the curtain would rise to show they themselves mirrored, or copied exactly on the other side of the footlights. They were determined not to believe what they saw, even if they saw themselves, acting out their lives a few painted yards away.

The swollen eyelid rose. A stage, tilted like a palette with a few lively daubs, was revealed. All over the world, in lamaseries, and in private orgies of paint magnates, men were watching the actors, the oracles which might speak of life or death. Some thousands of miles away the monkey god was expanding to save the hero from a realistic end. In London, or in Paris, men watched the little figures manipulated like lead soldiers, they cherished every word – did that gesture, this mixed metaphor, hold a truth by which they could live? – then, when it was all over, the arch hypocrites laughed.

They laughed, these men who had been desperate for revelation and solutions, lying and disappointed they condemned the tragedies and the epics as if they were not concerned with life. Self-consciously inadequate, they bayed out of the theatres, waving their leisured walking sticks as they prattled of 'the aesthetic illusion' and strode healthily away to vaudevilles and nightclubs, where they could share their neuroses with everyone else. Torgano at once felt himself drawn into the play; in that way, he was usually the first to dismiss anything which moved him, as untrue or irrelevant.

He heard the portentous recitative of the bass, the heavy weight which kept everything upright: 'Business is bad', the formal gestures to convey that this was the executive's grace, a puritan paternoster to dull the edge of enjoyment, to spur acquisitiveness. The man stood for the virtue of an ordered society, as seen and admired by its more insignificant members;

a cynical honesty which went as far as not cheating at golf; a comradeship which extended to all, without exception or reservation, to all those who fulfilled certain elementary and fundamental requirements of education, interest and income.

He daydreamed ...

Also, an artistic sense: without sacrifice or direction; it was a grotesque reflection of the man as beast, and as conformist; operetta, the more old-fashioned and laboured novels of neurosis and torment, paintings by futurists and Tadema, and, of course Chinese watercolours. A knowledge of how much there was to be done, how little he had helped in anything, was transformed into a belief that change was destruction for its own sake, and that the little he had accomplished made his opinions sacrosanct; the liberal imperialist, Torgano recognised him to be not a nice man.

His daughter: spotted with the marks of tragedy; Torgano identified himself with her; she sang a sad song to a choir of brass, the trumpets shining and sharp as mosquitoes, the trombones muted, weeping into their handkerchiefs. A song about 'Life – when it comes, it is so sad – life, fatal and inevitable – my father, alas my father stands over me, his skeletal legs are the pillars of society – life will no doubt get me eventually – until then, how sweet to think about nothing, dislike most things, and encourage others to persecute me,' and so on.

Then the assassin: the man placid and irresponsible, any opinion was good enough for him; subtly, he wrecked things, drove others until they came to terms with their own problems, and then, invariably collapsed at the realisation of their own impotence and exhaustion. He was the man who attacks others, insensitive and uncomplicated, he is easily repulsed, but his victims look at themselves and believe they are shattered, ready to destroy themselves. He came in to a brief sonata of percussion, the tympanist lay about him as if he were hammering nails.

To complete the main characters, there was another woman, definitively a woodwind type. She was piped in by recorders, to imply her innocence and a reasonableness which appeared to express itself in a fund of boring admonitions and pervasive moral motifs which rang through her conversation like an off-key clarinet. The play began to unravel itself: the brass irritated the spines of the front rows, the light swing everyone into a peasant world in which the virtues operate without the embarrassments of dirt and the vices.

The father and a hunchback fling about in some synthetic gopak; the daughter is oppressed by the father; she runs away, to the dodecaphonic remonstrations of choked trumpets. Away to the smoke which blurs the outline, the theatrical poverty into which every second act heroine is disgraced. And comforted by the other woman, who is, perhaps a member of an organisation devoted to that sort of thing: she seems to wear a uniform, but the smoke obscures much. Then a back projection of peasants dancing round their landlords: as a caption the heroine sings 'Better the evils of innocence than those of sophistication' to an accompaniment which has, so remarks the programme, economic overtones.

Little remained: the tragic had to be killed off; the young man makes the heroine see that her standards have declined since those days

> *'when you sat spinning*
> *Laughing at wind patterns in the dust –*
> *Now you come to the harvest*
> *Your head still too proud for the bitter blade.'*

Left alone, the girl condemns the bigoted economic outlook of small landowners, the horrible Kriegsspiel of the petty urban masters of capital. She throws herself under a carriage or a car – the period is insipid, perhaps late Austro-Hungarian ...

Torgano sat back disgruntled at the end; everything had started off so well, then it was all confused with music, technical problems of artificial smoke, which stagehand was to catch the revolver when it was thrown out of the window. They had started off promising to help his problem; every valve was oiled, every gold tube shone because people wanted to help him, wanted perhaps to say that he was exploited, that they would protest on his behalf. And this opportunity they had squandered: art, after all, was an act of self-sacrifice, the doctrine of 'nothing for oneself', it was the aggregate of the interest and attention of the audience, no one should expect to gain anything.

Gallista and the Director had subsided towards one another; they obviously had no thoughts for life or Torgano. Pierrina was ready to tell everyone what they missed in the lyrics and the symbolism – or was it symbolism? – of the action.

'I mean, surely the words don't matter – once you decide it is a parody, or a satire, you just sit back and let waves of pompous fun amuse you slightly.'

Torgano frowned, like a child who had been given praise when it wanted rewards; he was dissatisfied, conscious of being ungrateful: he saw, too, that Pierrina would not help the cause of the palace with her criticism. Indeed, Torgano himself was disgusted by his attempts to help preserve the palazzo. He had recruited a huge medieval army: monks had seized clubs and greyhounds, nobles had flickered through their hunting fantasies, had left dragons and women, abandoned a month's supply of fairy stories, to take arms to protect the ancient society and family of Tarrault. Torgano himself had pinned nosegays of sun-dried rags on the armour: in the colours of the household. Then, there had been a thunderstorm, everyone had run for shelter into the woods, in case they were rusted, and when the captains had boomed with their horns to recall the armies, no one came. They had all gone home because of the weather.

Gallista said, 'I'm afraid I didn't understand it, and if I did, I thought it not very good. I don't like things I nearly understand, it makes me feel inadequate. I much prefer it when it's all nonsense, and fights break out in the boxes, and all over the theatre, mistresses of the composer sweep out, shouting that they have been insulted.'

The Director said, 'Yes, a touch of the sordid pageantry does enliven the critical hangover in the weekly reviews. I myself thought the mediocrity of the ideas quite touching and stimulating: it made one realise how one too is an artist, how one can trample about on the rungs of the notes and scale passages as well as the professional.'

The Director paused, aware that he was not believed, nor loved. The four felt inward blizzards, they felt the need to shrink down inside themselves, to become small, prickly, and offensive. They had filmy visions of the future, in which they saw the seats ripped, the lighting torn out and coiled, like the intestines of fish, over the armed lady muses thoughtful above the orchestra. Could all this be swept away, and would their ill-considered opinions contribute to the force of the sharp destroying wind? Only, they thought, a sadist would imagine furniture piled in these streets, old noblemen and trade union leaders carried on wardrobes and traditional kitchen tables away from the invading horsemen, the obscure jumbled warriors riding calmly, tugging along toy gun-carriages and rocket launchers.

Into the open air the audience spilled, in the dark and cold, the groups congealed before moving off to restaurants and the flats of the polite but reluctant men and women who half disliked their friends. Gallista looked round, hungry for experience; the Director cowered in his overcoat close by her on an invisible lead. Pierrina moved about nervously: poised in her shoes, she seemed a fine balance ready to swing into soft action at a breath. She was wishing that Torgano would stop looking persecuted, would not continually make neurotic movements with his hands and feet, as if they had recently been twisted. People like Torgano, she decided, encouraged others to do all manner of unexpected things, to try to break away from the simpering foolishness of the weak and the sensitive.

And Torgano, because he was happy, thought everyone also must be equally satisfied. He stood silent, pointing himself towards the beached hulks of the extinguished food stall, then to the statues which stood head and shoulders above the official shacks of municipal engineers. Coloured bulbs sagged on hot ropes from the lampposts, dying lamps throbbed neon, there was a smell of overheated rubber. Sections of lighting went out; the main street lighting shone pink through the coloured lanterns in which it was installed. Posters became visible, men beautiful with the photographers' cosmetics frowned from the hoardings:

'Solomon Ardicek: fight socialism with passionate xenophobia and brotherly love for the lost colonies.'

'Passion Marden: socialists are communist failures: vote to keep the nation pure.'

'Empire, guarantee of the status quo: Party of the Common Man.'

'Theocracy, not mobocracy: vote for your Christian Church Party.'

'Reaction works: freedom is licence – empire is brotherhood – public ownership is state banditry – education is the prerogative of those who know – vote for the democratic nationalists.'

Gallista said, 'Something seems to have gone wrong: shall we tear them down?'

Patiently, and as if in committee, the Director explained, 'I admit our progress is slow; and if people live by the irrational, the conceited deception of the myth of progress through gradual fascism, it is only natural that they should finance such manifestations. We cannot speed up the process to what we believe is enlightenment without kicking down the meticulous frontiers of our principles. And nothing much helps us: for a start, men have seldom done things because they represented truth, if there are other reasons for welcoming it. In our politics, there is no such thing as the unpalatable truth; if something is true, and we dislike it, we pervert everything till the truth is surrounded by policies intended to qualify, inform or deceive. And our system, that too, perhaps, is confusing?'

Torgano nodded.

'You see, we are a coalition of the left; we were installed to allow the right to fight until it could form a government with a single party. That is what we think; but as the right is committed to a policy of piecemeal and incoherent reform, officials are not replaced. It would be tiresome; it just means that sometimes I am a minister, sometimes I am merely a servant carrying out a lot of orders I never bother to read. Some of my colleagues want reform to last for ever; so we go on, trying to form solid parties, while the men in power stay in power.'

Torgano asked, 'Then you are indispensable?'

'Alas no, there are many things to come to terms with, I continue, rather than support.'

'Then all this is unstable?'

'Again no, you ask anyone what they think of when they see a river. A big river; quiet stability, a small steep stream, speed and destruction. Yet more water goes down the river than the stream, it is infinitely more destructive. They look at our system, they say here is a reckless stream pouring itself away, but in fact, it is a river, with the capacity no stream could conceive. Our party fights can take a million lives in two weeks; yet we are stable, we are committed to a course, indeed now there no small governments, if ever there were. You must understand, that is what we cannot get the people to see: we have this solid foundation, it will survive most things.

'But because it is large, it can destroy anything, whilst retaining its outline. People laugh, they say the government does not matter, it is a trickle of brackish water which may overflow when a sheep dies in one of the pools. And when the water begins to rise, they laugh and buy funny hats, and have a holiday with guns in the squares. And when the floods come they quietly fill with water and hang so peacefully in the canals, little bent humans floating with their faces looking down, so seriously studying the bed of the canal.'

Pierrina said, 'But that only happens abroad, or in wars, or the occasional revolt in the provinces, or at elections, or when the currency is devalued, or when there is a strike.'

The Director reassured her, 'I doubt if any of us, or anyone in the capital will suffer in that way; it just pays, and here I commend to you the Chinese science of looking at water; it pays not to laugh at the river. Respect it, leave gifts of painted leaves and stillborn children by the embankments you would be wise to build, and remember that the gods who live under the right bank, and the left, are powerful, even if they do attract the occasional mermaid.'

Torgano was not impressed by this string of metaphor: it seemed to imply a warning; perhaps a general admonition not to forget that the outward playfulness of politics, the games through which all saw, were but ploys to obscure the working of men of power as absolute as any illiterate chieftain with astrakhan and a knout. Or perhaps it was a warning to Torgano and Pierrina not to interfere with an official, even if he were of the left. Chastened, the four said goodnight.

Gallista and the Director moved off into the false evening light of the squares, where cunning advertisements flashed and leered high above the crumbled facades of ugly buildings of theoretical historical interest.

Torgano took Pierrina home; they parted tenderly, almost.

'Till tomorrow,' Pierrina breathed as she clanged abrupt gates behind her.

Torgano wandered home; on a bridge, he stopped, looking into the slowly breathing water. His shadow, round-shouldered and anxious, lay in pieces among the ripples; he looked at his face as it jigged and shifted in the night breezes. Quizzically, he asked the shadow what causes, what ambitions prowled in the elegiac rhythms of those obfusc features. And the face lay, looking at the sky; and sometimes it seemed that the eyes were shut in sleep; sometimes that they were open in death; sometimes that they were not there at all.

Chapter 5

THE DIRECTOR AWOKE: without his suit, he was an old man, the eyes and lips tired and strained in the brash, delinquent life of a sporty government. 'I have served' could not be the boast of this early morning destitute. This troubled decrepitude of a ferine which had spent years in emulation and unlovely and non-spiritual self-preservation and advancement showed no trace of moral fulfilment or the beauty of a quasi-religious duty performed. It was the face of a defeated rowdy, of a warrior who had started fighting at an early age for the usual primitive reasons, and by rationalising his archaisms had bound himself and his contemporaries to a system, where otherwise there might be seen only an attitude, or an arrested development.

Yet, he might have been happy: success does not breed suicides, and the Director had been a successful rowdy, in that in his efforts to assert himself, he had adopted many worthy and morally defensible logical attitudes. Yet, as he half slept, it came to him that he had been so long acquisitive, that all he could do now that was beautiful or touching or useful was to give everything away again. And that was to make a mockery of his life, and the norms by which success was judged; besides, he had nothing to give away. He sighed.

Chilly slabs of dust and light moved stealthily round the room: visitors in a sick man's room, the gruesome waiting beams picked up here a vase, turning the sickly fingers slowly over the hideous fired industrial dragons glazed on the pottery, touched there a fabric, appraising it as the effects of a dead man. The Director swung half out of bed. An old man: he bandaged his feet. The patient tortoise gestures, the eyes resolutely not acknowledging the work of the hands. He reached surely for the bandages; yesterday's rags still, but he did not inspect them, with his fingers he rubbed and brushed them. Then, to the crippled scabby feet; he was trembling a little with effort and cold, and a familiar pain.

He sprinkled powder and cheap scent on the fungoid skin; swiftly, he weaved the bandages in loops and senile bundles over the diseased but exotically beautiful cultures on his feet. And as he did so, and as he hobbled about to go to the department, he thought of Gallista, that girl whose feet no doubt shone like rich, unripe fruit, and were soft and domestic. He longed for her to sit quietly by him, while he told her how ill he was, and how his feet had become worn out in metaphysical hikes in the valley of the absolutes. Just to be able to forget his maturity and nauseating superiority, that would be so pleasant.

He looked out of the window; beyond this park, a cemetery, beyond that, a tilted road down which sprinted the snarling camions. In the park, a dog was discreetly disrespectful, like a child in an empty cathedral full of the clutter and bad taste of the monuments of the departed. The cemetery each year grew its marble fringe, the pious strands of mausolea grew long, romantic and curled slightly at the ends, where they had to struggle up mournful contours. And the Director knew that, if he were lucky, he would be put in a church when he was dead; then at least, he thought to himself, I shall be able to escape the monotonous sight of all this insecurely and hard-heartedly buried suffering, this silent howl of the anonymous dead.

He prowled his house, to make sure everything was real: departmental photographs, like teams of athletes the grasping and the unfriendly buried their differences in a smile the exact duration of a time exposure. Metaphorically, the knees had been polished in honour of the occasion. Then photographs of buildings: caught in nonchalant poses, of an evening, or out of season perhaps, castles reclined, smoothed back their ivy with a retoucher's flattering skill. Mottoes said 'Relax'; the Director mocked them but relaxed. A postcard from a woman was tacked over the fireplace, a story about it was to be told to amuse or move the visitors, whom he never invited. The house was planned and lived in as if to summarise 'The great man lives simply'. The Director ate a little dry bread: his gums were tender in the morning.

Gallista, she was many countries, many cultures away; he felt like a professor who falls in love with a Chinese princess who appears in some barbarian legend. Bad enough thought the Director, to love someone who had lived in the wrong century – and in China. But someone whose very existence was in doubt, that came near to narcissism. He thought of Gallista as he fed himself with biscuits; she sat on the most rigid chairs, chairs which had no affinity with an Jazz Age, like a bird very high in a tree of apple blossom. And yet, so discreet and so impure, perhaps there was a Tuscan Jazz Age, a few of her dumb slaves might have tentatively thumped Egyptian rhythms on the harpsichord. Grimacing, the Director eased on his shoes.

*

Torgano shut his shop for a week. 'Perhaps I shall never open it again,' he frightened himself with morbid drama.

The other shopkeepers smiled sadly. 'All along, I knew this would happen; he was not one of us, he did not like us. But we, with our infinite contempt for the failure and the snob, we are sorry for him, because he was unhappy and effete. We will not sneer at him, for he is, we suppose, human; we will ignore him, but sympathetically.'

And the steamy nymphs in the hairdressers' found that a transient madness could be worked off by telling their customers that Torgano was certainly leaving – some insipid scandal, perhaps a woman, more probably professional ethic. But Torgano cocked his nose for the tendrils of scents which coiled white and sickly from the merchandise; the conifer tang of the ironmonger; the Baltic ropes for trussing up bushes; the enamels and the creosote slipped girlish labials into the chemical purity.

The butcher's assistants made of orange fat, their thumbs

bandaged, they tried so hard to hurt the dead animals; warm meat reminded Torgano of a sweet gamy decay, the smell interested only a few lazy bunches of flies which seemed to grow on the stumps of sheep's legs. The sweetshop: whipped sugar, essences of alcohol, cellophane, the face of luxury pressed towards a comparative poverty, which it envied, while refusing to come to terms with it. The synthetic smells of the street, more exotic than the organic composts of the countryside, Torgano snuffed them up: small pleasures were all the more necessary, now that Pierrina was walling up her emotions still more securely, like a saint's skeleton behind geometrically exact marble inlays, and precisely inclined Byzantine mosaic carpets.

Even when Pierrina seemed at her most friendly, it was a feeling quite self-contained, one which did not extend itself to him: when she was happy, he felt isolated; surrounded by, but not included in, a healthy impersonal bonhomie. Pierrina gave the impression, he decided, of almost tolerating him, merely because she was determined not to let him spoil things, not to let him persecute her with ugly romances.

Torgano wished he could rewrite everyone's character, change the lines already spoken; with the optimism of the utterly defeated, he thought that a magnolia sent as a token, a kiss sent on the back of a menu, this would change the world. One gesture, one grimace – rocks would split, mountains would roll like hot cats in the valleys; trees would change back into princesses; animal mascots and bulls change back into blind gods. Pierrina would be freed from the resented and generation-old spells which hindered a healthy and balanced acquiescence in Torgano's appetites.

Certainly, all that could be known was that prolonged effort had failed to produce more than concentrated indifference under a mask of decorous interest; so, all that could be tried now was the sudden masterful ploy, the trick between courage and fraud, cruelty and magic. Torgano imagined one stroke of the hero's antique sword, subduing fifty cities, winning a mountain of gold, and Pierrina: to win a girl, and save Europe. Both seemed equally unlikely. But as he went to the palace, obeying some quasi-royal commands, he thought only how he could find this action, the sick, destructive sacrifice to save a sick, destroyed victim. The dogs of the aristocracy fled before Torgano, the avenger and physician, who did not look where he was going, as he marched along.

*

Gallista talked to the proprietor of the nearby café; he was saying, 'You know, you understand these things, you do not try to advance yourself unduly, you are not a friend of the rich and influential. We all know that, and we are grateful; you are our intellectual, our artist, and I mean that as a compliment, you must understand. You are beautiful, but that does not stop you being sympathetic and helpful.

'Well, as you know, we have a nice crowd comes in of an evening. Friendly little girls still at school, talk to anyone, they would, they're that friendly; Kropec and his gang on their motorbikes. Very keen on the lost colonies, they are: that's the significance of the skulls on those surplus fascist jackets they wear.

'There's Benni, our novelist, when he's not at the Department of Health and Culture recovering from a weekend party, if you understand me. Then we get the casuals; all dropping in for a bit of music, some arty-crafty talk, or just to meet friends, or get away from them; and as you know, we usually cart them outside quite early, and they soon get up and go home again. Of course we get the odd complaint from those who can afford drinks by the bottle, and don't like their evenings made gay by those who like company, even if it is often too intellectual and fancy. And Kropec, well, you know what he's like in arguments; I admit I wouldn't like his knee in me when he's roused.

'But what I mean is, that these people have opinions, they

are leaders, they think, they're not standoffish, not unsociable; even senators come down here, and they tell me that as long as there are cafés like this, there's no need for state interference, and a lot of youth clubs spending money for us. You, you surely see that my place is an institution; it is the underworld of ideas and action; it is what matters.

'What I say is, if you can't have an elite to rule – I'm a monarchist myself of course – then you should have boys like mine with a bit of go in them. They would have fitted into any historical context: galley master, professor in the gymnasia for the sons of the rich; financier to any crusade or patriotic enterprise. Now, it's like this: not only you and I recognise it, but also our police. Bluntly, they want a premium, before they will let us carry on; they say if we don't pay up, they'll have us closed down as a Trotskyist cell, or I don't know what other nonsense. Gallista, we need your help: a subscription would help us.'

Gallista smiled without invitation; prettily she exaggerated her own importance. And left to squeeze money from the Director; then she would see on whom to spend it. As she went, Kropec himself wheeled over the road on his black tank; with his pennants, his badges, and a system of signalling by lights, he was a knightly figure. Always chewing, usually masked for his motorcycle, he was short, ugly, brutal, unthinking, given to moods and the artistic clichés of fringe journalism. He had one or two things to say in his moods, which concealed the emptiness and incoherence of his emotions. He found, too, that it was most boring, even insulting, when others took his mumbled alcoholic reactions and opinions for the gospel of a suburban leader.

But he did not mind the picture his flatterers painted: Kropec, chewing enigmatically, riding into classical cities, perhaps slightly wounded, cherished by women; perhaps one day he would have to prove the legend by sweeping across the continent at the head of a pomegranate people, fertile and coarse.

''Nice girl,' he mouthed at Gallista; she felt as if a saint had waved to her from a banner. 'Nice – you keep it that way. Tell 'em Kropec told you that: nice. Nice girl.'

The Viking hand raised in its gauntlet, the mask adjusted: the demigod chugged off serenely.

Gallista thought, 'One day we shall hear nothing but myths about him. He is just the sort we want: the benediction so enigmatic that it is meaningless. The approval which makes one tingle with xenophobia and patriotism. The ugliness, the power, the self-confidence; the motorcycle, emblem of the migrant, the inconsistency, the chivalry. And those eyes: tormented, shifty, tired; he had rejected everything, all systems, all values. Now he is alone, he wants the support of a woman, no doubt; but a few years and he will evolve some new code, a new way of life, which had affinities with the old but comprehensive promises not to repeat its mistakes.

'Kropec, dear persecuted Kropec, our martyr, the martyr of the poor and of the rich sadist, you live and die for us. Perhaps you will come again to us humbled, full of unselfish promises. But whatever you say, we all know you will demand our lives, every thought must be given to you. We will sacrifice ourselves to make us better than anyone else. Kropec, you are not a man of power – we know that; you are an outcast; we understand your failings; that is why we will go to any extreme to show that we will mutilate ourselves and others for the sake of humanity alone.'

Gallista sighed; she wanted to give herself away to a machine that would mortify her with naked charged wires in the name of love and family. With distaste, she saw that she was near the establishment where the army made its poison gas; the residents nearby complained of the smell, but government employees came round to tell them there was no danger. The officials were not used to it, and had to leave hurriedly, gasping into handkerchiefs. Gallista remembered the Director had told her smugly that he had tried to get it moved or abolished, but without success.

And she said, 'But surely, if we don't get the gases first, before everyone else, and their antidotes, our potential for peace, and our prestige will drop? Beside, poison gases are not dangerous, in small doses.'

And the Director had nodded to her, and smiled mysteriously, as if he had at least seven immortal armoured divisions mobilised in the next room. He smirked, as if to say: 'Yes, once I thought differently; now it is explained; weapons no longer cause pain – they are ideas. We have superior intellects, so we have the best weapons; I am proud of you, Gallista, for evolving so many eternal truths with so little reflection.'

And Gallista had remarked, 'All the trees near the factory have leaves like pressed lilac, shredded and purple, with thick sacs full of what seems to be pepper.'

But all this hardly mattered; she was to meet again this wonderfully impervious man who contrived to be both gentleman and aristocrat with women, and her mother had told her that these were rare indeed.

*

Turquoise opened the door of the palazzo, his shadow fell before him as he did so; it had been leaning on the door. He walked between ranks of packing cases, drawn up for inspection; the Director's assistant was making another inventory; he had been up on the roof, found two animals loose. He pretended that this was a criticism of the Director's efficiency; he had tried to push them into the canal's lumpy saliva, but children had been watching. Torgano went upstairs to look for Pierrina; the armour of renaissance gladiators was propped against the walls.

For a moment, when he came into the gallery where invisible warriors lounged in their iron suits, he could not distinguish Pierrina among the antique mercenaries. She was looking out over the water, across a wing of the palazzo feebly spread and angled over the canal. Seeing her like a nostalgic puppet at her stage window, Torgano wondered why he had spoken to Gallista. Pierrina, of course, knew that Torgano was there among the Teutonic and the Tuscan knights, childish and similar in their damascened boar hunts.

She was hating him today; she was tired of living in his pretence that she might like him; at times she felt in danger of forgetting the truth, that she disliked the intimate and beguiling creeds he represented. She wanted to be free from people, however pleasant they might strive to seem: why should she, however persecuted, regard a man as more than a complicated bundle of aspirations and failures, a friend, but no more, to be taken in small doses, a medicine occasionally necessary and always nauseating. That was why she might summon him, inspiring him to clean his shoes and his teeth, only to remind him once more that he was vile, not even a fine specimen.

'The zoo down the road has one just like you, but his horns grow tiny black orchids on this tips, and his hooves smell of Havana cigars and nightingales,' she seemed always to say, a polite but thorough humiliation; and wholly anti-romantic. Sometimes, when she was bored, she felt attached to him; he was after all, a sentimental appendage, but usually he stood in the way of some unlikely scheme, with his soulful demands.

'All my parties, the dances at which I am the only woman to be shared among regiments of hunched Napoleons, squat muscle-bound Hercules, ruined by Torgano's possessive unhappiness; I would rather be inferior, hence necessary, to a hundred men, than the equal of one, dominated by his kindness and passion.'

How could she have deceived herself into tolerating him so long? Yet, by refusing to recognise the existence of love, she had made it impossible to reject him on conventional grounds; she promised herself that when she had left the palazzo, she would treat herself to weeks of silence and loneliness. Meanwhile, there he was, gazing at her, his eyes always so full of trust that she felt an urge to drive spurs into the vapid jellies.

And Torgano thought, 'Does she not hear me? I will make a call out of the forest: she will turn and become a smile. I shall say, "Pierrina!" and our eyes will clasp like the heavy hands of crabs, incongruous, but compatible. She will stop telling me that there is no folly so deep as that of the truly sincere man. She will stop thinking I want to exploit her; she will begin to feel.'

On the canals, parties of English schoolgirls were instructed to look up at the palazzo. They were told: 'All the Romeos have gone now, I'm afraid (haha, well, after all it is holiday time). There was once a duke who forbad the building of balconies, because his steam yacht could not manoeuvre properly, or else Bolsheviks dropped bombs down the funnel, I forget the details. Look at the cat. In England we would not have so much pineapple; we import much fruit from nearby hills, where it grows in the black laps of a thousand reclining valleys.'

And the girls wrote, 'Pineapples' in their notebooks, drew some of the diamond shapes, faceted like monstrous juicy eyes, and forgot about it all, which was not unwise.

Torgano spoke to Pierrina: 'There is no need that we should ever stop looking out of windows together, you know.'

And Pierrina hid her irritation, saying that she wanted to be out there, splashing along in the water sometimes. Torgano wondered if she was changed: if she was coming to rely on him; now, it scarcely mattered; he was emotionally washed up, and was fit only for a long Swiss recuperation on the summit of a crystal mountain, with much bitter-sweet chocolate, and the comforting accuracy of mechanical cuckoos. But still he looked keenly at her long lips when she spoke, trying to examine the pictographs which sparkled briefly through her teeth: Pierrina was a lion into whose mouth he was never quite sure about putting his head.

It was all difficult and depressing that Pierrina should regard life as a struggle with beautiful demons; but no doubt, somewhere among what she said were the words he wanted her to say. It was all a matter of rearrangement: when she loved him, he would give her parties and champagne carnivals among the hollyhocks of some rustic square. He would hire peacocks: a truckful should arrive in the morning, with dressers and fitters to adjust their accoutrements. From nearby villages, enormous fish would be carried up on stretchers borne by four men; there would be a sound of scraping from the insides of huge carcasses on the lawn, where cooks would be collecting the materials for cunning animal compounds.

All day, succulent corpses would be dragged to the kitchens; a fruit would be pressed into a bowl and turned in a day to a plangent well-bred liqueur. Grotesque candles, like wax lanterns, would be brought; the moths would be polished, and set to fly nostalgically over the tables. Birds would be engaged to sing the latest waltzes: troupes of gipsies and musicians in tail coats would augment the resources of nature.

The square would be hung with ferns, the Socratic statues would be disguised with horns and tobacco plants. And the guests too should be of the best: drunk and promiscuous, they would shriek their intelligence from the shrubbery, they would smash things in the most amusing way. After a week, they would growl off in their limousines for a month in someone else's ship. They would leave the exquisite perfumes of wealth and responsibility behind them, also a few dead girls, trampled like orchids in the corners of the gothic square.

And Pierrina was thinking that she would stay with Torgano for perhaps a few more weeks, he was so helpless and reliable, it would not do much harm. It would be boring, but it would please him. When she had settled in, she would get rid of him; she would invite him to her parties, a subtle disgrace. She would invite artists, and be painted by them, have them insult her in novels. Politicians would relax with her, but never become disgusting, or permanent. She would be central, everyone would love her, people would die to subsidise her, she would flit through the life of everyone like a butterfly over a drowsy dog.

All would snap for her, try to catch her, but fall back and

grunt when they realised she was more beautiful, more swift, more ephemeral an illusion than anyone could hope to capture. Nothing would be sordid or intimate, because she would only look at what she wanted: nothing could destroy such profound and rewarding self-deception. She took it as a compliment when other women said, 'Ah, how I envy your detachment: I, you know, I am so indiscreet.'

She even thought people did not enjoy being indiscreet. Her flat would be on the slopes of a social vortex, gangsters called Emerald who bought Dürers, brewers called Esterhazy who shot pigeons with machine guns would meet and laugh together under her auspices. There would be so many romantic people round her, she would have no need for the terrifying, and, she suspected stultifying business of romance. When Torgano left her, the world would suddenly be illuminated; things emotional and irrational would expire; she would be free.

And Torgano could only say to her, 'The beginning of this week seemed bright and lucid: I remember taking special notice of everything, the canals, colour, food, sounds. But now, everything seems to have become bleak and diluted; the world has become a painting of a china insect pasted on a branch of a class of amateur painters. At the beginning we went to a carnival, where we were the characters; at the end we went to a play, where the anonymous played for us. Do you too feel exhausted?'

'What a horrible thought: I'm sure I never feel in any way as unusual as you seem. You seem to see life like a psychopath's drawing, full of heads with sneery faces.'

They stood, and were exasperated with one another; a cat walked in, pleased to see them, it whirred round them, making them forget all they had discovered. On the canal, a small steam coracle puffed by, carrying paraffin for palaces; a familiar sight, a new one was required often, for frequent explosions sent the vaporous vessels to burst starlike against the ducal facades.

Where the canals broadened, and the winds angled in from the sewage marshes by the sea, a careless captain might find a fire whipped up his only hope, to flop overboard, and watch the cascading ruby move slowly on, sending black webs of fume up nearby walls. The man at the helm shouted from time to time: haughty maids screamed back from delicious crenellations, which oozed cream stone, but he paid no attention. He was splendid, and potentially lethal.

'He is like a plague,' Torgano said, 'a nest of germs wandering about, inviting exorcism or fumigation, but receiving only frightened insults. One feels called to drop a ball of blazing resin on his head, and to show him the cross looted for the city from some cathedral, so that the fire would consume a heart in a state of grace, or fear.'

And Pierrina said politely, 'What I especially hate about you is your pride; you can't hide it from me; I know all about you, just what you are like. Pride.'

And Torgano knew he was not proud, whatever else he was; but one more injustice, one more daub of dislike in a huge mural of misunderstanding, what did it matter? Perhaps she just said this to hide her feelings. In many ways, things had been better lately.

'Wait, at any rate, for a few more weeks, before leaving her,' he thought, without enthusiasm.

Pierrina hung out over the water. 'A friend of mine is to be married this morning,' she said. 'Should we go and stand on the pavement and call benevolently to her, reciting chapters from the "Book of Witches"?'

'If you want – but please, do not lean out so far, or black marble dolphins will carry you off to be their queen. Do you remember those dolphins who came to the city early one morning, and crashed into bridges and at the artillery school cadets fired at them with revolvers? They lifted themselves out of the water like huge basalt saucers, one imagined them grunting as they wrestled with the corners, making themselves fleshy projectiles, but adaptable. And the old women screamed that here were the Turks back again. You remember?'

'Yes – nice.' Pierrina wondered if she could save the

palazzo; she waved away phantom ancestors who did not know the facts; if she filled the fountain with petrol and threw a branch of sticky fir in it, the building would pound upwards in smoke and spark. It would roar like a nightmare dog, the fingers of the armoured janissaries would straighten out and wave in the heat. The beams would stretch, push white-hot masonry into the canals reflecting their confused impressions of the mad scene. The woods would throw out green stinging sparks, the glass would burn off its enamel, and fuse into blue inextinguishable fires.

Perhaps the canal would be bridged by the collapsed façade: skeletons would tumble out of the foundations; the hands of dead firemen would beckon forward the rescuers in the black and red cube landscape, where gold and flesh were likewise spoiled. A glorious end, if expensive.

The officials from the Department of Public Monuments counted the heads of sixteenth century tradesmen cruelly sculpted on the beams: the puppet heads were scarcely human, but visitors recognised themselves among them.

Pierrina called to the officials, 'I'm afraid you will never agree on the total; some say it is inverse perspective; others that they are bewitched; others that there is a hallucination. The orthodox belief is that these were Florentines who came in some immigration scheme, but cheated their customers, so that now their numbers are so difficult to estimate as their weights were. They sailed away soon after, and fought for a republic of Corfu.'

The officials smiled patiently. 'Two hundred?'

'Yes, I made it two hundred.'

'Have you got these glass things down?' asked one.

'What, the vegetable set, those purple rainbows with the copper stalks, split down the middle, all whimsical colours and early spring angles? Yes, that's all done?'

'Shall we go out,' suggested Torgano hurriedly.

*

Gallista too looked from a window; far below, acutely sloping business men were comically distorted by the height. Gallista squashed them mentally; turning in towards the Director, she said: 'A café nearby wants some money to bribe the police with: may I have some please?'

'No.'

'I was so glad you said that; people always seem to think the only answer to frankness is a laugh, and acquiescence. Now, to convince you. It's a club really, where all may gather to bore one another, and fight without interruption. Politics and art, the pleasures of the connoisseur, such as coffee, alcohol, brawling, growing beards, all the occupations of the intellectual and the philanthropist.'

'Still no,' said the Director, 'but if you want, we can go to the police, and discuss everything with them. They live in a house with a delightful park; there are snakes and dragonflies in the garden; in 1911 a duke's son was assassinated there by small boys. The son was about nineteen, very romantic; there was a tree over a pond, and this gang of delinquent gnomes seized him, and swung him gently to hang from this tree over the water. He was found dying, and observed that he had seen a hatch of mayfly, he called it an exhalation of lively bubbles from the pond's mouth, and that he was glad to die at sunset when the lips of the roses were parted for a goodnight kiss. Very touching: the leader of the small boys died in prison, I believe.'

Gallista and the Director strutted through the admiring lackeys, who had chastely guarded the Director for years, and now flocked to Gallista, his favourite. 'We are a family': the department's boast permitted also the pervasive and ruinous tyranny of family injustice. Obscurely the Director's assistant felt that he, by right, by the inevitable hygiene and progression of official relationships, should have got Gallista's present position.

They walked to the police headquarters; in a chessboard of

marble vistas, each resolved by the ivory crown or the crimson cardinal, or was it a currant bush – the excavators of the landscape gardeners had enjoyed themselves. A hundred classical gardens were piled together; hills had been thrown up; soggy streams pushed here and there to preserve a feeling of natural artifice. Trees had been artificially shattered, as if by lightning, rocks had the faces of women as if struck by accidental winds, roses grew red and white to hide the more obscene statues. A generation of cats and squirrels acted out politics in the shrubberies, and the dilapidated greenhouses.

The Director extended a hand to show Gallista the sights; lightly, she thought of the murdered aristocrat, his brothers catarrhal and querulous in the suits of tiny generals; the father drunk and tottering behind his misshapen son. The grief of a family: the compulsory mourning of six regiments, the unfamiliar movements of the reversed-arms drill; young officers dropping their swords; muffled drums and muted brass barely drowning the angry conversations of the cavalry, horses overcome with grief or influenza, or whatever, lying down, or bolting.

Then, the guns firing over the grave, over the spotty poet who hated noise; the generals and admirals breaking ranks joyfully to become drunk in the mourning tents, the plumes on their splendid hats leaping in ecstasy, proud, tragic birds stimulated by imperial pretence. The relatives becoming intoxicated, just when the crowds in the streets had been made by journalists to feel guilty and sad. Those were the stirring times, thought Gallista.

They came to the police chief: short but well-hinged, he was reading the magazine *Detectif Ufficsor*; he swung his legs excitedly; in the uniform trousers they were like decorative sausages waving in the breeze of a mountain delicatessen. By the wall was a glass case: a skull full of shrapnel, a broken lute, a Chinese lion-dog mortar, a box of green chocolates, the ragged ends of lives.

When the Director greeted him, he grunted, then said, 'I

hear you are going to take over the Palazzo Tarrault; we get to know these things, you know, I have set a man to watch it: the canals hide all manner of men. Colonies of dog-eaters: they live in iron huts, drink a liquor brewed from plums and metal polish; assassins, they have a training school. They have built paradise by cementing together a number of large, unusual stones.

'Societies of women, those plant bombs in the slums, so that they can help the victims; they say there is not enough social work to do, so they create some themselves. I reckon there are at least fourteen unofficial religions, mostly sun and ancestor worship, in the town. And a number of complete moral codes! Sadists, who believe pain is a social purgative, they dress as clowns, nearly kill one another. The athletic clubs too: just a front – gang organisations which never break the law, just exist for the sake of being an organisation; they just make lists of café owners. And the real criminals flit through this make-believe underworld, like artists of talent through artistic society, rare and feared.'

The Director had heard all this before; it covered, with its talk of paradise for outcasts, an ability to detect crime. The Director asked if the police objected to Kropec: a conceited laugh.

'Well, now, how odd: we run that café, we pay the proprietor, not that he knows, to keep these cranks busy night after night. We even pay Kropec, secretly. It amuses us, it demonstrates our complete control. It does not matter that you should know, a little disillusion keeps things moving. We keep these people out of trouble, by subsidising them, encouraging them; talking and thinking are immaterial; we are not, thank God, "Thought Police" yet. The simple way to a criminal mind: pay him to be not quite a criminal: society must be itself slightly criminal to control evil.

'A sanctimonious snuffle into an immaculate handkerchief.'

And Gallista thought of Kropec, that blundered intellect, the child's attempt at a face, obviously designed for a primitive coin. She thought of the money spent by the government and its servants to create their own overthrow; a little disillusion serving only to ferment political and criminal activity, whilst an army of police watched putrid civilisations in the wharves and abandoned tenements by the canals. She felt insecure, she disliked this man, who spent his life encouraging vultures from the harbour garbage to this urban jungle, to flap off with a vole, or small, domesticated rat. Finding this weakness in herself, she resolved to watch the Director even more closely, in case he should be so unmanly as to show his feelings.

But the Director just asked, 'Why on earth watch the palazzo?'

'Just routine: no reason, but to impress you. And to warn you: we are everywhere. In the safest places, you will find a policeman. We could take over the government, we know so much, if you should all die, or suffer in some way.'

Kropec was dismissed: 'An interesting head, I often remark on it. If we had not put him out of action, he would have been dangerous.'

'Had you not better tell him he is no longer dangerous, in case he does not realise it?'

A polite laugh, they were sent away. They felt dirty, they hurried through the gardens, the cedar by the pond had its branches held up by hooks and chains. Some of the hooks had slipped loose, they swung one crooked rusty finger towards the lower branches, towards the heavily wattled birds greedy on the pond.

Pierrina took Torgano to the church, hoping he would not imagine she loved him because the two others were to be married.

'Soon,' she thought, 'I shall be freed from his love.'

And Torgano thought, 'Soon I shall renounce everything: a life of sacrifice, of purposeless and completely futile renunciation and resignation. That is what my life and my love have led up to, it is a gesture to obey the logic of fortune, the apparatus of chance. But it is all I can do: I must continue giving up pieces of myself, tormenting myself unnecessarily, growing slowly smaller, more spiritual, more unbearable, until I am wholly negligible, giving everything for love and a theory of personal justice.'

He decided to throw away his life: a noble, if barren decision. 'It seemed,' he said later, 'the most any man could ever do: it was not merely for Pierrina. It was a great gesture of protest: it was cowardly and mean, pointless and antisocial: but it was the greatest single thing I could accomplish. To extinguish myself before an abstraction; to say, "Love, politics, ambition: I gave up my body to you." I protest fiercely: you are corrupt, I fight you. But I am not living in a struggle with you all my life: I am throwing myself to be crushed by you, for if I do not, you will kill me anyway! It is an act of will, a choice, for the coward to rush forward in mock attack on the firing squad which is resigned to execute him.'

Torgano was glad to have settled his future.

They stood near the church door: a red banner, slit down the middle, framed the doorway: beautiful overdressed children climbed their mothers, by the silver limousines chauffeurs chased away class-conscious infants who were spitting through the open windows. Stewards were chasing away spectators who looked unlucky, a black cat in a cage was being teased by a police sergeant. A guard of tall girl soldiers were being formed, a trumpeter was squeaking down her instrument; the soldiers drew wooden swords, and began to sing nervously, accompanied by a man in morning dress on a mechanical piano. The uniforms might have been found in the baggage train of a moderately successful opera company; the braid had been fastened with pins, the lace was stained orange with the paint from hot necks.

'What does all this mean?' asked Torgano. 'Have we all been mobilised? Have the state cavalry gone off to charge machine guns in the lost colonies, sacrificing their ceremonial beasts at the whim of photographers for the patriotic papers? Are these the only soldiers we have?'

And Pierrina replied, 'The bride is a star of the theatre; she

specialised in nostalgic romances set to music, of the period of
the socialist proscription, the dynamiting of the memorial swan
pond, the murder of the four bishops with silver bullets as they
fought together on the cathedral steps, regarding some
peripheral dogma of the Copts.'

And indeed, the officials were slightly blurred at the edges,
as if they had worn away their souls with the constant
application of greasepaint. The banner parted like ripe lips:
beadles with clubs and leopard skins gave a blessing in
miniature. The bride and her man smiled sincerely, as if they
could not see the florid stage direction of their comrades who
ran like pigeons, their cloth wings neatly folded behind.

'Try to work up some enthusiasm, you photographers: fight
for position!' screamed someone in a whisper.

The girl warriors sang with embarrassment:

> *'Girls and boys, we all agree*
> *"Imperial welfare" makes us free*
> *But when all is said and done*
> *It's better to legalise your fun.'*

A platoon of fathers and uncles marched into the bottled
sunlight of the flashing photographers: an elderly reporter began
to weep by Pierrina, overcome by the spell he was helping to
cast.

'I like a real society wedding,' he said. 'Warm champagne
under pressure making an arch: a dozen rejected suitors
subscribing for a hearse, or pepper in the confetti, all the gaiety
of wealth and refinement of feeling. The bride perhaps
screaming that she is fifty, fed for years on animal gland, and
clinging to the knees of the adolescent bishop performing the
ceremony: the bride's father challenges a newsreel cameraman
to a duel. Dignity dies hard, sir: the true nobility will always
have it over the philanthropists and the scholars, sir.

'You see, a man like myself can see for himself: such men
are successful and generous. They give to charity as much as

one-hundredth part of their immense fortunes; they care about other people so much more than an impersonal government. That is why it is my mission, to report their weddings, and social caprices, to make them appear at once abandoned, and also inspired by the logical frenzy of the divinely intoxicated.'

Pierrina tried to leap above the flocks of admirers and advertisers to see the theatrical monarch, but they had gone off to their palace of gothic gauzes and thunder machines, leaving only the escort of girls to be wrapped in cloaks, and taken back to their theatre in a lorry. In the gutters were crunched flashbulbs.

'Nasty,' said Torgano.

The splendid couple had tramped to the cars on flowers: broken trumpets and gasping mouths showed how the flowers had suffered.

'Why not use dandelions?' asked Pierrina.

'I don't think milk and honey refers to dandelion milk,' said Torgano.

*

In a few seconds, when they had recovered from the experience of regarding two people who had been breathed on by a god, they moved back to the palazzo.

'I am going to sell my shop,' Torgano said casually. 'I think I shall try something quite different. It is no reflection on you, I just feel like a change; all I have to do is post this card, the auctioneers will come; eventually my antiques will become, as I have always hoped, bargains.'

Half bored with Pierrina, he frightened her; she said, 'But please, not for my sake, I hope. Stay with your shop, business will improve. In Scandinavia arms of ice will plunge down, slide their fingers thoughtfully along valleys, like a frigid young man who terrifies himself into unpleasant actions by caressing his face, they will prick the fat hearts of the Northerners. Salty snow will wear away the ancestral molars on the Rhine, the castles will be scrambled and sucked away.

'In England the chimneys of the houses will be full of snow; white owls will lay eggs in the dead stoves; a fox will dig for dead horses in the spring. In Belgium the mines will freeze, ice will block the shafts, men with ice on their lips will cut their way through. In Northern France the trees will be solid as the spikes of a rake; they will break off in the wind with light percussive twangs. From Russia there will come a million men carrying a city of fur and bone beams on their backs.

'All this it says in the newspapers; there will be a new ice age, men will flee from the anaemic landscapes and animals and come to us, for our sun, for your antiques; they will buy seeds from the floor of faince pyramids, sticky bark from the musky jungles in hanging gardens, and hoard them for the smell of expended sunshine. Please be sensible, dear: you may be a failure, but I and all my friends like you for being one. I assure you it is useless to try to stand away from your context.'

Torgano smiled at the frantic images and ambitions of the newspapers; possibly they hoped that tourists would stay on in the town, lest on their return home they should find that the cold ash of polar eruptions had turned everyone black and rigid one morning. But he posted the card:

'On Monday, I shall have to start thinking of what to do in the future, perhaps one of your careful rude friends you never mention will give me a job. I am sure I would be good at scraping gorse from the plump hips of their horses, or polishing the disgruntled faces of their clocks, or spending thirsty years naked in a boiler-room stoking their infernal fires.

'I am sorry if I too am rude, but you must realise that I relied on you and your palazzo for more than amusement. You women are all the same: you dress like musical instruments, and think that people are only interested in you as long as they can play melodies on you in irregular metres and distracting intervals. But of course, if you would enjoy seeing me wither and crackle up like a leaf in my shop, I have no doubt it could be arranged.'

Pierrina looked at him anxiously. 'I do not want to carry my dislike of you too far: be a waiter, observe the old elastic bodies propped at the tables, the grey, folded lips, the prickly teeth, the napkin tucked carefully round the well-nourished wallet. That would cure any man of eating.'

All the same she was concerned about Torgano. 'Come, help me move my furniture: they are coming for it soon, to take it away by boat: the Director will be there to watch, we shall all be delightfully spiteful, we will peck vaguely at each other's eyes. Come, Torgano, watch for a while these goldfish, they will stimulate our circulation, as they moon about like lost corpuscles.'

And they stood and watched the apricot leaves moving with fishy logic among the lotuses, or the lilies. A cat on a string limped with its owner to the pool; its swift eyes floated over the artificial waves, eyes like small curly yellow leaves, they did not worry the fish. White petals with traces of blood on the edges made boats for adventuresome insects on the surface; and the snub-nosed fish knew that they were somehow on show, and busied themselves in the pretence of hard work and other ambitious projects.

'These fish make me feel lazy and sad,' said Torgano. 'But really, they are grossly pampered, and spoilt for any decent occupation, even scavenging. Starving men throw their last sandwiches in here, and the fish don't care; they prod them, and mash them up, but they never eat them.'

Pierrina smiled distantly; the man walked patiently with his sick cat. 'Come on, Frederick, leave the poor doves alone; aren't they beautiful in the sunset, all flame and twilight heaviness? But my Frederick must have a drink, to cure his leg. I think I'll have a drink too, mine don't feel too good.'

The man sat on a bench and dragged the cat over him, to sniff the cosmopolitan luxuries which still smelled strong in the oily fur. He looked at Torgano. 'Not at our best today – my friends won't talk to me when I've had a bit of a party, because when I'm drunk I can't construct feathery mythological analogies and blas-phemies. And Frederick, I'm afraid he doesn't fit in: as a man, he would be merely stupid; as a cat, he's quite incoherent. I trod on his leg last night – or was it a week ago?

'Time goes so fast when you're unconscious; anyway, Frederick is wicked, getting drunk, and after his parents worked so hard to send him to college too. He'll never learn: selfish, and covered in thick hair; that's how I would describe Frederick. How would I describe myself? I write jolly music, and everyone says, "How beautifully naive and useless; what a precious poseur he is; he is as lifelike and enlightening as a husky purple star in the shape of God strung up in a tree of average size."

'And I laugh, and say, "You know how it is – I only write because I have to eat, and because I would burst with frustration and an enlarged heart if I did not. I only give you music because I am a genius and have something of vital importance to say to everyone."

'And they roar with laughter, and the women lean back so I can see all the way to the roots of their patchy, rouged tongues. And they say, "How funny you are: thank God you're not important and opinionated like serious artists."

'And then I go home, and dismiss the current wife and beat up Frederick, and cry for maybe three weeks or a month. Then I write some more music and it all happens again.'

Pierrina asked, and she sounded as far away as a lady should, 'But why drink for amusement?'

The man sighed. 'Why not? I suppose I could take Frederick with me to a concert; we could take a cannon worked by compressed air, and shoot balls of my manuscripts at the performers; and Frederick could laugh. Madam, what you call entertainment is my work: my entertainment is to destroy myself. All my life, people have called me selfish and crude; all the time I have been working to make things beautiful and true; I have been too preoccupied with the feelings of others to care about mine. But when I loved people they would never keep still, they kept moving about because my ideas excited them; they pranced about at the end of the wires of my music. All I have preserved are the scores of my own compositions, little stone children round an empty tomb, and Frederick.'

The cat grinned, tugged for its master to wander off once more.

'Not a very amusing man,' said Pierrina, pleased, however, to think that one day she could, hygienically, comfort him.

Back at the palazzo, they watched for the Director: Torgano hoped Gallista would not come too; she somehow made politics too ferocious and direct, and scarcely worthwhile. They sat on the cases; spiders found the landscape had moved; they saw no wormy wooden mountains, no pictures at the correct height for webs. They broke their homicidal silence, and with subtle interrogations suggested a provisional government, on their pointed feet they ran into organisations and leagues.

Pierrina knew the undertaker insects with the bloomy grape bodies saw her as a god, a distorter of the spider world, possibly the originator of a spider ethic, but she was frightened of her power over them.

Torgano asked if he could squash the community with the corner of a case, but she said, 'No – they rely on us, they eat the vermin we attract.'

The Director opened the door; it was like opening a book, dropping light over the characters sitting expectantly inside, seeing them gradually animated, beginning to brawl and argue in high literary voices.

'They look,' thought the Director, 'as if they have set sail on a thin island of moss, called Greenwich Village, and have found that all their rich and famous neighbours are, in fact, penguins. Undoubtedly, they think I am not at all the social mage they are waiting for: they wanted some disreputable uncle to come and conjure for them, shaking stars from the velvet sleeves of his smoking jacket, taking small bronze planets from the discreet wigs of bourgeois aunts. They are obviously disappointed by reality, they are unwilling to believe that their ruin may be the salvation of others.

'Ah yes, Gallista here would tell them that the benevolent conjurers were run over by trams as they left the charitable institutions of manufacturing relatives. The old gentlemen with the rubber rabbits lay for days in the mortuary, and no one came to identify them, let alone laugh and be puzzled at the primitive mechanics of their party tricks. The idea that revolution is the shabby uncle who never made the grade, never quite fitted into the family business, that, I fear, is quite wrong. I feel that I can refuse to read the nursery book, educational and colourful though it is intended to be, on the lives of Pierrina and Torgano and they will sit here and wait for me for ever. But perhaps that is my own nostalgia, a desire to have a childhood which would sound inviting, in my autobiography.'

Pierrina swept over to the Director, the hostess who is so friendly that she does not attempt to hide her rudeness and boredom.

The Director told her: 'Gallista and I would like to watch your move from a nearby bridge, to enjoy the scenery, the air, to give you room to move and rush about and scream at one another.'

Gallista would have liked to wander through the palace, sneering at the books, picking at the threadbare faces on the chairs where some clumsy wife had spilled the venom for her husband. But it would not have been in character; she must despise what she enjoyed; she must develop anti-cultural beliefs by the most refined aesthetic arguments. She was just too much educated and subverted by reason and truth, to be able to take the middle way, the way of negation, ignorance and violence.

When she was much older, she would come to see that she could not revolt against art by painting pictures, against law and socialism by formulating an artificial fascism, all genetics and economics, instead of natural brute stupidity. So she went on to the bridge with the Director: a man in an alleyway came down to look at the water.

'He seems to be looking for a meal in the water,' said

Gallista.

And indeed, from time to time, he would turn a loose vegetable over with his foot: as they floated along, he would try to appear interested in squares of flesh or fruit which other scavengers had rejected. Incuriously, the Director looked down at him: the man was crunched in a tunnel between two palatial slums, his suit was spotted with the droolings of lofty senile gargoyles. He looked up at the Director: he had a stick in one hand. With a crack, it burst into a furry red blossom.

And again: holding his right wrist with his left hand, shrinking from the noise, the man played a dull game with the Director. The black sparkling accessory crackled, and light sounds fell into the canals. Several times the man made his timid grimace at the noise and the recoil, abrupt as a reflex.

Pierrina and Torgano were pushing a case on the boat supplied by the Director. Gallista and the Director stared silently at the odd man who was concentrating on something so painfully childish and apparently serious, for him at least. He looked as if he was attempting some insult which was never quite audible: he looked guilty and fairly worried.

Then, it seemed to be all over: he looked at the bridge doubtfully, then put up his arm, and a fish jumped – or could he have thrown something? wondered Gallista. It was really too far away to see anything: some persecuted lunatic having a game, one dare not look too closely for meanings. One last glance, and the dissatisfied customer, having paid good money in his fairground game, had won only the derision of the stallholder and a memory of a tumbled summer night set with mosquitoes, scented with excitement – or was it heat rash?

'Quite a little mystery,' smiled Gallista.

The director laughed. 'Yes, he was so inefficient, he must have been a real gangster, a fake would have stood nearer. He might have hit anyone at that distance; we were as safe as anyone round here. He did not seem so very disappointed either. Perhaps a Director does not taste so good out of season; you have to cut out the most delicious parts before they are safe to eat, in the summer, I believe. For a lunatic, he had very little courage.'

Gallista was scarcely excited. It had all been such a misunderstanding, such an embarrassing failure, it was hard to become interested.

'Why did the police not stop him?' she asked. 'They say they watch the palazzo. And why could he not come nearer? Perhaps it was a sudden impulse, to try to frighten us?'

'I know the best way to frighten me is to shoot me,' laughed the Director, though now he was feeling less happy. 'I doubt if the police stay on duty at teatime; I know I should not. Anyway, they would only stop professionals shooting me, being professional themselves, they would not recognise amateur assassins. Besides, it was all so nonsensical, he might as well have been an admirer, trying to attract my attention. He even threw away his gun, so presumably next time it will be something more subtle: incantations, or cannibal stew, or some heavy, long-distance symbolism.

'Well, at all events, I expect he will get more to tell his children out of all this than I should. Not a charming man; notice the way he chose a highway for rats to sit around in, and then showed us the mechanics of his cowardice, but even so, it is unusual to meet a dangerous man who is so splendidly decadent. I suppose we should tell someone.'

He told Torgano.

'Was it really someone firing?' Torgano said. 'I thought it might be the fish climbing slowly out of the water and banging their tails on the resonant surface!'

And Pierrina thought how selfish it was of Torgano to laugh at the Director's moments of drama. If the absurd old man believed he was worth assassinating, he deserved to be told that men with silent rifles fired on him at least six times every day. Torgano was disrespectful to suggest poetry, where power had imagined death. The Director had probably imagined himself a duke: at a time when sensible dreamers were locked in their sweaty boxes, whiling away the afternoon sun with visions of molelike artisan kings in Spanish black, the Director had had his imagination stroked by the beard of an anthropomorphic sun.

For a moment he had absorbed a dripping gutter, a kneeling lump of iron quivering and exhausted: a patch of moss or creosote had fired at him. It was all so easy to understand. A man who had obviously been reading Italian political novels in bed, or in a café, panted over the bridge. Red badges of wine marked his shirt, a shirt reminiscent of woven nettles, and of stones seen through a sunset stubble, a wonderful shirt, a shirt full of coloured globules, anaesthetic nightmares, the muscles of syndicalist peasants.

All admired it; it was a garment to attract legions of thugs and rejected consuls. His face was clumsily constructed, he was trying to look so foolish that all would assume he was shrewd.

'Yes, gentlemen,' he said, 'you admire my shirt? My boys all like my shirt: I make them myself. Good cloth, you'd like one perhaps? You'd never get hurt, you know, not by my boys, if you wear one of my shirts, and support the rallies. Shirts: that is the history of the inspiring movements of the world: religion, nationalism, fascism, communism, all shirts. One day, people with shirts like mine will lounge among the marble eagles, writing meaningless notes on the new banknotes, and sending them by duchess to their friends. And everyone will wear my shirts: I shall be rich, and have two shops. I shall be dictator, and have four sewing machines.'

The man paused; the Director saw that he was little practised in the lunatic ambitions of adults. He obviously saw government as a schoolboy excursion into a land covered with small saffron cakes and photographs of varicose legs on a spotty seafront. He did not realise the sacrifice and heartbreak required of one official, the life of a public servant, necessary to pay for the smallest delight of empire, the least enjoyment of power. He did not appreciate that the brief campaign abroad to procure half-caste entertainers, cardboard cities, a regiment of naked oppressors, would mean that colonial officers would melt like ivory idols; wet and yellow they would fall into the slimy forests, to die in the ambiguous service of native and master.

It was only long enough for a brief meditation on the justification for empire, with special reference to its observed effects in the lost colonies, before the man continued:

'Well, I was going to tell you. Me and the boys were trying to get a couple of rats to fight, in an old warehouse. We were wearing our pointed hats, as is our custom, and an agent from the lost colonies was there, so we laid bets on the rats. Well, Mascak had on the gloves, he is newly promoted our Venerable Antisemite, you know: and then I heard a crackling, like rats in the bones, and a breathing like the rustling of garments on a rack in August, when they breathe with difficulty, swelling like burst lungs.

'Anyway, I lifted the sacking which covers a hole in the council chamber, in the wall owned by the Shadow Department of Agriculture: it makes a hiatus in the bronze shirt-sage commissioned by us from Brunelleschi, so the Minister of Education assures me. I lifted the sacking: then there was a man there, firing at you, frightened, and you were so well composed on the bridge, I wish I had been in his position, I wouldn't have missed, I can tell you.

'Well, the boys all agreed that it might not do to interrupt him, seeing you were gentlemen together, likely to conduct business in undemocratic and lofty ways, unknown to the Committee for Liberating the Lost Colonies – that's me and the boys. So we let him get away, and then they sent me for the reward.'

The Director looked in the strawberry eyes for a joke. 'Reward? Pointed hats? Brunelleschi? Committee? Are you all mad, or have you and your ministers mined our government officials with immense magical fireworks?'

The man smiled. 'Oh yes, we have a large quantity of arms – and the reward?'

'You have the reward: it is your weapons which are the reward, the weapons you have been at once encouraged and forced to rely on. We were evil, in a mild way: and now you are mad, gently deranged. It all follows, until you believe that all that matters is that someone would try to shoot me. We should have made it clear, that everything about that assassin mattered, every opinion was important, could probably be refuted, that all his belongings were the fruits of theory and the development of political actions. But we never encouraged you to think in terms of theory: we wanted you to laugh at theory, which we sneered at, as a highbrow form of truth.

'We said, "Don't look at our ideas, look at our achievements; don't bother about our policy, we make it up as we go along, but see how successful we are!"

'At times, we might point to the idea of justice which underlay our actions; but we feared argument, because we thought you would not follow it, merely call us tricky. So we relied on statements to give an impression of sincerity; on action, where a speech would have made things clear. We surrounded ourselves with the ritual of "what we think you want", until we forgot what it was that we wanted.

'We are right, but we forgot to convince you that we were: it was so much easier to give you more money than discuss politics with you, and be frank. So, now it is necessary that we should be shot, be harassed by petty armies which revolt with banners and razors on November nights, and ride away before morning on the moon.'

The Director looked sad, a little frightened: the gangster general strutted off, his shirt lively and threatening as mature gorse.

Gallista said, 'I don't know why you bother to explain, he was not a child. As you grow older, you seem increasingly to want to change the systems by which you live. You are the legendary goat who leaps to the top of a mountain pursued by wolves, black and steaming on the erect, drab structure. In the valleys woodcutters have been cutting down trees which contain witches or werewolves; grandfathers have been describing the incestuous politics of the village to battered tourists in the filthy hotels.

'But everyone wants to help the goat, stuck on the mountain; it is a necessary animal, like the enchanted bears of Switzerland; it attracts and placates the critical. An army of diseased villagers forgets its preoccupation with tubercular Scandinavians, inbreeding, demons in the mountains. Inspired by the necessity of preserving this special beast, the mountain people forget that they are characters in a fifth-rate Nordic opera; they march up the swarthy iced chimney.

'But the goat has a vision, or an ulcer: it grows and vomits. Very large it grows, full of lightning, silver and black like grapes, it bursts over the valley, and a cloud of sulphur and broken mountain smashes all the villagers, and creeps over the roads, and squeezes flat the diesel bus and a division of cows. People are ready to respect you, help you; don't spoil it by becoming coy, or unable to digest the friendly sandwiches offered by, say, the enormous children of the English.'

Pierrina and Torgano went back to help the loading; if there was to be a quarrel, they wanted it to develop freely, without embarrassment or restraint. The boat provided was made of bark, covered with scum of paint: possibly it was a melon skin preserved by a local boatbuilder, himself long ago cut out from an inferior tree, allowed to live because as timber, he would be useless, unworkable. The boat was powered by a biscuit tin full of alcohol; as the director remarked, 'It was the most like a funeral pyre I could find,' and indeed Torgano came to think of the pungent engine as a sooty mouth which might spit blisters and raw flesh all over his face.

One or two helpers who had been preserved in crumbled vellum in some forgotten dowry chest in an attic, crouched like birds with needle feet in a fragile nest. They only avoided being called mentally deficient by refusing to speak. They were not employed because the department pitied them, but because it could exploit their silence and be admired for it.

Perhaps they had been abandoned by the Flying Dutchman on one of his romantic idylls; perhaps after a riotous weekend burrowing in the graves, they had failed to make the necessary transmogrification, to return aboard the stormproof ship. They certainly looked as if they missed those winter nights blowing on chromatic foghorns into vertical waters, bellowing bovine exhortations through long demon tubas at the weather. Or perhaps they had rotted in the sea; or else they belonged beneath the sea, and had gone mouldy, as all the mermaids used to, when kept for long in the domestic cosiness of eighteenth-century estates.

All this struck Pierrina, as she realised how the Director must have wanted to impress Gallista with his unsympathetic handling of the Tarraults. Briefly she thought, 'And Torgano, how strange, that he seems to fear Gallista, ashamed, yet interested. I remember my grandmother looked like that when an old man came to the palazzo selling ballads, who had one eye red, the other green.

'I recall it so well, one eye red with brown veins, the other green and a pupil with a picture of a curled lash in it. I was three at the time; it was all confusing; it turned out he was an imposter; but the eyes were genuine, for I believe they cut them out as punishment. But then, Torgano is too insensitive to worry about Gallista's eyes,. and she is a big, well-fortified woman; he would be afraid to know her, in case she battered him with the silver crusts round her wrists and ankles.'

Gallista was dressed very correctly: like an elephant, she wore spiked collars round her arms and legs. 'To keep the wolves off,' she explained archly.

'A very beautiful elephant,' the Director assured her. 'A toy elephant, just the right size to sit on my mantelpiece for always, and curl its trunk up for kisses, like a pair of lips on the end of a powerful worm.'

And Gallista, even Gallista, wondered whether the bitterness of experience, the maturity of a man of power and self-sufficiency, merited such similes; but when not fiercely in love, the Director quite enjoyed disgusting images, so both were tepidly happy. They watched Pierrina lifting tapestries rolled on their poles, the feather hats of Chinese generals, and the satchels of banners they carried on their backs. Smaller objects: wooden roses, chess sets in which the pieces were cats in various national costumes, motor cars made of shells.

'You are letting her take everything, all the treasures are being taken.' Gallista was angry.

Occasionally things fell into the water: a set of china eggs sank to make an interesting composition at the bottom of the canal. The cats shopped around, anxious to get their old lives packed up and forgotten. Timid dogs sat in the bedrooms, weeping a little, perhaps tearing up old photographs.

Pierrina was too irritated by the Director to be sad; which pictures was she allowed to take? She snatched a few, hardly caring which: some anonymous peasants bounding before a peasant artist, while other peasants hovered nearby with whips and infuriating condescending, taking care not to appear in the picture itself. Some horses: expensive bosoms, triangular boards poised over the pure shirt-fronts and the rainbow sashes; their excellences, the racehorses, hooves like claws. In the backgrounds, the chimney-pot hats of the classless spectators, a thousand cardiac faces throbbing with greed as the animals prance round them.

She smuggled into the boat a few mail suits for children: one never knew what the interests of one's family might be. A set of wooden trumpets, of various sizes: and Gallista saw these and said, 'Horns to announce the liberation of the lost colonies? Perhaps she is a spy, and has archives of microfilm of the bullfrogs in the premier's artificial sea, leaping into oriental hats at subversive fishing parties.'

The Director was listening to his heart, in case he had been shot without noticing it. Torgano grew miserable; he dropped a case of exquisite rubble; the Director started exaggeratedly, and in one cheek a half-buried muscle kicked briefly to be born to a world of irrational fear.

Pierrina pushed people, stuffed and preserved Asiatic limbs and heads, the starving dogs, leather wallets full of black silver junk, to the bottom of the boat.

'Should we switch off the fountain?' asked Torgano, and Pierrina cried, 'And dismantle the statues, in case they strain themselves? And order the suits of armour to rest after meals in case they are beginning to decay, as warriors will? And beg the stone animals not to go too near the edge of the roof to admire themselves in the water? Really, Torgano, there are times when I wish I could have pushed you through the boat, through the canal, to some communist antipodes, where everyone would call you a brother, and you could be flogged by fathers or confessors in the sanctity of churches, or your bedroom.'

And Torgano was bored, at last, with the emotional arguments which so amused all who overhead them, in buses, or restaurants. He resolved never again to spoil the taste of shy, scavenging crabs with the bitterness of a burst love. Meals would be once more abstract, with fresh, pungent titles, like 'Foxes of the Forest Fringe', or 'Interlocking Balances under a Striped Awning: Three', or, his favourite, he always thought, 'Tantalising Panthers on a Spring Ceiling'. So he merely replied to Pierrina, for whom he had not yet planned his final wilful sacrifice:

'Why do you think communism should be an affair of Catholicism and the conformist oppression of the older brother, and his arch-conspirator, the father? Yes, we know it is an organisation with the disadvantages and advantages of a family, the sons being sent to found an empire because they refused to part with their pet bears, or seduced the inflexible family servants. All that is there: like the college or the monastery, no detail of the succession can be left to chance, or personal choice; all the children may promise to respect the terms of the will, and to bow daily before the portrait of the chairman of the board of Directors.

'The purity of the infant mind must be preserved – filial piety, cruelty, all the old Roman catchphrases. And yes, religion is there: mortify the affections, the real enemy is humanism and humanitarianism, that is why churches attack the good godless man, rather than the evil mystic, the satanist. Yes, both systems are, comparatively, classless, managerial perpetuations of myth: the miracles, the ceaseless fight against the good man who does not agree with the system, but strives for substantially the same ideals.'

But Pierrina could not be troubled to reply, and the boat moved out, under the Director and Gallista whose faces were blotchy and hard as saints', stuck away on some church in a pine forest, near the electric storms and the unkempt nests of birds. The household steered itself on towards an artificial sunset; a thousand city householders were celebrating the weekend by burning the garbage and dust libations of the past week. A thousand bonfires climbed into mushroom shapes, and a false dusk formed at about the level of the higher triumphal arches, and the more stunted commercial skyscrapers.

Women saw the twisted hearts of the fires, saw the limbs of dead shrubs sweating, giving off a few aromatic sparks. The little hygienic families were secure in the sunset they had made; they went contentedly to read about machines which could extinguish the sun, if so desired.

Soon, the evening drinkers would make a neon glow in the sky which would reassure the old and the weak; everywhere people were making smells, lights and sounds, to reassure a nation of the timid. The politicians and the authors were frightened too, for it was themselves they had to fear:

'It's not religion, and it's not dogma; what we need is not any old drug, nor the merely beautiful woman. We are too far gone for any of that; we need the potion in the toy cupboard of the most heterodox magician, one who has been burnt, but unsuccessfully, by all the crowned heads of Europe. And the woman must be ugly, her face full of valleys in which lurk abandoned civilisations, a few smoked Indians mortified with lumps of cactus, or Thai processions with guards of satin elephants; all this for our amusement lest we are bored. And a woman to dominate, to drag us to humiliating deaths, with ropes of flowers. Yes, we all are so unromantic.'

And when Torgano had finished, a woman scavenging in the rich green mud – was it for skeletons, or bait, or antique silver? – shouted over to them: 'What we need is protection from worms, freedom from pollution. You and your sort, pouring out your petrol vapours to dirty the mud, and kill my worms, or take all the flavour out of them. Disgusting: and me and my sort, digging in this rubbish – if we were pigs, we wouldn't stick our little petal noses in this, I assure you – all we find now are colonies of worms either dead, or thin and convalescent, taking only gentle exercise and gruel, as my husband used to say.

'If you were a fish, you wouldn't touch those poisonous brutes: no, you'd swim on to the next principality, where the unions do something for the worm gatherers. All we want is a system of priorities: as soon as we were within sight of a decent life, everyone got tired of the petty human details, and started saying, "Ah, the lost romance of it all; the brain is a prison, it erects its own frontiers. Let us make our cells decorative and somewhat ornate, then we can open a vein, relax till our life runs through the floorboards."

'You said this, just when we were getting a national minimum for our worms: and now you just drive about on your couches languidly dangerous, saying, "It's not out fault, we weren't interested any more. Besides, in a generation, we will all have killed ourselves." Surely you see, it doesn't give us much of a say.'

The woman did not look, reflected Pierrina, the sort who will talk loudly to no one in particular for an evening in provincial pharmacies; she whispered apologetically, 'I'm sure we're not to blame,' then 'At any rate, the city centre would disintegrate with all the grace of a thirteen-syllable poem in the next war. Torgano, do you remember the last war?'

'I was small – but patriotic. When the bombs came, there were not many. I used to go out and look at the bodies till they were taken away. That was because it was not national policy to acknowledge the existence of aeroplanes, because we could not afford them; so, of course, logically we had to ignore bombs and precautions against them. And then there were the parades: all those horse tails; on the helmets.

'And the painted officers, no officer was allowed to have white hair, nor the horses with curly legs. And the artillery which was mounted permanently in ambulances, and the pictures of atrocities committed by our colonials, to show how desperate was the struggle. And the taste of the food: the coffee made of powdered wood, the sugar distilled from the sweetness of aircraft dope.'

Pierrina told him how dull and ordinary were all his memories, but because she was soon to be rid of him, she felt fond of him. 'When I pass him in the street, I shall not pretend that I have not seen him: I shall just walk past as if he were a sycamore shoot, presuming to penetrate a city pavement, a nuisance till sprayed with venom. And he will feel disliked, but not really hated.'

Gallista knew she was important: the Director was watching her; as she smoothed her wings in her reflection she was aware that what she equivocally called 'generations of official birds' were interested, in spirit, in her progress. It was time for the humming bird to kick around in the nest, to show the kind professors that the skinny beak could draw blood, and draw like a diamond on the glass walls of the cage. The Director must be shown that his new pet had a definite personality and sharp feet.

Gallista knew he was as conceited as only the very nicest men were allowed to be: so she thought it only an amusement to irritate him. For everyone had told her he was covered all over with ivory plates, quite impenetrable.

'You seemed quite surprised that they should try to assassinate you: you always told me you were so important that it would be almost indecent and disrespectful if a day passed without its scents of death. The iron filings in the coffee, the acid in the roses, detonators thrown like myrtle beneath your feet, all this you told me: yet, you were quite pale when that man failed to make you a national holiday, or an international incident.

'A man fires at you, and you say it is an interesting idea, probably wrong; you are not merely a coward, for that is just restful, a physical allergy, like those people who hate cats. No, you are an intellectual myrmidon, a time-server; you play at being not very clever, you despise all the right things, such as creative activity, women, English music, yet you try to seem a theorist, a man of culture heroically setting fire to social jungles set with rice-paper temples.

'But when you are faced with danger, you fall back on the old nonsense; to avoid doing anything, you say "Well, we must provide an incentive for private charity," or "The nation tells me we require lethal gases to safeguard unborn generations and preserve an illusion of democratic control to terrify communists and Africans."

'You want us to believe government is difficult, but because you yourself are small and timid, you always fall back onto the easy solution, the act of violence, the great Aegean heritage of particularism, the mystic injustices of Platonic fascism, and the mechanics of city politics: assassination and the constitutional status quo.'

The Director said, 'Well, even that is difficult sometimes – to make things stop still. As the French might say, "Everything crumbles"; as our political opponents so often find, the institutions they want to preserve cannot be kept still; they grow stronger so long as they are important. A truism, but eventually they find that the strength is absurd, and as they require majority support, they find that the strong institutions always tend to become monopolies of power.'

'The fourth precept of "The Intelligent Slav's Guide to the Anti-Fascist Front, with a Personal Message from the Chairman of the Socialist-Syndicalist League". I know it well,' Gallista said.

She watched a duck with sealing-wax wattles looking at its mate and thinking, 'Love – love on the canals is like freedom in a drain. Why does he never flap away to the mountains, and reign there to make the world safe for ducks of all kinds? Then I would admire him; for I would enjoy being his queen, and to grow another suit of feathers, more in keeping with my qualities as wife and mother.

'Ah, the mountains: larger even than the largest of the local buildings: so admirably blocked they are; great flaps and rolls of mountain material. Or the marshes: the ducks of the Western marsh have six toes on each foot, and carry beaded evening bags to musical evenings with American bankers. But love on these canals, what an excess of domestic cliché and poverty!'

And Gallista smiled; whimsical nobles had imported these angry birds to sit in boats and sleep; like cushions, they were to hide dirt and exercise the eye.

The Director saw that Gallista wore a crazy smile to show she was having a historical fantasy; he said, 'Surely you know we are no longer connected with the syndicalists? And you must know that our problem is what the innocents and the tourists call drunkenness, but is really drugs. At night, anonymous peddlers creep in in boats; like fulfilled wishes mysterious parcels appear in the half-dreams of the drugged romantics. Perhaps they do not even know what they are doing; they see these animated statues beckoning, whispering, chuckling, and leaving these bundles of leaves, or polished bamboo syringes; and they use drugs, as others use dreams – natural releases which occur in the early morning.

'My colleagues are drugged: please do not believe I speak figuratively; I do not mean they live by illusions and frothy entertainment, and the lily smell of distilled women and old funerals – they would do that anyway. No, I am not primarily a moralist in this; I do not condemn life because I can rise above it. These people take drugs, and they seem to be drunk; because of course the symbolism is there.

'From the start drugs are a way of life; drink may be merely a habit; and men are now more concerned with ways of life than habit. Many in the government have the look of nocturnal animals; you will see them dressed as admirals in their committees, all braid and huge tossing faces; they preside over everything wonderfully. Occasionally to preserve their air of immortality, they sniff delicately at cocaine flowers in their buttonholes. What can we do?

'They are not unreliable, they rely on their surreptitious chemicals for relaxation; in some cases it seems to be only a mild auto-eroticism, a change from the self-torture of former ministers who used to ski themselves into crevasse tombs every year, or were shot, mistaken for hares, as they hunted in their tall hats among trophy-filled grass. You see, because people are worried and bored they must destroy themselves to give an illusion of happiness. You will have heard them saying, "I forget my problems when I am happy; if I am always happy, I need never bother to solve anything."

'And of course, their ruin comes all the quicker for never being miserable; the more wretched people feel, the more likely they are to survive. We can no longer say, "We hold a balance, we are the centre of a world," for everywhere is in the middle; between two opposed millstone forces. In addition, we have to guard against as ideological schizophrenia – I fear I have always nearly suffered from this. But please don't be alarmed: many of those who appear to be drugged are in fact only drunk.'

'Self-pity,' said Gallista, 'and dramatic father-play; you take any series of tragedies and comedies; you invert them, combine even a retrograde version of it all, and expect to reproduce the same moods, the same self-glorification each time. Surely you are too old to play in this way, to impress with the same techniques, to pretend that because you are old and carefully treated, you are beautiful, that every word belongs on velvet with all the other ministerial creeds on their godsized patio.'

The Director was tired and he felt small and not at all quarrelsome. He wanted to curl up in Gallista's pocket, to be taken out and looked at only in a poor light, or when beautiful imagery music was being strummed on cedarwood guitars.

'Please don't. Please don't destroy the atmosphere of trust:

please don't begrudge me this last friendship before they wall me up in a cathedral with their little gold trowels and the department's alloy wheelbarrow. I have come so far for you – it is necessary, desirable, imperative – the road of bones and histrionics so tiring – the heat, the illnesses to be endured, only to be wasted because at the last, Gallista, you, my Gallista . . . I know you were amusing yourself to make me angry: I am unreasonable, you are just.

'But not now: I am too old – Pierrina and Torgano, perhaps I have made them also feel something of the urgency of my last desperate years. Gathering speed, the last years, the last feet to negotiate so carefully, so skilfully, such experience helps me make the years pass more quickly. Do not be so full of scorn, because I am old, and want you for my last playmate. My brother walked into the canal one night long ago, a tourist into death, he said all he regretted was those swans, too conceited to have to die. When they found him, he was covered with soft pearls, and his hair was full of butter; they supposed it was from a case damaged during the riots.

'Well, I always regretted my brother, and when I saw you, I thought, "To spend the last months with her; I could not envy my brother if I did that."'

Gallista sighed; one accepted that men were not strong. But surely this should not always happen? Every time she found some social bandit, and armed him, sent him out to prove his strength and worthiness, he came back and wept about, 'Ah, the mothers and their crawly children, and the old mangy dogs – so human. And you, you are so strong, protect me from my monsters and my ambition and vanities.'

It was too bad: her ideal was the hero, the man who does not feel, but acts as if he does. He always does the perfect thing, because he has no emotion, no weakness to dissuade him. And now, she had touched the Director, and instead of being tough, he had collapsed, into tenderness and sentimentality. Perhaps he took drugs?

She said, 'I hoped you would not think of me in that archaic manner; I want love more than anything, but it must be a free gift, an intellectual surrender, not just because you need me. I can't explain: I want everything I can get from love, don't misunderstand me, but it must be love as passion, the essential love of an emotional equal. I don't want it mixed up with psychology, if you understand me, not a business of trust and respect, possessiveness, jealousy, not a couple being attracted because they are weak and deficient, and need someone else to rely on. I don't want to become a part of someone else's deficient life: I'm not like Pierrina, frightened to be committed.

'No, I want all I can get, on the spiritual level, of course, but I want to remain myself. I don't want you to collapse all over me like a mined castle the minute I touch you.'

The Director had assisted in too many humiliating dismissals to attempt to argue with the processes of a logic which was usually anti-human. He sighed, and though they remained together, with great strides, as in a duel, their imaginations went off in opposite directions, not looking back. The Director looked in the canals, as if they had been the bottom of his glass after an evening's drinking, slowly watching the dancing women turn into elephants, then into obsessions, flowers with long red noses, which finally crawled away on the ceiling with many pairs of blurred legs.

And again it was night: above the railway station, a black sky mocked with its heat; nuns locked themselves in the waiting rooms and prayed to be released from the dark warmth. The Director lay on his bed; occasionally a breeze caught him and he lifted and rustled like a leaf on a catafalque. Had he not been notoriously impregnable, Gallista might have thought he contemplated the sooty algae of unhappiness which flourished on the underside of the brain, that he thought of his brother, the church, or her.

But Gallista prowled the streets once more; and the Director thought only how old he was, how unwillingly self-sufficient still. Soon, he got up and boiled himself an egg: 'A sort of gesture,' he giggled to himself, and 'no more decisions today', as he took extravagant care of himself.

'If someone really knew the answers to anything, they would force everyone to believe them,' he thought, so he munched his supper, an old performing bear whose circus is bankrupt and uninsured.

And Gallista too had her regrets; but, she thought to herself, she had the living creed, the creed of humanity. She had merely to search for love, that mystic communion with the unreality of the socially incompatible, the semi-divine sympathy between opposites, the discovery that everything is compatible, complementary. The last enormous myth, she knew she had twenty years before old age invalidated her assumptions. Because the most optimistic, so the most misleading: her philosophy would induce an early devolution of the body. The mind would delegate its power to the magician and the writers of rhymed prose; the body would give its tasks to a young executive class, to exercise its blackening sinews in the pursuit of slogans which meant as much as an animal call.

Gallista was bound for a boarding house senility; she would have her reputation to play with; a reputation only because it was a list of failures, the endless permutations of the unsuccessful and the insatiable. Perhaps this was why she felt sad, and tired. The sharp dialectic of the Director had defeated her, but she knew she had wounded him; and now, it did not seem either a very difficult nor a satisfactory thing to have done.

'My life is winding up!' groaned the Director. 'The time till tomorrow is too long to live through: Gallista, my child, she has gone once more, and I am too old to grow older, to receive still more unwanted experience. I no longer want to have to grow up, to be burdened with the grief of maturity. Yes, I am a socialist, but I want a personal status quo; I want to freeze my life at yesterday, disregarding its little feudal appurtenances, the idealist kings who walked through my heart from time to time.'

He was tired: the images no longer came easily to him. As he slept, he mumbled: and was lonely, that there should be no one to share his unhappiness; he quoted the old saying, 'From *nada*, to *nada*, we are *nada*,' but Gallista did not come to tell him this was not true.

Gallista had met no one: back in her room, she knew only that it was hot, that all people were small and rather crinkly, outmoded as last year's pine cones. She sat till it was time to sleep, as if she were waiting for a death. She remembered her childhood, how she had loved the world of sleepy cats she called aunts, the old wooden toys who had been her parents.

'There is no freedom in my life unless I am successful. That is what my parents never needed to consider: if I fail, I shall be so lonely, and not at all a well-regulated enterprise.' She sighed: as the days became more ugly, so they were longer, and occupied more of everyone's time. It was distressing.

Torgano had found himself: his decision was made, to make himself unhappy by whatever means presented themselves. Pierrina cared for him, if he took more care of himself and did not creep around like an extinguished lighthouse in mist, she would, one day, have placed her metropolitan hands on his head, and murmured the usual polite phrases. But that could not be: Torgano was not foolish, nor unusually self-centred. But he believed he had established a tradition, of frustration and the near madness of an impossible love.

He would go away, not because Pierrina hurt him, for that had been his imagination, and the results of Pierrina's fear. He would go away because he did not believe in logic as a source of action: all he would find around him was a mannered degeneration, the compromise which leads to death and extinction through a confectionery countryside. Long ago he had said to himself:

'I must make a stand against the corrupt and the deceitful, by refusing to recognise them: if necessary, I will leave Pierrina as a useless gesture against the society which produced her, so that I can honestly say, "Look, our society, your society, made me lose Pierrina." I will desert my life because I do not approve of it. I do not like myself enough to want to be changed.'

He told Pierrina, 'I am going away. It is not your fault, you understand.'

'Of course not. How could it be? But dear, you will come back? I may become bored with my life spent crouched over a gargling samovar, listening to the flattering gossip of White Russian confidence tricksters.'

'You may indeed.' Torgano smiled sadly. 'I am leaving you because I am disgusting. I, unworthy, will take myself away to be polished. A revolution, the occasional act of charity or violence – they are often allied, you know – and my spirit will become shiny, or at least blunt, the edges bevelled, beaded with heads of curious birds. I will return. Perhaps. And save you all, or talk to you about things I have seen and considered while I have been away. I will travel, you know, abroad, and in the next valley too.'

'But you hate travelling, and you have no money.'

Torgano thought, 'But all that was in the days when I was a creature of convention. If you renounce things, you become quite different. Laws and so on no longer operate.'

Pierrina smiled: for a joke this was entertaining; for a future it was ridiculous. 'But to leave me now, when I need your help to unfold myself in this disgusting little flat to which it hardly seems possible I can have come, that is too unkind. You can be cruel, you know.'

Torgano looked round him: they had not pressed Pierrina's flat into the mould of lovers' whimsy; everything was anonymous because everything had a name: chairs were chairs, and that told you nothing about them. In the palazzo, chairs had been galleons, mahogany swans, landscapes of straw and leather, anything but mere chairs. Now, the names came too easily: there was no freedom because there was no choice.

Flatly, he said, 'I am sure you will manage without me. But if you miss me, that will have justified my leaving you: the more you miss me, the less I shall want to come back, so that when you die, you will know you loved me.'

Pierrina was thinking that in a few minutes in a few minutes only she would be left alone to cry, if she wanted. But she longed for Torgano to leave her, so that she could weep for him. There was no light, there was nothing to observe; the people had extinguished themselves a little prematurely. Some tragedies had ceased to be relevant already; there would be no climax; the heroes would all die just before they could switch on the lights. It was no less sad.

They stood silent, prevented from saving the things that mattered by their belief in the integrity of the characters they believed they were representing. Wisdom, pity, affection, everything but sense; emotions scraped together like old sabres, decorative and rusty. And yet, Torgano saw himself not merely as self-destructive, or narcissistic, but rather as the one who must always lose because he has no values,. no criteria with which to judge success. The only victory of a man without values can be that he should convince himself of the reality of moral standards; until then 'meaningless but true' must be the reaction of Torgano to life and achievement. And spoiling even this simple pleasure was the knowledge that truth, save as an emotional conceit, did not really matter.

He looked at Pierrina, saw that she was beautiful: the last chord of the symphony is full of nostalgic regret for the completed and unheeded beauty of what has gone before, and that was how Torgano saw Pierrina. She had become an artistic whole, because he was seeing her for the last time. He was saying goodbye, he realised, and no should ever have to say goodbye.

'It is not right that we should part,' he said.

'Then why—'

'Because you want it: I want you to want it, it is right to part, because you are not happy with me.'

Pierrina wanted to say that because of a sort of hatred, she could not live without Torgano: she wanted to say that they were not sophisticated animals like the Director and Gallista, forever doing little dances for one another, or building synthetic bowers out of old books and cellophane wrappings. She wanted to say so much; she stretched a hand.

'Memories ... regrets ... chaos into light ... return ... alone,' mumbled Torgano, hardly listening to what he was saying. He was wishing her the same lonely existence to which he felt himself condemned. They were infinitely kind to one another. A beetle ran across a panel of the door, and Pierrina showed it to Torgano; they let it run across their joined hands. They laughed because to have considered their coming separation would have destroyed them. Torgano had been right after all, he had exposed Pierrina's feelings, but only for as long as he was unable to enjoy them. 'It is not ironical, just sad,' he reflected.

'When will you go, dear?' she asked.

'Now!'

They moved apart.

'I knew Gallista before, you know,' said Torgano suddenly.

'It doesn't matter. Don't go.'

'I can no longer be weak about my decisions.'

Pierrina whispered, 'Remember always,' but Torgano sighed.

'Nothing to remember, except what I am.'

'But be happy when you think of me,' she said.

'No, not happy. There is no happiness in being firm, in doing the silly, reasonable thing; no hypocrisy, but resentment of myself, longing for you.'

'We could have talked like this always if you had wanted.'

'You didn't want, though – it only works at the beginning and the end.'

'But we've scarcely tried . . .'

An Illusion of Sun

THEY COULD HAVE talked forever. Torgano went downstairs, and wandered to the water. The night was full of Pierrina; when he breathed, the air and his lungs were full of her name, so that he coughed; breathless and nauseated, he leant on hydrants. Only slowly did a few scraps of life return: the Director and Gallista trying to hurt one another to prove something, really wanting security, obtained by the submission of the other. Pierrina hurt by his belief that she was wounding him: there was somewhere a unity.

And the Director's politics: Torgano hoped the country would continue its inscrutable development which seemed at once so denaturalised and depersonalised, even though the Director seemed more sure of the theory than the practice.

'Your leaders are old men,' thought Torgano, 'but they are not decrepit nor senile, which is perhaps a bad thing. If statesmen had to be sat in the sun and fed with soup five times a day, and allowed to play with their grandsons only after tea, perhaps theory could be allowed to come into its own.'

The station: it was a country proud of its railways: the little stall, the offices, the newly rich pushing their ancestors in handcarts, it was another capital, another complex of custom and constitution. The cathedral roof, the money changers, Torgano dazed in the midst of enquiring glances, yet at home in the most obviously diabolic circle of what the Director had called 'this commercial hell'.

What was this roof? Quickly, thought Torgano, describe it before our social conscience has the better of us. The quick splendid description, to raise us from the banal: a roof of old stone spar pendentives, fingers bursting like steel quills, coming undone from the wrist; the lively gloves of the verminous and the destitute strapped over the marshy exhalations of iron

217

beasts.

Torgano sighed. He had proved nothing, except that he was exhausted; he was an old European who would go to the East not from curiosity but boredom. He bought a ticket, selected a train.

Everywhere there were soldiers, parachute troops and military police: military notices were relayed over loudspeakers, without complaint the men occasionally removed or modified pieces of equipment on the orders of the presiding officers. There was little light here: men slept on the benches, animals dozed in their trucks.

Torgano climbed into his carriage. He looked at the strings of mechanical baggage trains, the steel cages which held the rifles of the conscripts, the priests with their platoons of reluctant boy scouts. Old men carried their culture, their homes, in a few paper bags: a customs officer forced the lock on a case. Men danced milk churns into wagons, carefully they waltzed them on their rims, smiling and powerful.

And Torgano thought of those he was leaving, no longer friends, but individual: the Director, now as remote as tomorrow's date on a calendar; Gallista, of all the searchers the most easily rewarded; and Pierrina, her detachment and common sense always preventing her happiness. Perhaps it was worse to think they were not unique. It was bad enough to believe that in the future discoveries, could only be made by those whom their contemporaries would call neurotically aware of themselves.

It was a miserable thought, that intelligence was a questioning of values which meant that the half-mad thinker and visionary would always be in advance of any social organisation in which they could be happy. It meant that the scientist, the musician, the philosopher would be called not dangerous but deranged: it condemned the original to a half-life, the life of the intellect alone, an intense and impregnable personal unhappiness.

Even worse did it become for those with intelligence but

without originality, those without values, whose only success in life would be to question the usefulness of what they did. Men like himself would be called mad, because they were intelligent, because they despised without contributing alternatives. So, thought Torgano, because I am aware of things, because I cannot be happy in a status quo, yet have not the power to improve it. I must suffer the loneliness of the leader, without sharing his achievement.

Was this always so? Has it always been true that the increased psychological perception, the heightened personal awareness, of the men of knowledge has made them fundamentally unhappy? Is it a probability that those who increase knowledge do so at the expense of themselves, of their emotional ambitions? Is all human development bound to be at the expense of suffering, no longer perhaps physical, but mental?

Torgano carefully considered the railwaymen in the sticky dusk: they were slow and beautiful, dispatching with light rhetoric and sentimental regret the travellers and the migrating warriors. They must have had the impression that their city was always emptying, to be filled almost at once with another tired invasion. Torgano curled himself in a corner: the gently turbulent chemistry of loneliness lulled him; he wanted to sleep, and wake among mountains.

Men and women filled the compartment; they wept briefly and prepared meals. The engine roared; more soldiers. A general, so large he seemed to have won promotion by successful individual combat, inspected his troops; they carried blankets, chattered together like typewriters.

'So very tiring,' thought Torgano. 'Soon we will be away once more, seeking the regenerating forces, returning to first principles. It is ironic, but perhaps just, that these soldiers should go with me, the semi-divine source of moral rearmament is so often violence.'

The train moved, and in receding, the idea of Pierrina became more clear, because it had become an abstraction whose reality could no longer even be treated by physical contact; as an idea, it swung like a star, a faith. What Torgano had tried to leave, he now took with him as the only principle of his new life.

The sky was ribbed with green stalks of cloud: like a bomb, an old can had burst behind the station, pouring steam and a few wings of exploded pigeons over a contracting sky. The last birds fluttered to land; the lights of the town felt their way round the obfusc angles of destroyed buildings. In the tenements by the line, a thousand families waited for the train to pass, so that they could sleep. By the canals, pumps clanked, in the basements of the palaces a few inches of water mixed with old wine was never quite sucked out by the long black limbs of the drainage system.

The city was settling down for the night, the tide was bringing in surreptitiously a few more inches of the water which was to destroy the buildings. Torgano began to doze: relief that he had escaped, but to escape was to destroy himself. Everything was there to start a new life, except the new man; but he was too tired to be depressed. He would sleep like this for years, he decided; it needed only a ticket to go anywhere. Somewhere he would find it, that reason which would persuade him to go home. He slept, frowning, his cheek drawn up, like a nervous child's, to support a headache.

An illusion of sun remained; soon there were more stars than lights to be seen. The city became dull and amorphous, a spot of rust on the fertile iron of the countryside. People became concepts; life was the train, as it crashed along beside the trees and towns. After a time, the sense of movement troubled no one; the lights were extinguished, except for the tiny blue lamp which, itself feeble, gave the passengers the ugliness of exhaustion, near-death.

Written in 1959–1960

About the author

John Fraser has lived in Rome since 1980. Previously he worked in England and Canada.

An Illusion of Sun, the first of his eighteen published works of fiction, was written in 1958.